PRAISE FOR *THE 11:11 WISH*:

"Debut author Tomsic infuses Megan's first-person narrative with lots of personality and a distinctive voice, and secondary characters are all complex and multidimensional. Light fantasy firmly grounded in the realities of middle-school emotions."

—ALA *Booklist*

"Readers will empathize with [Megan's] tenuous position and her tenacity despite the hilarious situations she gets herself into. A fine, funny fix."

—*Kirkus Reviews*

"Tomsic puts a *paw*sitively magical twist on middle school mayhem. Whimsical and wacky, *The 11:11 Wish* is a romp of a read."

—Ingrid Law, Newbery Honor winner and *New York Times* bestselling author of *Savvy*

"Full of unexpected twists and turns, this sweet, funny book is pure magic."

—Tara Dairman, author of *All Four Stars*

THE 11:11 WISH

KIM TOMSIC

KATHERINE TEGEN BOOKS
An Imprint of HarperCollins Publishers

To my daughter Noelle, who kept me laughing
throughout her middle school years

Katherine Tegen Books is an imprint of HarperCollins Publishers.

The 11:11 Wish

Library of Congress Control Number: 2017954126
ISBN 978-0-06-265495-3

Typography by Katie Klimowicz
19 20 21 22 23   PC/BRR   10 9 8 7 6 5 4 3 2 1

First paperback edition, 2019

CHAPTER 1

If Dad had just dropped me off on the middle school side of Saguaro Prep, I would have had a 96 percent chance of arriving on time and avoiding the zap drama.

But no such luck. He asked me to walk Piper into the elementary school first, and my little sister can make her brown eyes as pleading as a golden retriever's. That only left me with T minus eight minutes before the first bell.

We rushed from the heat into a cool office where music played from overhead speakers. The song was "Better Together," one of Mom's favorites. I darted a glance at Piper but couldn't tell if she noticed the song, too, so I flicked her pinkie with mine. "You good?"

"Yeah. You?" No signs of worry. Typical Piper.

"Yep." *Be confident no matter what.* That's what *HSMS*, the *How to Survive Middle School* blog, had said in its current post, "Fail-Proof Formula for Winning Friends." I rubbed my thumb over the guitar pick I kept hidden inside my pocket. "Yep."

"Happy Monday, girls." The elementary principal walked over to us, her heels clicking.

"Thanks," Piper said. "I love your shoes."

Mrs. Butler said something to Piper while I glanced around for a clock. One hung above the door. T minus five minutes.

She finished talking, and I gave my sister a side hug. "Okay if I get going?"

"Oh," Mrs. Butler said, "wouldn't you like to meet Piper's fifth-grade ambassadors?"

According to the information given to us when we'd registered on Friday, we'd each get an ambassador to meet us at the start of the day and show us around.

"You don't have to wait, Megan. I can already tell we're going to love it here." Piper's attitude shone like the stars on her sneakers: sparkly and happy.

"Okay. Seeya." I turned to leave.

"Hold on," Mrs. Butler said to me. "I have some

printouts for you." She picked up a porcelain cat paperweight and grabbed the printed sheets from underneath it. "Here you go. School holidays and contact phone numbers."

I stared at the papers, stuff that should've gone to Mom.

"I hope you and Piper like it here and get involved. Saguaro Prep has many fine clubs and 'traditions.'" Her eyes twinkled as she put air quotes around "traditions."

"You'll especially enjoy our upcoming Spirit Week."

"Thank you." I glanced at the clock. T minus two.

"Right," Mrs. Butler said. "You should run along. The fastest way to the middle school office is to cut across the lawn."

I hurried out and rushed back over the dried grass, nearly tripping to avoid a pile of dog poop. Dog poop! As if the first day at a new middle school wasn't hard enough.

By the time I got inside the building, sweat was running down my neck. It also didn't help my look that after staying up past midnight, reading *HSMS*, I'd overslept and hadn't had time to dry my hair—now it was in a ponytail of half-wet frizz.

Add to that, I didn't have an ambassador waiting for me.

Then the tardy bell rang. T minus zero.

Great.

A student office assistant smacking a wad of pink gum filled out my late pass. She glanced up, holding her pen against the paper. "Name and grade?"

"Megan Meyers, seventh."

"Reason for the tardy?"

"Uh . . . first day."

The girl's eyebrows popped up.

I didn't want to come off completely clueless, even though the odds of me seeming chill were equal to the probability of a meteorite landing on my roof (182,138,880,000,000 to 1). Still, I managed to say, "I already got my schedule and everything on Friday."

She cocked her head. "Did you go to any classes then?"

"Um, no. It was late afternoon when—"

The girl jumped out of her chair. In a flash, she grabbed my hand and scribbled a single word in blue ink across my knuckles—"ZAP."

I pulled back my hand. "What does this mean?"

She shoved the late pass at me. "Go. You're late, remember?" And then under her breath she added, "Rhena will finish that later."

"Who—"

"Next."

CHAPTER 2

I spent all of first and second period obsessing over what "zap" meant and why that girl had written it on me. I was afraid it was some kind of hazing ritual. Or her way to tell me my teeth needed whitening—*Hey, girl. Time to zap those chompers*. And who was Rhena? Saguaro Prep was starting off weird to the tenth power.

I really needed to start focusing on the new me. As much as it sucked moving to a new school in a whole other state, at least it gave me a clean slate—nobody here knew me as Miss Science Fair, the girl who snort-laughed when she spoke in public. That was in the past. But between the zap and being late, I was so thrown off that by third period algebra I hadn't even worked up the nerve to talk to anyone yet.

And not to be braggy or anything, but I'm good at math, so everything should've gone fine when the teacher called on me. If she had just asked me to solve for x or calculate five to the seventh power, I would've been golden. Instead she pretty much said, "Everybody look at Megan. Let's make her feel super-awkward."

Okay. She didn't exactly say those words, but same difference, because what she actually said was, "Welcome to Arizona, Megan. Why don't you tell us a little about yourself?"

The entire class shifted to face me, which sent my stomach bungee-dropping to my ankles.

A tall girl with a high ponytail sitting on my right smiled and nodded encouragement. Then her eyes traveled down my arm, and at first I thought she was checking out my T-shirt, my favorite from the Humane Society. It said Woofstock instead of Woodstock, which I thought was hysterical. But in about a half second I realized she was staring at the blue ink on my hand.

"Megan?" Mrs. Matthews said, her tan sandals clacking as she walked to her desk.

I met the teacher's gaze, eyeball to eyeball, and tried to send my best SOS look. Teachers back home knew better than to ask me to speak in front of groups, because I'd either clam up or babble. Like at last year's sixth-grade welcome assembly when I'd tried to recruit people for Mathletes with the motto "Join us. We have pi." Because pi and pie.

Hardly anyone had gotten it, or they acted too cool to get it, so I had kept yakking. "You know. Not apple. I mean we could have apple. Pie that is. But I'm talking about 3.14. Get it?" I couldn't stop the word vomit. And worse, that's when Brooke Sutherland and Ronald Miller had started calling me a dorkjob.

But that was last year and Mrs. Matthews couldn't have known. So I took a breath—*I can do this*.

The posts on *HSMS* had said stuff about being bold and outgoing, as if that would ever happen. But the blog also gave me a formula so I was prepared for this moment with three simple steps: Say my name. Make them laugh. Say something impressive.

What's "impressive," though?

"Megan?" the teacher said for the second time.

"Well . . ." My voice wobbled. "I'm Megan, but you know that." Step one—check. "Um. Do you know there's an *Idiot's Guide to Twitter*, and an *Idiot's Guide to The Walking Dead*, but not an *Idiot's Guide to Being the New Kid*? I sure could use a book like that."

I laughed and everyone laughed with me, so I sat up and steadied my hands.

"That would come in handy for a lot of kids, I'm sure." Mrs. Matthews gave me a friendly smile and took a sip from her coffee mug. "Go on. Tell us whatever you'd like."

Now I just needed to say something impressive. "Well, I moved here from Colorado, and . . ." I cleared my throat and planned to go with the fact that I ski black diamonds and like to volunteer at the Humane Society, especially with the dogs. I can actually see a mutt and name its breed 9.5 times out of 10.

A boy near me yawned.

I looked around. Was anyone else yawning?

"Megan?"

"I ski black dogs," I blurted. "I mean . . . black diamonds." Then my signature snort-giggle leaked out.

I froze. So much for a clean slate.

The teacher nodded, waiting for me to add more to the story, but shutting up seemed like the best action plan. I stared at the sharpened end of my pencil.

The silence in the room cued Mrs. Matthews to move on. She put her hands into the pockets of her neon-yellow capris, tilted her head, and said, "Okay. Great. Good." Teacher code for "You are odd."

Eventually the bell rang, and I shot out of the classroom.

A clamor of sweaty students spilled into the

hallway, zipping around and chatting about import-ant stuff, like what they did over the weekend and where to meet later. I speed-glanced at faces. *Do I look at people and smile, or would that be creeper-ish?* I should've Googled that, too.

A crowd of girls blazed by in flowy skirts and cute tops. I smoothed down the pockets of my cargo shorts and hurried to the bank of red metal lockers where paper signs had been plastered everywhere—the fronts of lockers, the sides of the water fountain, and even on the ceiling. The one on my locker had a sketch of a hamburger and read, "Spirit Week! Vote Eric Burger." Doors clanged open and shut all around me.

"Hey. Can I see your hand?" someone said from behind me.

I turned. It was the tall girl from math. "Hi?"

"It's Megan, right? I'm Ally Menendez. We just had third period together."

"Yeah—"

"Your hand," Ally said. "What does it say? Can I see?" She leaned in, her ponytail falling forward.

I didn't know why she was asking. She'd already seen it. But I held it out. "Zap."

"That's it?"

"Um, yeah?"

Ally's mouth fell open. "Nothing else?" She grabbed

my wrist, flipped it over, and inspected my palm.

Huh? I tilted my head and looked at it, too.

"I can't believe it! An unfinished zap!" She freed my arm and started frenzy-digging inside her backpack. "Who wrote it?"

I shrugged and acted all chill, telling her about the girl from the office. Really, I just wanted some answers.

"Was her name Rhena?" Ally asked, yanking a pen from her backpack.

"No, but she said Rhena would finish it later."

"Figures." Ally's mouth twisted.

"Okay, honestly," I said. Students shuffled through the hallway, streaming in both directions. I moved closer and lowered my voice. "I've been dying to ask all morning. What does 'zap' mean, anyhow?" I hated letting on that I was a girl who wasn't in the know, even though clearly I was that girl.

"Of course you wouldn't know what it means," Ally said. "It's a newbie ritual here. When somebody writes 'zap' on your hand, they get to write a dare, too. Then you have to do the dare by the end of the day."

"Ooooh . . ." Dread seeped into my pores.

"It's been Saguaro Prep's underground tradition for as long as anyone can remember." Ally continued on about zaps, and I hung on every word, getting sucked in by her breezy sureness.

"Zaps are about fun," she said, and I nodded.

"They help new kids get to know everyone." She smiled and I smiled.

"Consider it an introduction of sorts." Her grin grew wider, and of course mine did, too. How could it not? She was like one of those girls in a shampoo or tampon ad, marching down the sidewalk with so much confidence that people start following her just to see where she's going. ". . . and since Rhena hasn't finished the job her worker bee started, I will. Do you mind? Here." She held out her hand.

I wiped my clammy palm down the side of my shorts. "It's a little—"

"Yup. That's August for you. Monsoon misery. Sticky hands, humidity, thunderstorms. You'll get used to it." Right on cue, a rumble of thunder vibrated the hallway windows, followed by a crack. Squeals and giggles busted from a cluster of students. "Monsoon season will move on in a few weeks. Now come on."

I surrendered my hand like she was a palm reader. Ally scribbled across it and then squeezed my fist closed. "Remember. You have to do it by the end of the day. Okay?"

I nodded while the worrier in me cranked to full blast—what if the dare says I have to shave an eyebrow, or eat a cockroach? Or what if I'm given a costume to wear—or worse, what if I have to wear a bikini in the lunchroom? As a seventh grader with less boobage than probably anyone in the entire school, including Piper, I'd rather go for the eyebrow shaving.

"I'd better run," Ally said before heading off.

I hurried and opened my hand. It read, "Do something EXCITING by 3 p.m. today."

My optimism lasted a full nanosecond and then, *yhish*. That might be a problem, since the biggest thing I'd ever made happen at my last school was Math Jeopardy, which had started out fun but ended in public humiliation.

And now this zap. I kept staring at my hand. "Exciting" had been written in all caps and underlined three times. Outside the hallway windows, another crack of thunder boomed. I looked up as lightning tore a line in the Arizona sky.

A smile inched across my face.

This was my fresh start, and Ally believed I was the kind of person who could deliver exciting!

CHAPTER 3

I leaned against my locker. A cluster of nearby students buzzed about the upcoming Spirit Week election. One girl who looked like a teacup poodle compared to the guy next to her ripped a Spirit Week sign from a locker door.

"You cannot vote for her," the girl said. "Can. Not. She'll make our lives worse than reality TV."

"Yeah," the boy said. "But maybe she'll have her parents throw us a pizza party."

"Get your stomach in check, Tank." The girl gave Tank a playful shove. "Seriously, though. It's not worth it."

Okay?

I waited at my locker for my ambassador another few seconds before I decided it was pointless—she had no-showed all morning and wasn't breaking trend anytime soon. I glanced left and right, wondering which way to go this time. The layout felt like Saguaro Prep's architect had teamed up with a video game designer to plan the hallways as a super-maze. The challenge: find your classroom and stay on your side of the invisible line dividing the lower and upper divisions.

I tightened the straps on my backpack and chose a hall draped with red and white streamers and a poster that read, "Spirit Week! Think outside the Bun. Vote Eric Burger 8th Grade Rep."

I found my history class and walked into a room that smelled like kettle corn and rain. On the side wall, rays of sunlight slanted through long windows coated with lines of drizzle.

The only open seats were toward the back. I chose one behind a boy who was using a teeny-tiny screwdriver to tighten the sides of his glasses. On my way down the aisle, a few people smiled, darting glances at my hand.

I hung my backpack on the chair and took a seat. The Smart Board was angled at the front of the room, and near it on a pearl-green wall was a black-and-white cat clock with moving eyes, timekeeping whiskers, and a ticktocking tail. And the weirdest thing, it looked exactly like a clock my grandma used to own. I squinted. Even the tail curled at the end with that familiar, whimsical star etched into its tip.

The tardy bell rang, but the teacher, Mr. Kersey, seemed oblivious to the bell and kept messing with controls on the Smart Board. His polka-dot bow tie and hipster glasses sat crooked, and his spiky blond hair looked like it had been styled by static. "Ugh. I'm grabbing new batteries. Quiet discussions, people." He scooped up his bottle of fizzy lemonade and headed out of the room.

When the door clicked shut, the boy in front of me dropped the screwdriver into his backpack and turned around.

"Hey. What'd you do? Switch classes?" He pushed his glasses up his nose.

"No," I said quietly.

"I don't remember seeing you in here the first two weeks of school. And I'd remember you."

Heat splotches crept up my neck. "Um, okay?"

I dropped my gaze to the buttons on his blue-checkered shirt. He'd missed one. When I made eye contact again, he was waiting like he expected me to say something brilliant.

"Um, I'm Megan."

"Turner. You been zapped yet?"

"Yeah." I placed my hands on the desktop and leaned forward, lowering my voice. "I have to make something exciting happen today. Any advice?"

"Hmm," Turner said. "Just don't end up like this kid Eldon from the eighth-grade class. His zap was a major fail, and I mean major. Now he's homeschooled."

"What?" I sank in my seat.

"Oh. I mean, I don't think the zap had everything to do with that."

"Maybe I should back out." At least that's what the swirling in my stomach was telling me.

Turner shook his head. "No way. That would be worse than Eldon." He seemed ready to say more, but then a latecomer walked down the aisle and his backpack swayed into Turner's shoulder. "Ow!"

"Sorry, T," the boy said.

"Geez." Turner rubbed his arm and then twitched off a few flexes at his bicep like he needed to test if it still worked. His thin arm made a little muscle bump with each flex. "Okay. Guns are still working. But watch where you're going, dude. You could've messed up my Frisbee-golf arm."

Turner and the boy continued talking, and it seemed like everyone was chatting with somebody— except me. The old me wanted to slouch, but I knew

I wasn't going to win friends looking miserable. All I had to do was say my name, be funny, and be impressive. Easy.

I took a breath, steadied my elbows on the desktop, and shifted to the girls on my right. The one closest to me, a pretty girl with a bundle of colored pencils poking from the side pocket of her backpack, focused on doodling on the cover of her notebook. The other girl flicked soft brown curls from her shoulder, then folded her hands on her desktop. She spoke to me before I even said anything. "I'm Shelby. This is Yoona."

Yoona glanced up from her doodles and smiled.

"Megan." I smiled back and readied one of the funny lines I'd practiced. "Did you know there's—"

"So, Rhena zapped you already, huh?" Shelby said.

"No," I said. "I haven't met Rhe—"

"Hi. Excuse me," someone said, tapping my shoulder.

I turned around and looked up.

The owner of a solar-bright smile stood in front of me, twisting the straightest and shiniest hair I'd ever seen, glossy with shades of brown and cinnamon. The room had gone silent.

"I'll go ahead and finish the zap now." She motioned for me to give her my hand, her silver and stone bracelets clattering.

I must've just stared, because she lifted her eyebrows and added, "I'm Rhena."

Shelby crossed her arms. Other students jumped out of their seats and formed a circle around us. Somebody passed a pen to Rhena like a nurse putting a scalpel into a surgeon's grip. The circle tightened. People leaned in.

"Oh, actually the zap is already done," I said as if it were a chore that had been taken care of for her. I even held out my palm to show the writing.

Someone gasped. Another whispered, "Wait, what? Who then?"

Okay, clearly I'd broken some rule. "Um?" Sweat trickled down my back. "But you can write something, too."

"That's not how it works." All the friendship in Rhena's face twisted into annoyance. Her words came out measured. "It's one. Zap. Per. New person." She closed her eyes and took a breath, rearranging her expression back to neutral. "Who wrote your dare? Was it Ally?"

"Umm." My face must've given the answer.

Rhena narrowed her eyes. "Figures," she said, sauntering back to her second-row desk and tossing a look over her shoulder. "Good luck." Her tone sounded like code for something, but nothing to do with "good" or "luck."

Everyone returned to their seats, talking low and trying not to look at me.

I whispered to Turner, "What just happened?"

He leaned in. "It's basically an unwritten rule. Rhena's in charge of our class zaps, and it's best to stay out of stuff between Rhena and Ally."

"What stuff?"

"For one thing, they're both running for seventh-grade Spirit Captain."

"Okay?"

"No. Not just okay. Spirit Captain is big. Major big. Every class gets one rep, but the seventh-grade class gets to send forth the school Captain, and that's where the real power is at. For a full week, the Captain is in charge of what we wear, what we eat, how we cheer. Shoot, if the Spirit Captain wants us to eat limes for lunch, wear babushkas to gym class, and do down dogs in English, then lime-eating-babushka-wearing down dogs is what'll happen."

"Wow." I laughed. "Really?"

Turner stayed serious. "What the Captain says goes. Period. And the administration completely supports their reign. We even get graded on participation, because the teachers say it educates us about politics." His eyebrows lifted.

"You know." He nodded, urging me to get it. "By making us experience the benefits or consequences of electing leaders."

Ugh. I sighed. I hadn't really noticed the election except for using posters as GPS; I had been so focused on my plan for making friends—a plan I'd just derailed.

Turner shook his head. "Every year it's a competition with Rhena and Ally. Who'll be captain of the swim team? Who'll have the best grades? Now this. I'd just stay out of the middle if I were you."

A little late for that advice.

The door swung open. "We're going to forget the Smart Board presentation," Mr. Kersey said, "and talk about the Temple of Apollo."

I heard none of the lecture, too busy trying to figure out a formula to make this right. Should I tell Rhena I was sorry? That I didn't know the zapping rules? I squirmed, wondering why Ally would put me in this position, but knowing I'd never ask that question. Confrontation wasn't my gig, and *HSMS* strongly advised against it.

Outside, wind and rain whipped against the classroom windows. Even though the air conditioner rattled like it was pumping full blast, I was sure it was broken. The room felt like a sweat lodge, and I would know since Grams had taken Mom and me to one once.

Drips of sweat trailed down my neck. But Rhena, sitting catty-corner in the front, looked absolutely weatherproof—all cool and comfortable with her Oxy-clear skin and flatironing skills. Her blue jean shorts and cute shirt made me rethink my outfit. I'd been going for comfortable with a touch of "Look! I love animals!" Now I wondered if my cargo shorts would've been a better choice for a fishing trip.

Rhena took out a tube of gloss and flipped her smooth hair over a shoulder. I lifted a hand to my head and felt the frizz, wondering how she stayed so put-together like it wasn't a thousand degrees in this room. She opened her gloss, dabbed on a layer of pink shine, and then let it drop to the ground next to her flip-flops. When she leaned down to grab it, she slipped a note to the girl behind her.

The paper changed hands down the row of desks, finally landing one row over in the palm of a boy wearing a Cardinals hat. He unfolded it and I saw "ZAP" written on the top line. My skin prickled. I leaned forward to read more, but the boy caught me and shot a glance my way. I tried to fake like I wasn't creeping in on his note, then changed tactics and zipped on my best I'm-sorry-for-snooping smile. He scrunched his eyebrows and sent a death-ray glare my way, so I tried to look anywhere other than at him. Out the window, at the wall, back at the cat clock.

At this exact moment it clicked to 11:11 and jarred loose a memory of Grams saying a rhyme: "Pop. Click. Seconds tick. Wish at eleven-eleven, and watch it stick."

Grams had acted so strangely the day I'd walked in on her wishing on that clock, and the next day it had been replaced by a cuckoo.

Now I was sitting in a classroom with a clock identical to Grams's, stressing over how I was going to make something EXCITING happen before the end of the day. Not to mention the fact that I was stuck in a power duel between the two most popular girls at my school.

Why not wish? I thought. *It might be my only chance at making a good impression at this school.* I always wished on birthday candles and shooting stars. Eyelashes and dandelions. I even wished with watermelon seeds and green M&M's! Just then my signature snort-laugh slipped out.

Mr. Kersey darted a curious glance my way but continued lecturing.

I slid low in my seat. Still, I kept my gaze on the clock's face. Thirty seconds left. *If I could truly have a wish*, I thought, *it should be for something epic for the zap. Something really good.* Then people wouldn't be annoyed with me for breaking the zapping rules. Girls would pass notes my way; boys would smile instead of shooting me death-ray glares.

Another drop of sweat trailed down my neck, and I'm not lying when I say my brain cells felt fried by the August sun. It was so scorching here that my mind went to thinking a break from the heat would be exciting—and especially exciting for anyone who had lived in the desert their whole life. I squeezed my eyes tight. Thunder clapped, and I silently mouthed, "Pop. Click. Seconds tick. Wish at eleven-eleven, and watch it stick." Then I launched my 11:11 wish at the universe. "I wish it would snow today."

I opened my eyes. A flash of lightning filled the classroom, and I felt a surge of hope. I sat up tall. Middle school, Arizona, this zap—this was my big chance. New school, new opportunities, new me. With a few seconds left on the clock and another crackle of thunder, I added, "And give me some magic, too."

The rain stopped and the classroom was quiet, everyone writing in notebooks. The air conditioner rumbled, churning and chugging out puffs of lukewarm air like it was mocking me for wishing for snow. It was 110 degrees outside, nowhere near the freezing point of water. I leaned my forehead on the back of my hand. What was I going to do by three p.m.? Wishing wasn't going to help with a zap dare.

The teacher's voice registered in my brain. "Megan, are you okay?"

I looked up. Mr. Kersey and twenty-nine students were staring at me—yep, two classes in a row of awkward, gaping attention. "Ahh, yeah, I'm good." I bounced my head up and down for emphasis, a move well played if I was going for the bobblehead look.

"Okay." He patted the air, trying to press down everyone's muffled giggles. "Megan," he said in a confidential tone, which of course made everyone listen extra carefully. "You've got ink on your forehead."

I looked at the back side of my hand. The "ZAP" had smudged thanks to a sweaty forehead, which probably meant I had a twin "ZAP" or "PAZ" or something blue and inky plastered above my eyebrows. *Ugh.* I rubbed it off with my thumb.

"Class," Mr. Kersey announced, "our quiz on Wednesday will cover the chapter on ancient Greece. It will count as five percent of your history grade, so I expect you all to make a positive start to the school year." He looked at me again. "Megan, since you've missed the first two weeks of class, you're not expected to take the quiz unless you feel prepared."

"Excuse me?" Turner raised his hand.

"Yes, Turner?"

"I don't feel prepared. Can I take the test later, too?"

Mr. Kersey exhaled. "You're welcome to come see me during office hours, or you can study with a friend. Which brings me to my next point: it'd be a good idea if everyone could find study partners."

The bell rang and Mr. Kersey plopped a pile of papers onto his desk. "Take a study guide on your way out."

Turner shoved his notebook into his backpack and turned to the guy with the Cardinals hat. "Lunch, dude?"

"Sure," the boy said.

I wondered if I could just turn to one of these girls and make a lunch plan that easily. I looked at Yoona, testing out my best hopeful smile.

Yoona dropped her gaze to her shoes, her licorice-black hair covering her face.

Shelby shook her head. "You made a big mistake on that zap, new girl." She turned to Yoona. "Come on." They gathered their stuff and headed out.

Suddenly, the reality of being saddled with a zap dare hit me hard. I had to make something exciting happen. Today. Or my reputation as a dud would be sealed for the rest of my life.

CHAPTER 4

When the classroom emptied, I headed to my locker, alone. Again.

As I rounded a corner, I nearly bumped smack into a girl carrying an oversized leather messenger bag.

"Ah, good," she said. "I finally found you."

I stopped. "Me?"

The girl unsnapped the bag hanging at her side. She lifted a tan leather flap and the sweet smell of tangerines filled the air. "Yes, you," she said, rummaging inside her bag.

For a half second, I wondered if she was my missing ambassador. Maybe she'd help me with the zap or save me from facing the cafeteria alone. But she looked too old to be a student. And her lens-free glasses, pigtails, and gold nose ring told me she wasn't a teacher, either. "I think you've mistaken me for someone else. The office is just a few doors down. I'm sure they can help you find whoever you need."

Her almond-shaped, green eyes matched the cat's on her T-shirt. "Nope. No mistake. I'm looking for you." She gave me a smile that was probably meant to be reassuring. "Seriously," she said, returning to scrounging through her bag, "I should get organized. Maybe if I arranged things alphabetically, or by location, or by wish."

"Huh?"

Her sentences spilled out in a rush. "Now, let's see. Where is it? It would be tragic if I gave your package to my previous delivery." Her eyebrows popped up. "Can you imagine how horrible that could turn out?"

"I really think you've made a mis—"

"You are Megan Meyers. Right?" She tucked her chin, looking in her bag, both hands now sorting through it.

"Does this have something to do with that zap dare?" I looked around to see if Rhena or Ally was hiding behind a doorway. "Or the Spirit Week elections?"

She giggled and the fluorescent light overhead

flickered. "Nope. At least I don't think so."

My mouth went dry. What was going on?

"Ah, yes." She pulled a thin box from her bag and held it out. It looked like it had been meticulously wrapped in a paper grocery bag and measured a little larger than a spiral notebook. "This is for you."

"Are you sure?"

"Yep. Yep. Yep," she trilled. The light overhead sparked and then hummed.

Again, I glanced both ways down the empty hallway, before looking at the box in her hands. Shiny golden twine wrapped the outside of the package. The folds were perfect on every corner. Everything about it seemed to sparkle, even though the paper wrapping was dirt brown.

She pushed it forward. I took it and the hair on my arms spiked. I swear the package vibrated. "Whoa!" I said, dropping it on the floor. "Sorry." I knelt to pick it up, and as I did, I noticed the glamorous and curlicued writing, like calligraphy on an invitation to an actual ball. And there under elaborate stamps and markings was my name. Miss Megan Meyers.

Who would send me a package? And who would know the name and address of my new school other than my dad?

"Did my dad send this?" I asked.

"Your dad? That would be crazy. He's a bit too scientific for something like this. Am I right?" The girl laughed like we were in on a joke together.

"How did you get my name?"

"From the delivery roster, of course. Oh, and one more thing." She reached back into her bag and whipped out a scroll, adjusted her lens-free glasses, cleared her throat, and began reading. "No returns. No guarantees . . ." Her words flew a hundred miles a minute, like a radio announcer at the end of a used-car ad.

The speeding chatter ended with ". . . does not include tax, title, or license." She shoved a golden fountain pen into my hand. "Please sign here, accepting terms and delivery."

"But—"

"I know you think there's a mistake, but there's no mistake. It's your package. It says so right here. Now, quick quick. I have a full bag and a busy day."

I signed, glancing at the return address. It had been written longhand: *1111 Desear Lane, Pique Z. & Phair. E. Conservatory, When You Wish for Magic We Deliver.*

Maybe it wasn't from Dad after all.

"Who . . ." I looked up, and the girl was gone.

CHAPTER 5

The bathroom reeked of lemon Clorox. I ducked into a stall and sat on the toilet seat lid, backpack squished between my feet and package resting on my lap. I pulled out my phone and thumbed a text to Dad, asking if he'd sent something to me.

Dad: No. Why? And please tell me this is your lunch hour and you're not texting in the middle of class.

Okay, not from him. I picked up the package and examined it more closely. The bottom left corner had something written in elfin-sized print. I leaned in and squinted. It said:

LEGAL NOTICE: UNWRAPPING THIS BINDS YOU TO THE ENCHANTED CONTENTS AND CHARMED OBLIGATIONS. IF YOU CANNOT MAKE SUCH A COMMITMENT, DO NOT PROCEED. DO NOT UNFASTEN A SINGLE PIECE OF TAPE, OR UNTIE THE TWINE. SIMPLY DEPOSIT THE UNDISTURBED PARCEL IN THE NEAREST POSTAL BOX. HOWEVER, IF YOU ARE ALLURED BY THE PROMISE OF MAGIC, AND CHOOSE TO REMOVE THE TAPE AND UNRAVEL THE WRAPPING, UNDERSTAND THAT YOU ARE PLEDGED, AND RESPONSIBILITY WILL REST IN YOUR HANDS TO BE A GOOD CUSTODIAN OF THE MAGIC.

"What the—" The main bathroom door scraped open.

"Do you think he was looking at me?" a girl said.

"Yes. He is so crushing on you," another girl replied.

"Seriously? I hope so. Should we go back and hang out with him or wait till he comes over to us?"

I sat motionless in my stall and tried to make sense of everything. Not whether the guy was crushing on the chatting girl—I mean, science can go only so far in predicting attraction—but enchanted contents? Charmed obligations? Ummm, yes, please. I could absolutely positively use some magical help.

I rested the package on my knee and started tearing open a corner. The girls stopped talking, maybe because all the crinkling noises in my stall made it sound like I was struggling with a giant tampon wrapper. I froze and stayed still until they left, which gave me time to think—*maybe I'd better not open this at school in case it was a prank*. Who gets real magic other than Disney characters?

Still, that delivery girl knew my name *and* she had said "wish"—I did make a wish at 11:11, after all, so that left a few options: either everything was a colossal coincidence or a practical joke, or this package was . . . magical?

The legal notice felt like a big fat warning sign, so I pushed the tape back into place, whipped out my phone, and dialed my grandma—she'd love this. Plus, she'd give me advice without thinking I was nuts—nobody loved talking magic more than her. Voicemail answered on the first ring. "You've reached Esmerelda Meyers. I might be at the top of Kilimanjaro or eating pasta in Pisa, you never know. But if I were you, I wouldn't hold my breath for a return call." *Beeeeep.*

"Grams. It's Megan. I know you're traveling, but please call me as soon as you can."

I stuffed the mystery box with its torn corner inside my backpack and stepped out of the stall to stand in front of the mirror. Not only was there a new zit on my chin, but I was also suffering from a serious case of the frizz. I tried to smooth my hair in place, when my phone rang, blasting the theme song from *Mission: Impossible*. "Grams!"

"How are you, dear?" Static filled the line, then music and laughter.

"I . . ." My mind raced with where to begin.

"Honey," she said, "are you there?"

"I'm here," I answered. "Where are you?"

"Paris, of course!" Her words bounced out like a song, all vibrant and happy. "Just finishing champagne and appetizers on the Seine and then off to a restaurant in Le Marais for dinner."

"Dinner? What time is it there?"

"Around nine. Now tell me. How are you? How is Arizona?"

"Good." I didn't tell her I was camped out in a school bathroom. "Good."

"Megan. Don't play poker. Everyone knows you're fibbing when you go repeating yourself. Give it to me straight. Your voicemail sounded urgent."

Dad would definitely lecture me about a dare, but not Grams, so I unloaded, telling her about my day and how stressed I was about the zap. "This dare could either make or break my reputation. If I get it right, I could have a bunch of new friends. But if I bomb . . ."

I shook my head. "I'll get 'the look' and everyone'll think I'm lame."

"Okay, I'm not sure if I believe that." She laughed. "But go on."

"Anyhow, at eleven-eleven I made a wish like you did that one time. And—"

"What?" She stretched the word apart, her tone tipping to uneasy.

"Umm."

"Sweetie," she said with an odd quiver, "what did you say you did?"

A knot curled in my stomach, and it only now occurred to me that she could be mad I'd messed with that rhyme—the rhyme I'd accidently heard her say in front of her own cat clock. The one she'd told me never to repeat. Still, I needed to push forward if I was going to get answers, so I took a deep breath and kept my voice all faux-carefree. "I made an eleven-eleven wish. And on a clock that looks just like that cat one you had in your kitchen when I was little. Isn't that hysterical, and—"

"You wished on a cat clock!" Her voice rose. "What exactly did the clock look like?"

"Just like yours. It . . ." An ambulance siren blared from somewhere outside the windows and down the street. Layers of alarm crawled up my back. "It had the whiskers to mark the time."

"Three of them?"

"Mmmhmm."

"Was there a star?" she said, now frantic.

I gulped, wondering what was wrong.

"Megan. Was there a star?"

"Yeah? On the tail."

"Oh, Megan!"

"And I said the rhyme," I confessed, wanting it all out. "The one . . . the one you'd never talk about. The one that goes, 'Pop. Click. Seconds—'"

Breaking glass rattled through Grams's side of the phone line. "How in tarnation did you remember that?"

"I don't know. I just did."

"Is Piper with you now?"

"No, but—"

"Good. You cannot tell your sister any of this. Not a thing. She'll be too tempted to use the clock. Okay? And furthermore, everything from here moving forward is for your ears only. Give me your word on that."

I didn't answer right away. I may fib here and there, but Grams and I never broke our promise when we actually said we gave our word. She knew it. And I knew it.

"Megan."

"Okay. All right. You have my word. I won't tell Piper."

"Or anyone."

"Or anyone," I said, and as I agreed it occurred to me that this was special. Just between Grams and me. The apprehension crawling up my spine melted. She had a way of making everything I told her seem important. I smiled. "I love you, Grams."

"That's nice, Megan. I love you, too. But it's time to focus. You've combined a magical cat clock with an eleven-eleven wish, so there's no messing around. Tell me everything—every detail."

My scalp tingled. Grams had just said "magical"— just like the delivery girl and package label—and I hadn't even mentioned the package yet! My heart pumped fast and filled with hope.

"I need to know what you've triggered," Grams said. "So out with it."

"I wished it would snow today." I snort-laughed. "Like there could be a winter wonderland right here at my school in Arizona. Ridiculous, right?" *Please don't say "right."*

"Winter wonderland? Okay. Okay. First wishes are generally free and people make weather wishes all the time for weddings and sporting events and such. No problem. We can deal with that."

"We can?"

She didn't answer. "Was that the whole wish? Is there anything else?"

I crossed my fingers. "I also said, 'Give me some magic'?"

"Oooooooh, Megan." She sighed all dramatic, doom and gloom.

"Come on, Grams," I said with a laugh. "You can't seriously be upset. I saw you wish on your own cat clock and nothing bad happened. And my wish was just for fun. A little wish."

"There's no such thing as little wishes when it comes to that cat clock. Frivolous wishes will cost you, and lazy wishes—mmmhmm, don't get me started." She clucked her tongue. "That's why I took mine out of the kitchen."

The hair on my neck rose. "You really think my wishes are going to come true and my teacher has your cat clock?"

"Of course your teacher doesn't have my clock," she said. "Mine's stored in the attic in a chest and under lock and key. But the clockmakers crafted eleven magical clocks, and this clock sounds the same as mine. It could very well be one of the eleven, which would mean your teacher is the owner of a timepiece crafted by the infamous Bellini brothers."

"Who?"

"Giuseppe and Remy Bellini. Italian clockmakers. People say they dabble in wizardry and have a wicked sense of humor—not a pleasant combination. They like to lure their victims with the promise of magic, only to have high costs attached. You'll get your snow, Megan. I'm not fretting over that. It's the other wish I'm worried about."

The quiver in Grams's voice had disappeared. She was all business now, using her matter-of-fact tone, and it lifted my hope from a simmer to giant bubbles.

The odd delivery and snow-day magic may actually be real and could cinch my future at Saguaro Prep. Or better yet: "Grams, if this is legit, I could wish myself to Europe with you." Pause. "Or I could rewind the clock a few years." I reached into my pocket and felt for my mom's guitar pick, running my thumb across its smooth top.

"Oh, honey." Grams's voice filled with so much love and sorrow it squeezed my heart. "There's no such thing as wishing away the past. Wishing has no power over your mom. It also means moving is a done deal, too. And honey, if you disappeared to Paris, your dad would panic."

The whole time Grams had been talking, the logical side of my brain had been trying to find a numerical explanation to make everything add up. But statistics, science, even the hypergeometric distribution of probabilities couldn't cancel the weight of Grams's words—she was 100 percent certain I'd found something magical, and I was on board. That's the way it was with Grams—and now the more she talked, the more I was convinced I had Italian wizard clockmakers on my side. My heart raced. My smile spread.

"Megan. Are you listening? You could be in trouble."

Yeah, the most exciting trouble ever!

CHAPTER 6

The smell of grilling burgers and french fries filled the cafeteria. Low-set windows lined the walls, and streams of yellow sunlight made the place seem cheery. The food service counter was set up at the entrance. Inside, students gathered at long bench tables in the four quads. Kids from my morning classes sat in the front on the right, so I guessed that's where the seventh graders hung out.

The line inched forward. I grabbed a cold bottle of water and a red apple, scanning the room and hoping to spot a friendly table before my turn at the cash register. The boys behind me laughed and shoved each other.

"You're new, huh?" the first boy said, bumping into

me. I turned around and he pointed at my palm where Ally had written "EXCITING."

"Is that from a zap dare?" the other boy said.

"Um. Yeah." I cleared my throat. "I have to—"

"Excuse me," the first boy said, sounding all concerned. He leaned in confidentially. "Did you know your wenis is showing?"

His buddy did one of those bogus laugh-coughs.

"What?" I faked an itch and wiped at my nose—okay, no danglers.

The first boy leaned closer and whispered, "We can see your wenis."

I yanked up my shorts to make sure they hadn't plunged to plumber depths.

They exploded in laughter. Now others in line were looking at me. Heat blazed from my stomach to my face.

"Go," someone said, pointing.

I spun to face the front and realized I was holding up the line. "I'll have a burger, please," I mumbled to the lady with the hairnet and speed-scanned the tables again. Across the room, a girl from my first-period class caught my eye and smiled, and for half of a half second I had a lunch table to join. But the boys behind me busted out laughing again, and my courage dried up.

"Actually, never mind," I whispered to the lunch

lady, my throat tight. I tossed five dollars toward the cash register, scooped up my water and apple, and bolted for the exit.

"But dear," the lunch lady called, "you forgot your change."

On my dash toward the door I practically plowed into Ally.

"Hey, I've been looking for you," Ally said, plopping a lemon wedge into her drink. "Come on. I'll show you where the seventh graders eat." She grabbed my elbow and directed me toward a long bench table.

I didn't know how I felt about her after she'd put me in the middle of her feud with Rhena, but I followed her anyway.

The wenis boys passed us, mumbling, "I'd cover that up if I were you."

I cringed. If Grams could see me in my new-girl glory, she'd get why I needed magic. She'd probably encourage me to use it.

"Ahhh," Ally said. "I take it Nick and Jason hit you up already?" She hollered across the room to them, "You guys need to grow up. That's so fifth grade." Then she leaned close. "Just so you know, a wenis is the skin under your elbow. They try to embarrass all the new kids with their lameness. I should've warned you."

I let out a breath.

"Come on. This way," she said.

We arrived at a packed table. Ally set down her drink in the center. "Hey, guys. Can you scoot over a little and make room?"

Girls and guys scooted each way and a spot opened. "Here you go." Ally gestured for me to sit next to her. "Megan, this is everybody. Everybody, this is Megan."

I nodded at a sea of smiling faces while my body did its standard large-group reaction—blushing and butterflies. I forced my shoulders to relax and reminded myself that these people didn't know anything about my snort-laughs or how my mouth fires on autopilot when I get nervous. They certainly didn't know about me trying to be a big shot last year during sixth-grade Math Jeopardy—my jokes had been hilarious, my answers had been correct, and I was Miss Popular— or at least I'd thought I was, until Ronald Miller said, "You'd probably have more friends if you didn't talk so much." Then Jerry Plinker laughed, Sanji Bose laughed, and Brooke Sutherland held back a giggle (but not really). I sat super-still, trying not to cry and hoping nobody would notice the burn on my cheeks. When I told Hannah, she said, "Forget those jerks."

But like Grams said, the past was a done deal. That was behind me.

Ice sloshed from Ally's drink to the table as she swept a hand in front of the three girls closest to us, two on their phone and one with a book in front of her nose. "Specifically, this is Noelle, Erin, and Mia."

Noelle set down her phone. Her hand had an intricate geometric pattern drawn across it.

"Nice henna," I said.

"Thanks." She held it out and admired it. "It's a mandala. Took me an hour to do this one."

Mia dog-eared a thin book she was reading called *Metamorphosis*. She set it on top of three other library books, adjusted her tortoiseshell glasses, and said, "Noelle can draw anything. On your birthday, she'll make whatever henna you want. But watch out for Erin." She elbowed the girl next to her. "Erin likes to slam people with her infamous produce slurs."

"Huh?" I said.

Erin laughed. "Don't be an artichoke, Ally." She smiled at me. "Nice to meet you, Megan. I hear you're the zappee."

"Yep," Ally said. "I zapped her, and Megan's going to make something exciting happen today. Right?"

"Uhhh." The butterflies in my stomach doubled and tripled. A minute ago, I'd felt certain about the snow. Now I had a sinking feeling that I needed a plan B. What if that clock wasn't an authentic Bellini clock, or what if Grams was being dramatic? I couldn't bet my future reputation on magic that might or might not be real.

"What's your three p.m. plan?" Erin asked.

"You guys. Stop with all the pressure," Noelle said. "Can't you see you're freaking her out?" She tucked a wisp of her white-blond hair behind an ear. "Sorry. Everybody here gets stupid-crazy about zaps."

"You guys get that many new students?" I asked.

"Not really," Noelle said. "That's why Rhena's going to be ticked when she finds out Ally zapped you."

"Looks like she already knows," Erin said, lifting her chin as Rhena rumbled toward us like a storm rolling in.

"Hi, ladies," Rhena said, a frosty look on her face. Shelby stood to her right, and Yoona shuffled behind them. "Nice to see you, Ally." Sarcasm danced in Rhena's tone. Then she turned to me and plastered on a magnificent smile. For a nanosecond, I thought everything was going to be okay. "Hi, Megan."

"Hi." I held my breath.

She turned to Erin. "Hello, Ellen."

"It's Erin." Erin huffed. "What a crock of cabbage. We've only gone to school together since kindergarten."

"Whatever." Rhena twitched her gaze back to Ally, who stood up.

The buzz in the seventh-grade quad went silent. Even the slurping from straws stopped, and attention sizzled on Ally and Rhena.

Ally broke the quiet. "So. Good luck in the elections on Friday."

"Right," Rhena said. "Well, I just wanted to thank you for taking care of the zap." Her smile and sweet tone didn't match the simmer in her eyes. "Coming up with a creative zap every single time we get a newbie has been such a chore for me, so I appreciate you stepping up and agreeing to take on the challenge for once."

"Agreeing?" Ally scoffed.

"Like I said. So kind of you to do it for me. Especially with the pressure of it all. I mean, everyone here"—Rhena paused and graced a hand and a smile across the crowd as if they were her personal fan club—"everyone here knows I've never ever had a zap go poorly, so your first zap must make you feel a bit trembly, especially right before the election. I sure hope it goes well for you and Megan."

Rhena was like a tropical storm that deserved a ranking on the Saffir-Simpson Hurricane Wind Scale. **Category One. Wind pressure 80 mph. Very Dangerous.**

"Right, you hope it goes well." Ally rolled her eyes. "Trust me, it will. And it's not like you're the boss of zaps."

"Nope. You're in charge of this one. So listen up, people." Rhena turned to the crowd, pausing between sentences to face each and every packed table. "Ally zapped Megan," she said, rotating to face a new direction. "The dare: make something exciting happen today." She turned again. "As you all know, I've never had a zap *not* go perfectly exciting. Now we get to see what happens when Ally's in charge, especially since Megan says she's going to deliver something Coachella-Lollapalooza fabulous right here after school. Right, Megan?" Her smile cranked up the flurry.

Category Two. Wind pressure 100 mph. Very Dangerous.

"Unless you don't have anything planned. Had I zapped you, we'd have the details worked out by now."

I nodded like a moron, making a note to self to Google the Coachella and Lolla thingy. Then I fuzzed out, wondering if I could really pull this off, and if I couldn't, then what?

"Just so you know, Megan," Rhena said, "you're expected to deliver big."

"Colossal," Shelby added.

Storm upgrade:

Category Three. Wind pressure 112 mph. Devastating Damage.

"Exactly," Rhena said. "We wouldn't want to lead up to Spirit Week with something drab."

47

Category Four. Wind pressure 130 mph. Catastrophic.

"Megan's clever," Ally said. "She's got this."

I looked at Ally and took a breath.

"If you weren't over here trying to nose in on our squad goals," Ally said, "we'd probably have it all worked out by now."

"Whatevs," Rhena said. "It's your name, not mine." She turned to me again. "You know Ally's reputation and the election are tied to your zap, right? What *are* you going to do, Megan?"

Alert!

Category Five. Wind pressure 157 mph. Catastrophic Damage and Destruction.

"Calm down. We have it handled." Ally smiled at me.

But with all the hot air swirling around, a word slipped from my mouth.

"What's that?" Rhena said.

"Snow," I repeated, my voice barely audible. "I'll make it snow today."

"What do you mean, snow?" Shelby asked. "As in outside?"

Yoona hugged her doodle-covered notebook.

Ally looked worried. Speechless.

"Umm." I glanced toward the windows. Not a cloud in the sky. The rain was long gone, leaving just a blazing sun. Even the ice that had sloshed from Ally's cup to the center of the table had turned into a puddle.

Then Ally said, "Ohhh." She winked at me. "We wanted to keep it a surprise, and we were just about to work out the details, but we're thinking a snow theme, like a snow cone truck or something, right, Megan? We're calling it Spirit Snow Cones. Or Chill Out."

I couldn't stop my mouth. "Um. Not snow cones." Typical me, nerves power-driving my jaw. "Just snow."

Ally's expression landed somewhere between confused and embarrassed.

Rhena looked toward the bright rays glaring off the windows. "Snow?" Her voice was patronizing. "In Scottsdale, Arizona?"

Even the puddle on the table from the melted ice seemed to jiggle with mocking laughter.

"Well, Ally," Rhena said, "now you get to show everybody what kind of mentor and leader you are." Shrug. "Or aren't. I sure hope you don't disappoint."

I wanted to backpedal, but I'd missed my moment.

Ally dropped her chin and sunk back onto the bench. All I could do was hope that I wouldn't ruin the election for her, not to mention my entire social life.

CHAPTER 7

The only word I wrote in my notebook during my last class of the day was "snow." Snow, snow, snow, snow, snow. Line after line after line. Like that would help. The odds of it snowing today were even worse than the odds of me dying from heat exposure: 1 in 10,784.

The only thing that kept me going was the fact that Grams had never lied to me. But no matter what power she claimed for her own clock, she didn't actually know if the clock in the history classroom was made by those Bellini brothers. I looked at the timer on my phone and gulped—I'd find out in exactly 3,480 seconds, aka fifty-eight minutes, every one of them grueling.

I was sitting in English class, watching a film version of *Macbeth* with the blinds closed, my heart flopping around in the pit of my stomach. As the minutes inched along, the room felt cooler and cooler. Maybe the air-conditioning had finally kicked on, or maybe—

The bell rang, crackling my nerves. The moment of truth. I shoved my notebook inside my backpack. *Please, God. Please.* Even before the lights flipped on, I rushed out the door and raced toward the end of the hall, past high windows where I could see the sun hovering bright in the sky. *That's okay,* I told myself. Sunshine didn't have to mean a snowless ground. There were plenty of days in Colorado when it was both sunny and snowy.

At the end of the hall, I flung open the school door. The wall of heat smacked the breath out of my chest. And there, the dried yellow grass at the end of the walkway sat snow-free, portending my social suicide. I sunk down on a bench. Students blurred past.

Utter failure. I'd be Motormouth Megan again. The girl who talked too much and delivered zilch.

"You Megan Meyers?"

I looked up. A beefy man in a dark blue mechanic's uniform stood in front of me. His sewn-on name tag read "Bruce" and his eyes were as green as the delivery girl's.

"Yeah?"

"I'm Bruce," he said. "From Backyard Blizzards. Right this way, miss."

I stood up. "Uhh?"

"Megan!" My name erupted from voices behind Bruce. "Megan!" Ally, Mia, and Noelle ran to my side and words flew at me, about a hundred miles a minute.

"I . . . wha . . ." They grabbed me by the elbows, pulling me along and saying stuff like "awesome" and "never seen before" and "whiteout." Bruce turned left at the end of the front walk. We followed to the back side of the school, where squeals and happy screams rang through the air.

And the ground. It was like my magical Colorado fairy godmother had waved an enchanted wand and created the most perfect sparkly scene. In defiance of the 110-degree heat, the back lawn of Saguaro Prep sat coated in brilliant, white, fluffy snow. Snow!

"I can't believe you managed this!" Ally said. "I'm sorry I doubted you. But I mean, how in the heck? Do you have a wealthy grandparent or something?"

I must've nodded, because Ally said, "Lucky!"

A boy from my history class, the one wearing the Cardinals hat, ran up to me. "Megan!"

"Yeah?"

He lifted me in the air and twirled me in a circle.

"Thanks! This is awesome! You're awesome!"

Ally and Noelle laughed. He set me down and ran over to Turner, who said, "Dude, we can do a sledding Frisbee toss!"

"Anything else you need?" Bruce asked. "We aim to please."

Five trucks labeled Backyard Blizzards spurted out the stuff, and from the looks of things, they'd been at it for hours.

"Everything's . . . perfect," I said, my voice catching in my throat.

"It really is!" Noelle said.

"I know, right?" Ally agreed. "You've got everything. A sledding hill." She gestured toward a small hill where workers dressed like Bruce handed each student a plastic red sled. "Snowmen-building competition. Snowball fights."

"Hot chocolate with giant marshmallows," Mia said, holding up a cup.

"Even free gloves!" Noelle said.

"Definitely the most exciting thing that's *ever* happened at this school," Ally said.

I caught sight of Piper across the white lawn and smiled. She was laughing and building a snowman with another girl. The last snowman we had built had been with Mom.

"Well, well, well," Rhena said, striding up with Shelby, Yoona, and a few other girls. "You made this happen?"

"Mmmhmm." I nodded, crossing and then uncrossing my arms.

"Nice." Skepticism edged Rhena's tone. "But there's something I'm not getting about you. Am I right?"

"Whatever, Rhena," Ally said. "Just admit it. Megan nailed the zap dare."

Ally smiled but Rhena kept staring at me, like she was trying to see under my skin. I don't know why it made me nervous; it wasn't like she could know about the wish.

Could she?

"Come on, let's be honest." Ally flung an arm across my shoulder. "Megan is uber-creative. Probably the most creative girl at this school. This is better than anything you or I could've managed."

Noelle and Mia smiled at me.

"The snow is good." Rhena shrugged and talked to Ally like I wasn't even there. "But the most creative? Maybe Megan's just a one-hit wonder."

"You've got to be kidding. Look at what she's pulled off." Ally turned to me. "Tell her you're not a one-and-doner, Megan."

This would've been an ideal time for me to clam

up, but no; I'm Megan Meyers, Motormouth, Rambling Rookie, Yak-Attack. And so I said, "Ahhh . . . one-hit wonder? Ha!" The "ha" banged out too loudly, but I blitzed on. "Yeah. You should've seen me at my last school. I was *always* making fun stuff happen." What a fat lie, but I had to impress, right? Sure, some articles on *HSMS* had said I should be myself, but that hadn't worked out for me in sixth grade.

"Like what?" Rhena asked.

"What?" I stammered, all deer-in-headlights.

Rhena crossed her arms. "What fun stuff did you make happen at your last school?"

"Well . . ." Throat clear. "Once, I got lunch extended by ten minutes."

"Wow. So exciting," Rhena deadpanned.

"Ummm . . . and this one time, I turned the class into a game show."

Rhena twisted her mouth to one side.

Ally nodded. "That sounds fun."

"And . . . and . . ." I swallowed a gulp the size of a Chihuahua. What else could I say?

"Well?" Rhena said.

Ally smiled and put a hand on my shoulder. "You don't owe Rhena your résumé. You've obviously had plenty of practice creating exciting events."

Ally believed in me. She trusted I was all kinds of

interesting. But Rhena narrowed her eyes. *HSMS* had said to impress, so maybe if I made up something good enough to impress Rhena, this inquisition would be over. Who would it hurt if I lied?

"And another time"—I cleared my throat—"another time I did this covert scavenger hunt at my school." That whopper made Rhena's eyebrows lift, so with a little more confidence I said, "It was huge. Like ten-to-the-tenth huge. A blast. Everyone called me the Fun-meister." *Ugh*. I needed to stop before this turned dorkier.

"Really?" Ally asked, her face bright. "That sounds super-fun."

I nodded.

"Hmm." Rhena looked me up and down. Impressed? Skeptical?

Everyone stared at me like I really could be known as the Fun-meister. Turner ran over holding up bright red gloves. "Look what they gave me for free!"

Mia held up her hot chocolate again. "She's thought of everything."

"They called her the Fun-meister at her last school," a boy said to Turner. The girl next to him nodded.

I felt weightless. Floaty. Joyful. Across the snow, a girl from my Spanish class waved, and I gave her a full arm wave back.

Ally was amped, talking fast. ". . . and we've never done anything that interesting to kick off Spirit Week. Could you do one here?"

My body stiffened.

Rhena raised an eyebrow.

"Huh?"

"A scavenger hunt? Or some big event like that?" Ally asked.

"Um." Swallow. "Sure?" I said, my voice too high. I cleared my throat. "Sure. Of course."

"Not a scavenger hunt. I'm doing that at the mall on my birthday," Rhena said. "But something. I'm sure you have plenty of ideas, since you're the 'Fun-meister.'" She added air quotes.

"Sure. Okay." My voice squeaked.

"How about on Friday?" Ally asked, all animated and hopeful. "Can you do something for the Spirit Week election?"

"That would be perfect," Noelle agreed. "You could do a big event, then everyone votes for the Spirit Week Captain at lunchtime, and then the principal will announce the winner."

"And then"—Rhena placed her hands on her heart—"I will make the speech to reveal my themes for next week."

"Or I will," Ally said.

This felt like dividing by zero. A no-sum game.

I stared blankly, wondering how to backpedal, but Noelle must've thought I was wondering about Spirit Week, so she continued.

"The themes aren't announced with the campaign," Noelle said. "We have to wait until we get our winner. Mr. Scoggins says he doesn't want it to be a popularity contest. He wants us to vote simply based on character and leadership skills."

"TBH, the themes are the best part," Ally said. "Every day we dress up and show school spirit. Like last year we had Mardi Gras Monday and we wore beads, and face paint, and feathers and stuff. And then for Tie-Dye Tuesday we all made shirts, and—"

"Yeah, yeah, yeah," Rhena said. "Can you do something for the election or not?" Her eyebrow arched to maximum doubt.

I nodded, feeling sick. Words squeezed from my throat. "Of course."

Rhena made one of those laughing *harrumph* sounds and said, "We'll see." Then she marched off with her crew.

Snowballs flew and screams and cheers echoed from every direction.

Ally patted my back and said, "Number one rule here, ignore Rhena's snarkitude. You've got this,

Megan. I can tell you're full of surprises."

Maybe Ally was right. Maybe I had this in the bag. My first wish had come true. The snow party was even better than I'd asked for, so the second wish would have to be just as good or even exponentially better!

Erin ran over. "Why are we sitting here like a bunch of grapes? Let's go build a snowman."

I started to follow when the smell of tangerines hit my nose and the green-eyed delivery girl sidled up next to me.

"Hey," she said, checking something off the list on her clipboard. "The snow turned out great, so wish one complete. Now wait till you see what's in the box for wish number two."

CHAPTER 8

On my way down the sidewalk toward the Humane Society, I texted Grams about the snow. Her reply came right away.

Grams: Glad it was fun! Now be on alert and put a stop to anything out of the ordinary before that second part of your wish is granted, the "give me some magic."

The green-eyed delivery girl was 100 percent out of the ordinary. I should've mentioned her to Grams. But I didn't, because the way Grams was talking, I knew she'd make me throw away the package, and that was a hard no. Why would I cancel magic when I'd pay any price to make middle school easier?

Still, I'm not going to lie, Grams's warnings and that caution label on the mysterious box made me hesitate. I left the package tucked in my backpack and planned to do a cost-risk analysis at home before I opened it.

I texted back:

Me: OK! On red alert, Grams.

When I arrived at the Humane Society, the gray-haired lady at the front desk was talking on the phone. Her name tag read "Mavis." She glanced up and smiled, and I was happy to wait. It gave me time to casually look around for Mystery Guy.

Mystery Guy had been at the Scottsdale Humane Society on Saturday, when the place was in chaos— cats had been let loose in the rabbit sanctuary, and they were sprinting after the bunnies. The poor, wild-eyed rabbits bounced in every direction. Naturally, I jumped in and helped gather up the cats. That's when I saw mystery guy, the cutest boy I'd ever seen in real life, wrangling bunnies in the middle of the mayhem.

Our gaze connected, his eyes light brown with flecks of gold and hair messy in just the right way. He smiled at me, and a dimple appeared, making my knees actually wobble. Then we got propelled in separate directions. After it was over, he had been whisked off to first aid to have his scratches cleaned up, and I had been thanked and asked to please just come back Monday.

"May I help you?" Mavis said, hanging up the phone.

"Hi. I'm Megan Meyers. I stopped by on Saturday to check out volunteer opportunities, and the personnel coordinator asked me to swing by after school today. Can you direct me to her office?" I smiled. "She said she needed to take a photo for my name badge."

"Sure, honey." She lifted a penciled-in eyebrow. "Saturday, huh? Were you here when those doorknobs snuck cats into our rabbit sanctuary?"

"Oh my gosh, yes. Did you guys catch who did it?"

"No. But I'd like to ring their bell." She held up a blue-veined fist.

I smiled. "Me too."

Mavis directed me to human resources, and on my way, I looked around, still hoping I'd spot my mystery guy.

The director gave me the orientation schedule, details about volunteer opportunities, and papers for my dad to sign.

Afterward, I walked home, photo done. Schedule

in backpack. Cute-boy sighting a bust.

At home, Archimedes swished through the kitchen doggie door and ran to me. Dad says Archimedes is a mutt, but I think he's a Schnocker—a mix between a schnauzer and a cocker spaniel. Mom used to say the lighter fur around his mouth and nose looked like a mustache. She called him Theodore Roosevelt's twin. Then Dad would argue that he looked more like Einstein. I didn't care. He was mine and loyal to me no matter who he looked like.

"Hey, Archie." I sat on the tile floor, and he rolled to his back, ready for his belly rub. "Good boy. Did you miss me today?"

He panted and stared at me like I was the most important person in the world.

"Aww, I missed you, too." I got up and refilled his water and food bowls. He followed me and rolled to his back again. My backpack beckoned, but I said, "One more rub, Archie, then I have to get down to business." I gave his freckled belly a good scrubbing and then plopped my backpack on the kitchen counter and yanked out the mystery box. Archie rubbed against my legs, but I stayed focused on the package, half expecting it to burst into flames. The clock had delivered snow in Arizona, and the possibilities for the second part of my wish—"give me some magic"—felt limitless . . . and scary.

I did the mental math: factoring in the snow (a positive), Grams's warning (a negative), the package label (another negative), and the delivery girl (neutral), there was an 82 percent chance of an unfavorable outcome.

But then I recalculated, considering the cost-risk analysis. It was as simple as zero times zero equals zero. Zero risk multiplied by zero benefits would equal the same old me. But a simple wish multiplied by a little effort could equal infinity.

My hands shook. I turned the box, feeling its weight. Grams's words spun in my head—*Nothing in life is free, including wishes.*

But school had costs, too. Big ones. And middle school had its own set of rules. I should've asked questions when I was zapped, but since I didn't, I'd ended up stuck in the middle of something between Rhena and Ally. Ally seemed super-nice—even though I didn't like that she'd stuck me in the center of her feud, she'd also included me in lunch. And as for Rhena—I didn't want her kind of attention. Maybe I could use the magic to get out of the middle of their rift.

I took a breath and cracked my knuckles, hands shaking. I tugged at the twine. It wouldn't budge. I opened and slammed kitchen drawers, looking for scissors. No luck. I gave the twine another hard tug. It held fast.

The front door whooshed open, making me jump. Archie took off to the sound of Piper's voice.

What was Piper doing home? She'd texted me that after sledding she was going to a yearbook club meeting, so why was she back so soon? I set the box aside and headed to the front door to see if she was okay.

Piper glowed as usual. She and a girl sat on the slate floor in the foyer, yanking off their shoes. The hand-drawn star on the girl's sneakers told me Piper had met a fashion-lovin' soul mate.

"Hey, Pipes. Everything okay with yearbook club?"

Archie licked Piper's face as she struggled to remove her Converse. Not the regular-folk Converse, of course, but custom ones she had designed on the internet. They were Hubba Bubba pink with blue crystals on the tongue and stars. The laces were white silk ribbons decorated with super-tiny pink polka dots.

"Yep. It wasn't really a meeting. Just a quick sign-up. We'll have an official meeting tomorrow. I wish you'd come—we're getting matched with middle school buddies and you could be mine if you join." She beamed. "And can you believe the snow today? That was amazing." Piper smiled. "This place is awesome. Everyone says the Scottsdale Fashion Square Mall is a quick bus ride from our school. And all the clubs sound like a blast. My homeroom teacher, Miss Powers, is the yearbook club's adviser. And she asked if I'd help with Reading Buddies in the younger grades. Oh, and she's getting married next year, and she has the prettiest hair and wore the cutest jeans ever. Didn't you think so, Barett?"

Barett yanked off one of her shoes.

"Oh, Megan, this is Barett. Her mom drove us home." My sister didn't stop until she ran out of breath—classic Piper.

Barett, practically Piper's twin with her honey-blond hair and genuine smile, dropped her shoes beside Piper's. "Wait. *You're* the older sister?" She tilted her head sideways, as if Piper was trying to pull a fast one.

Annoying.

But I couldn't blame Barett for wondering. My "little" sister already had an inch on me.

"Yup," I answered. "Piper, do you know where I can find scissors?"

"I think I saw them in the dining room." Piper grabbed Barett's hand and headed upstairs. "Come on, Archie," she called.

He glanced at me.

"Go on," I said, and he trotted up behind Piper and her new BFF.

I marched back to the kitchen, snatched up the box, and took it into the dining room. I deserved good things, too.

Large moving boxes labeled "china" were stacked in the corner. Scissors sat on top. I plucked them up and set the package on the table, looking again at the wrapping and words—shimmery twine and beautiful script. I considered Grams's warning one final time. But this package, warning or not, made me feel like things could be easy for me, just like they were for Piper, if I embraced the magic.

"I'm game," I said out loud. "I've already moved. I'm already the new girl. I've already made more promises. What's the worst thing that could possibly happen if I use *some* magic?"

I pulled on the twine, lifting it so I could slip the scissors underneath, but it was like my words had done an *alakazam* on the ties, because this time they easily slid apart. Brown wrapping fell aside, revealing a shiny red box. The room felt static-filled. My pulse quickened. I lifted the lid, pushed aside purple tissue paper, and removed the contents.

All I had in my hands was a magazine.

I dropped it on the table. All this buildup for a magazine? I'd been duped. Like Grams said, the clock-makers were tricksters. They'd gotten my hopes up for nothing.

I picked up the magazine, ready to chuck it into the garbage. Then it quivered! Goose bumps traveled up my arms and my eardrums buzzed. With shaky hands I peeled back the cover and a handwritten note fluttered out:

Hi, Megan! Thank you for choosing Pique Z. & Phair. E. Conservatory as your 11:11 wishing resource.

If you've got a dilemma, we've got your back . . . Mean girls? No prob. Beauty help? Yup! Wardrobe? Duh!! Just ask.

You've heard of genie in a bottle . . . well, that's old-school. We're your concierge-pixie in a book (or magazine, but let's not mince words when there's important magic at hand). As long as you find the problem in these pages, you're covered. You've signed the scroll, so let's get started!

I looked at the magazine's name—*Enchanted Teen*. And the line under the title read: "For girls who need *some* magic."

CHAPTER 9

I ran to my bedroom and hopped on the bed, sending blue and green pillows tumbling. Still clutching the magazine in one hand, I clamped the other over my mouth and held down a squeal. *Can this be real?*

Music and the sounds of Piper's and Barett's giggles filtered through the bedroom wall. I unclenched my death grip and stared at *Enchanted Teen*. It had a picture of Hollywood's rising teen star, Marlo Bee, plastered across the cover, and a yellow blurb that read, "Find Your Five Best Looks."

I flipped to the index on the first page: Fashion Advice, Dating Dos and Don'ts, Hair + Skin +

Makeup, Fun Stuff, Health + Fitness. One heading asked in green bubble letters, "Do You Have the Best Back-to-School Style?" The next read, "Are Your Lips Kiss-tastic?" It seemed like any other magazine until I turned the page.

Surgeon General's Warning: This publication is potent and meant to be enjoyed like a rich dessert. Small tastes are luxuriant and rewarding, but too much in one sitting can leave you feeling nauseous. No binge browsing, please. If you experience dizziness, headache, sweating, or vomiting, close the pages immediately. If symptoms continue, drink sweet peppermint tea and read a few pages of a novel. Normalcy should return within an hour.

Hmm. Maybe this was the cost Grams had warned me about—nausea, headaches. Big whoop. All I had to do was be careful about how much I looked at the magazine. Done. Now, show me the magic!

I turned each page carefully, then stopped at a photo of a teen model done up with purple pigtails and dressed like a waitress at a fifties diner. Her name tag read "Mac" and the photo showed her roller-skating down a school hallway, getting pulled by cats. She clutched their leashes in one hand and held a sign in the other. It read: "Imperfection is beauty, madness is genius, and it's better to be absolutely ridiculous than absolutely boring—Marilyn Monroe."

"Sure." I grunted. "Doesn't ridiculous equal embarrassing?"

Currents zipped up my arm. "Ouch!" I rubbed my skin. "What the— I'm just saying who wants to be ridicu—"

"Owww!" Another shock wave rippled through my arm, making me drop the magazine to the bed. My heart thudded. "Wow. Whoa." With the caution I'd use to approach a skittish dog, I gently reached for the magazine, ripped out the picture of the model with the Marilyn quote, and tacked it to my wall. "Good?" I looked at *Enchanted Teen* and waited for some sort of sign.

Nothing.

I took a few breaths, working up the nerve to pick up the magazine again. "Okay," I said in my soothing dog-whisperer voice. "Be nice, please." With two fingers, I plucked it up. No shocks this time. I let out a breath and plopped back onto the bed, flipping pages with shaky hands. After a few more page turns, I came to another picture of the same model. This time, her eyes were painted like butterfly wings, and she was dressed in layer after layer of purple, pink, and blue sheer wispy fabric with a set of wings on her back. Her warm brown skin shimmered with glitter, and she posed like she might take off. I looked at her eyes.

And she winked.

I squinted and blinked. Was it a holograph? Could I make her wink again? I flipped the page back and forth but nothing happened.

"Okay?" I said to the picture. "You're giving me a message. Right? With the Marilyn quote and the butterfly wings? Snow was ridiculous, but that turned out great, right?"

No response.

"Are . . . are you showing me magic?" I asked.

Again, nothing.

I ran my fingers over her fancy eye makeup. The page sparkled and glowed like I'd plugged in a string of LED lights. I pulled my hand back and the lights faded. I touched her butterfly eyes again and this time felt drawn in, like I was being sucked right into the page. My skin rippled and my vision went hazy, then purple, pink, and gold colors swirled in front of my eyes. Sounds melted away like I'd dived underwater. My finger felt glued to the picture, but when my head went dizzy, I yanked my hand back.

A clammy layer of sweat washed over my chest. Wow. Magical-ish.

But shiny lights weren't going to help with a new school. I sighed. The sides of my head started to hurt.

Headache. Sweating. Next could be nausea. According to the Pixie General or whatever, it was time to stop looking at the magazine. I snapped the pages shut. My eyes itched. Sound resurfaced, and I realized my phone had been ringing. I looked at the caller ID and snatched it up. "Hannah!"

"What's up, Megs?" she said.

"Magic" was on the tip of my tongue, but I had to hold it in. Hannah and I had told each other every secret we'd ever had since kindergarten. She told me about her fifty million crushes, and I told her whenever I faked sick to get out of stuff. Stuff like backing out of our sixth-grade play because after the Math Jeopardy failure I'd overheard Ronald Miller and Brooke Sutherland laughing about how dumb I sounded when I practiced my lines. Hannah said I didn't sound dumb, but that's what best friends are supposed to say. It was my middle school heads-up not to draw too much attention to myself.

I had tried. But it didn't matter. After the first month of sixth grade, the judgy looks had spread like a pandemic, and somehow every student had earned an unofficial label—the athletes, the computer whizzes, the choir kids, and the dorkjobs. Hannah had become popular, and no matter what anyone said, she'd made sure I was included in stuff with her. Whenever I snort-laughed, she'd laugh harder. Whenever I acted like a dorkjob in front of a group and then apologized, assuming I'd embarrassed her, Hannah would put an arm over my shoulder and tell me she wasn't embarrassed, not even a little bit.

Now I had the biggest good news of my life: I'd found a magical wishing clock, I was going to reinvent myself, I was going to be impressive—at least I hoped I would. But I couldn't tell Hannah a thing. I'd given my word to Grams.

The magazine lit up and flopped. I smacked a shaky hand on the cover and held it down till it stopped moving.

Hannah continued talking a million miles a minute, telling me about her day and asking about Saguaro Prep and the people I'd met.

"Can you believe I've already made a few friends, sort of?"

"Yes," she said, as in *duhhh*. "You were the only one who worried you couldn't do it. Are you using that three-step plan of yours? What was it? Be friendly, make 'em laugh, be impressive?"

"Yep." It had actually turned into "lie if you need to" and "get yourself into a big jam." Ugh. Hannah never minded when I dorked out. But she hated— *hated*—when I lied.

I went on telling her about Saguaro Prep and Arizona. "And of course, Piper already brought home a new friend."

"That's good. I still don't think you need that checklist." Hannah rambled off her usual comments about being myself. "Hey, my mom told me your grandmother is on another one of her adventures."

Hannah's mom was Grams's travel agent.

"Yep," I said. "Paris this time."

"I wish that were us. I hear tomorrow she flies to Avignon for a bike tour called Seniors in Provence. How about Teens in Provence? Wouldn't that be fun?"

"Bike tour?" A wave of panic swam over me. What if I needed to ask questions? "You think she'll turn off her phone?"

"I don't—"

"Oh, geez. I hope it's not going to be like when she went to Machu Picchu. Phones still work in Provence, right?"

"Probably. Why?"

I rubbed the back of my neck. "You know, this move and all. I'll want to talk to her."

Hannah and I chatted for a little longer until I could hear her mom calling her in the background. "Gotta go, M. Love you."

"Love you, too." When I clicked end, a group text

popped up from a number with an Arizona area code.

Pizza and study party, tomorrow nite 6:30 pm
4142 e. becker lane. xoxo Rhena

An invitation! From Rhena? She must've gotten my phone number from the student office helper. Still, that didn't make sense. Rhena was annoyed with me about the zap. Now she was inviting me to her house?

Maybe I didn't just get a magazine; maybe magic had helped me land this invitation, too.

There was a knock at my door. I yanked out homework papers from my backpack and threw them on top of the magazine. "Come in."

Piper sprang into my room. "Hey, I'm going—whoa. How did you do that?"

"Huh?"

"Your makeup. It's awesome. Look, Barett."

Barett poked her head in the doorway. "Wow! Will you do me up like that one day?"

"Yeah. Both of us," Piper said.

"Ummm." I'd barely worn anything, a little pinkish-gold shadow on my lids. The rest of my makeup was in an unpacked box in my closet—new and still in its packaging. I scratched at my eyebrow.

"Ack! Don't mess it up," Piper said.

I stopped mid-scratch. Why was she being so weird?

"So listen. I called Dad and he said it was okay that I go to Barett's house for dinner. Unless you want me to stay?"

"That's okay. Thanks, though."

"All right. Later," Piper said. "But will you make sure Dad has something healthy to eat?"

"I always do."

"Later," Barett said.

The door closed and I went straight to the Jack-and-Jill bathroom I shared with Piper. "Aieeeeeeee!" I screamed at my reflection. "What the what?" I leaned close and touched my face. Somehow my makeup was identical to the model's in the magazine. Smoky eyes and then shades of purple, blue, green, brown, and gold dotted and lined my face from cheekbone to eyebrows.

Science could explain man-made snow, and there could be a rational explanation for the delivery girl finding me and giving me a package addressed in my name. But nothing in real life could explain how I suddenly had runway-esque butterfly eyes drawn on my face.

I was dealing with real magic. And that meant anything was possible.

CHAPTER 10

I took Archie on a long walk. Afterward, I made a spinach and kale salad for Dad and covered it with plastic wrap. For me, I did as the magazine had instructed and brewed a pot of peppermint tea. I also cooked a package of organic mac and cheese, dancing from sink, to stove, to refrigerator. I had magic. Endless possibilities. Middle school survival!

I still wasn't sure how the magazine worked, but the snow from the wishing clock had been perfect, and it was something I'd specifically asked for. So maybe that was the ticket: stick with specific wishes to get what I want—easy. The hard part was figuring out what specifically to wish for next.

If I wished to fit in, would the magic be literal, making me fat, skinny, or angular so that I'd fit into the precise space in a room? Or maybe the magic would work like a radio in my ear, telling me what to say and how to act. That'd be freaky. Or what if it helped me fit in with fringe groups, like suddenly I fit in with adrenaline junkies, and the next thing you know I'm skydiving or streaking at a football game? Ahk!

I filled a bowl with noodles and forced myself to calm down and settle on a stool. Archie curled up at my feet and snored while I read several pages from *Macbeth*. My English teacher said she'd planned the film and the reading to go with the election since it was all politicians and power goals.

The front door creaked open and Dad walked into the kitchen.

I prepared myself to talk about homework, or Saguaro Prep's science lab, or algebra, or whatever school question Dad would ask.

"How's my favorite oldest daughter?" he said, giving me a goofy look.

Huh? I had washed off the makeup, but the way he stared at me made me wonder if I'd missed a spot. "Um, fine?" I scooped up a bite of noodles.

Dad's wrinkled blue shirt had seen better days and his blond/gray hair looked as frizzy as mine. Piper had worn the same shade of blue today, and I couldn't help but think how she was turning into the spitting image of Dad (minus the frizz), but her personality was everything I remembered of Mom—bubbles, and frosting, and music; whereas I looked like Mom (except for Dad's frizz, thank you very much), I was Dad through and through—equations, and science, and snort-laughs.

He picked up the pen and the permission forms from the Humane Society that I'd left on the counter. "Here we go," he said, signing. "Says here orientation for new volunteers is after school tomorrow."

"I know." I smiled. "Thanks."

He poured a glass of water and took a long swig. "Piper called and told me she was having dinner with a new friend. How about your little sister? Her first day at a new school and she's already at a friend's house."

"Mmmmhmmm." Big surprise.

"So it's just you and me, kiddo." "Kiddo" fell from his mouth all awkward, like someone testing a foreign language. "Did you get enough to eat? I could cook something more." He swung open the refrigerator door, staring at the mostly empty space.

"I'm good. I made your salad. It's in the crisper drawer."

"Food police put you up to that?"

"Yep." I smiled. "She did."

"Thanks. I'll eat later." He shut the door. "If you've finished your homework, we could play cards. Or even . . . Monopoly?"

I teetered. Monopoly? That was a blast from the past. Something we did with Mom. A lump lodged in my throat and I managed to say, "Okay?" I stared at the bottom of my noodle bowl and hoped he'd say more, like how funny it was when Mom cooked, because she'd leave every kitchen cabinet open, or how Mom was the only one who could get Archie to dance for treats, or how he missed the smell of Mom's cinnamon perfume.

"Or maybe," Dad said as he raked a hand through his hair, "instead of Monopoly you'd like to . . . talk?"

My eyebrows lifted.

"Your grandma says we should talk more."

My spoon dropped. "You spoke to Grams today?"

"No. Not today. It's just lately she's been telling me she thinks you and I don't talk about what's important. And I'm wondering if we should talk about this move."

This wasn't a Mom conversation after all. I reached into my pocket and squeezed Mom's guitar pick. Dad wouldn't talk about her. But he was acting totally awkward, and I wondered if she was on his mind, too.

Mom had taught music at the elementary school—she could sing and play four different instruments, but she loved the acoustic guitar most, and Saturday mornings in our house had been the best place in the world—Mom singing and strumming old songs like "Banana Pancakes," "Better Together," or "If I Had a Million Dollars" and the rest of us humming and laughing as we went about our chores. Sometimes Piper would take out her guitar and play along, and then Dad and I'd kick back on the couch, singing off tune with Archie in my lap. Then we'd stop trying to sing and just listen to Mom and Piper play, me resting my head against Dad's shoulder and Dad saying how lucky we were to have front-row seats.

Since the accident, Dad had packed away everything of Mom's—her clothing, her cinnamon perfumes, and her guitar. Two weeks after the funeral, I lay on Piper's bed and asked her to play one of Mom's songs, and next thing we knew Archie was howling—Dad was having a heart attack. Doctors said it was an arterial blockage, but Piper and I were sure it was grief. It seemed like Dad's grief lightened if we acted like those Saturdays had never happened, so Piper stopped playing music altogether, and we erased Mom's name from conversations, like we could stop the sadness if we didn't talk about her—I came to think of it as a game we played to protect each other. And Piper—who's usually the most honest person I know—played the game with gusto. She never opened her guitar case again, and she never mentioned Mom except in the middle of the night.

Secretly, though, I kept a jar full of Mom's guitar picks hidden in the back of my closet.

"Megan." Dad cleared his throat, returning to his professor's voice. "I know moving is tough, but this job at the university has been in the works for quite some time." He settled his gaze on my shoulder.

I walked to the sink and sponged my bowl clean. "I know, Dad."

"And your mother . . ."

I sucked a long inhale—the weight of missing her pressed into my chest. I held my breath and stared holes through the sink basin. And even though Dad was standing right here, I missed him, too.

"She and I . . . when she was alive . . ." His voice hitched.

I looked over. Dad gazed at his hands, twisting the wedding ring he still wore. A burn hovered behind my eyes, but then Dad scrubbed a hand across his chin and cleared his throat, turning himself back into the man who'd earned a doctorate in engineering. "We'd always planned to live in Arizona. I'm sure you'll come to like it here, too. And—"

"It's fine. Honestly." I faced the sink and flicked on the garbage disposal before I sniffled.

"I just want you to know I realize how hard all of these transitions must be for you." He put his glass in the dishwasher and patted Archie on the head. "I know this is awkward. Sorry, Megs."

I turned off the garbage disposal and nodded. Awkward. How did losing Mom somehow get reduced to that?

Dad walked out of the kitchen, his shoulders sagging.

Thinking about magic was so much easier than this, so I added sugar and ice to the peppermint tea, poured myself a glass, and headed back to my room with a to-do list in mind.

Goal *numero uno*: find out how the magazine magic works.

Goal *numero dos*: figure out what to wish for next.

Archie bounced into my room as I was setting my full glass of tea on the desktop. My arm wobbled just a bit, and a tiny splash of tea jumped from my glass onto an open page of the *Enchanted Teen*. Just like that, the magazine slammed shut.

"Whoa!"

I stood still for a moment and then clicked the bedroom door shut. Archie whined. I petted his sweet face until he rested his head on his paws. "You think magic will help me?" I searched his eyes. "Archimedes, you know you're named after one of the greatest mathematicians of all time." I sighed. "He'd think I'm nuts, wouldn't he?"

Archie yawned.

I went back to my desk and picked up *Enchanted Teen*, the self-proclaimed authority on clothing, hair, and life's dos and don'ts. I'd just spent a day sporting frizzy hair, a faded T-shirt, and shorts with more pockets than the combined total of pockets in the school; *maybe that's why I got this magazine—it thinks I'm a makeover emergency.*

Okay, goal *numero tres*: get style help.

I hopped onto my bed, talking to the magazine. "You claim you can help me. Let's do it."

The pages pushed themselves open, and Archie backed away, letting out a low, rumbly growl.

Enchanted Teen flipped to a spread of Milan Fashion Week. The first photo was of models on a runway decked out in see-through shirts, odd-looking drop-crotch pants, and crazy puffed-out forms that were probably meant to be dresses. More photos showed models dressed in orange bodysuits that zipped from neck to ankle; others wore leather jackets with black-lace swimsuit bottoms—I snort-laughed.

85

"Who wears stuff like that other than ice skaters and rock stars?"

I thumbed forward until I got to a clump of pages that had stuck together when I'd spilled the tea. They seemed cemented in place, so I skipped ahead and found the section titled "The Best Back-to-School Styles." Ahhhh. More my speed. Shorts, skirts, jeans, and a bunch of shirts, both flowy and fitted. And there was Mac again, now wearing blue jean shorts and a jewel-green sleeveless shirt with crocheted panels across the collarbones and shoulders.

Love it. I grazed my thumb across the bottom of the photo. Right away, my vision went blurry like a smeared watercolor painting. Archie whined. Pounding and buzzing clanged inside my ears. A rush of brilliant green swiped across the room. Sparks fired to my left and right. I slammed the pages shut and felt like I might throw up, but I caught my breath and the color storm and noise settled. When my vision cleared, a new outfit lay at the end of the bed. The blue jean shorts and the jewel-green shirt.

"Whoa!" I picked up the shirt and ran a hand over the fabric's soft texture.

Maybe it's the touching that makes it work.

A sear of pain throbbed at my temples. I dropped the shirt and grabbed the sides of my head. *Oooowww.*

Tea. I needed mint tea.

I grabbed my glass and gulped it down. My headache lightened. Carefully, I picked up the magazine again. Maybe I'd already had too much browsing time for one day, but I had to know if touching a picture was how the magic worked. I opened the pages, holding on by the corners and flipping forward until I came to an ad for a T-10 hair-nourishing blow-dryer and diffuser.

The T1-0 blow-dryer cultivates healthy hair. Made of ceramic tourmaline, our negative ion technology seals in moisture and nourishes hair with each use.

Yeah. I'd always wanted a T-10, but the price tag—geez—was way outside my allowance budget. Maybe now I didn't need money.

I smacked my hand on top of the ad and the room darkened. Wind whipped my hair. Swirling sounds charged at my ears. I closed my eyes and held on to the magazine until the pushing at my eardrums was too much, then I forced it shut and dropped it to the bed. My head throbbed. When I opened my eyes, a brand-new T-10 and its specialty diffuser were sitting beside me.

"Sweet!" I squealed, ignoring the nausea in my stomach. It *was* the touching! And I could touch *anything*. I quickly scanned the list of articles; too bad there wasn't one on winning "instant friends."

The yellow blurb on *Enchanted Teen*'s cover lit up like a flashing neon sign. Now it said, "Find Your Two Best Looks."

Two? The blurb about finding your best look had gone from five to two. Now I understood—the magazine came with five chances to use magic, and I had already used up three: one with the butterfly eyes, one with the new outfit, and now one with this blow-dryer. Only two left.

I shrugged and took a breath. "So what?" I said to Marlo Bee, the Hollywood star whose photo was on the cover. "I can go back to the clock when I need another magazine."

Marlo Bee's expression changed from a smile to a scowl.

Huh?

Marlo Bee wasn't a scowler. Even when she'd tripped at the VMAs with a zillion people watching, she smiled, took off her four-inch heels, and said into the microphone, "You've got to admit, these are smoking-cute shoes, but next time I'm wearing flip-flops." What a recovery! She'd know how to handle a new school and magic.

I leaned closer to the photo, trying to read her eyes. "Are you making a face at me?"

No answer came.

I shook my head. None of this was going to be easy to figure out, but one thing I knew for sure: my head hurt. I hid the magazine in my desk drawer and looked around my room. What a mess! Homework papers were scattered.

Archie's tail poked out from under my bed. I knelt down. "Poor Archie. Did that scare you?" I tried to coax him out but he wasn't having it.

My book and clock radio had been blown over, and the frame on the side of my bed had fallen to its side. I sat back on my ankles and picked up the photo of Grams and me posing on a beach in Hawaii. We were wearing grass skirts and flower leis—me with one and Grams with several stacked on her neck. She'd won extra leis for being the best student in our hula class.

"Don't worry, Grams," I said, glancing at the new blow-dryer. "I can handle this." Then I lay on the floor near Archie, one hand hugging the picture to my chest and the other reaching under the bed to pet him. "Sorry you got scared, Arch, but between the clock and this magazine, I'm going to impress the heck out of this school."

I just needed to learn more about the magic. The methods for scientific problem solving started ticking in my head: ask questions; do background research; construct a hypothesis; test with an experiment.

I took out my thin, orange Moleskine journal, and in no time I had a strategy written down. I was ready for another turn with that wishing clock.

CHAPTER 11

"**M**egan?" My body startled; a hand rested on my shoulder. "Megs?"

I opened my eyes. My sister's outline hovered over me in the darkened room.

"Piper?" I glanced at the clock. Two a.m. "You okay?"

"I . . ." She sniffled. "Can I sleep in your room tonight?"

I scooted over, and she slid under the sheets, Archie snoring at our feet.

The moonlight reflected a tear on her cheek, and I reached over and wiped it away. "Another bad dream?" I asked, finding her hand and taking it lightly in mine.

"Uh-huh."

"Tell me."

She stayed quiet, her body tense.

"Come on, Pipes," I whispered, channeling Mom. "Our words can take away the power from things that worry us."

I waited until she finally spoke, her voice small and strained.

"This time, I dreamed Mom was alive after she was thrown from the car. And she was alone, lying in the snow and calling for us to help her, but we didn't come. So she was lying there cold and shivering and we never came." A hiccup escaped her throat.

"Oh, Piper." I squeezed her hand. "I'm sorry." I paused, swallowing the sadness rising in my throat. "That's a horrible dream, but you know that's not how it happened. The police said she didn't suffer."

"I shouldn't have begged Dad to ski longer. We should've all left together."

"Mom and Dad still had their separate cars at the lodge. She would've been driving no matter what. And she would have hit that black ice whether you were in the car or not." It was the thousandth time I'd reminded Piper of this.

"I know, but maybe I would've seen the ice and could've warned Mom. And maybe Dad—"

"Nothing about Mom's accident was your fault, Piper." I squeezed her hand again. "And Dad is going to be fine. I promise."

The alarm blasted. I rolled to my side and smacked it off, opening my eyes just a slit. Piper had already slipped out of bed, and I heard her banging around in her room. Archie was gone, too, probably in the kitchen eating half of Dad's breakfast.

Ka-thump!

Something hit my floor, and then *fthipfthipfthipfathipfathip*. Pages turning?

I bolted up. The window shades were mostly closed, yet the room glowed like a rainbow. Beams of light shot straight to the ceiling. *Enchanted Teen* flapped in the center of my floor, a burst of color rising from the opened pages.

What the . . .

I flopped out of bed and carefully picked it up. The rainbow disappeared and the lights in my room returned to normal. The pages were covered with before-and-after photos of models with makeovers, and the title read: "Avoid *Cat*astrophe: The Dos and Don'ts for a Flawless Face."

That would be nice. I rubbed my chin where yesterday's zit had now doubled in size. Far from flawless.

I hurried to the bathroom. Ponytail up. Face washed. Pimple inspected. I leaned close to the mirror, thinking I could magic the zit away or even touch the magazine for a full makeover, but skipping an early-morning head pounding felt like a smart idea. Hannah and I'd gotten our faces done a few times at the mall—it couldn't be that hard.

I searched for makeup stuff in the boxes still waiting to be unpacked and buried in my closet. I dropped one box at a time on the floor next to my pile of laundry. The first was stuffed with Halloween supplies, including the Lincoln mask I was supposed to have worn back in the day for that school play. Another box had the stack of my favorite books from when Mom read with me. I picked up *The Wonderful Wizard of Oz* by L. Frank Baum and tried to remember Mom's voice. Some of Grams's favorite books were piled in there, too, *Healing Plants* and *How to Make Tinctures*. Finally, I found the box with the bag from the Sephora shopping spree I'd had with Hannah before moving, everything still unopened. I clicked on my radio for some getting-ready music, shoved my books from the desk to the floor, and then unpackaged a mirror and little boxes of lip gloss, eye shadows, and brushes and stuff.

In no time, I camouflaged zits, stroked shadows

on my lids, and brushed color on my cheeks, finishing with gloss and mascara. I stared in the mirror. The girl staring back looked pretty good. *Really* good. But I didn't have experience with this kind of stuff, and I had no idea how long makeup lasted. Maybe a light layer lasted an hour and more would last all day. I added extra mascara and a few bonus layers of shadow. It made me look older, like an eighth grader. I swished on another layer. Maybe I could look like I was in high school.

The scent of cinnamon floated upstairs, probably Pillsbury rolls knowing Dad's sweet tooth. Voices blasted from my radio. "This is Will and Jer on KYMN-FM. It's seven fifteen and time to . . ."

Seven fifteen. I rushed to my closet and put on the new jean shorts and green shirt. Then I shoved one of Mom's guitar picks, the red one with gold writing, deep in my pocket.

Piper poked her head in the doorway. "Dad says it's time to . . ." She paused and stared at me before blinking and looking away. "Um."

"What?"

"Uhhhhhhhhh." She pressed her lips together and darted glances at the corners of my floor. "Well . . . it's just . . ."

"What?" I asked louder. I gazed in my full-length

mirror, turning side to side, checking to see if the new shorts and shirt fit okay.

"Oh. Not your outfit. It's super-cute. It's just your makeup, Megs." She looked down again and fiddled with her bracelet before softly adding, "It's way too much."

"Are you sure?" I leaned closer to the mirror and looked at my face. "I kind of like it."

"You might want to open your shades all the way. Or come here." She grabbed my hand and pulled me to the bathroom, flicking on the lights. "See." Her voice dropped. "It's way too heavy."

"Crud!" She was right.

"You could—"

"Just go." I didn't know if I was more annoyed that I had to wash it off, or that my little sister knew more about makeup than I did. I turned on the faucet and scrubbed cleanser on my face. "Tell Dad I'll be down in five."

She stared.

"Go!" I said louder.

"Don't be mad. I just think you're way too pretty for all that."

I sighed. Logically, I knew it was dumb to feel grumpy at Piper when my makeover disaster wasn't her fault. She was just the messenger. And the message was loud and clear—I couldn't survive being the new girl without magic.

My door clicked shut.

I had to hurry or I'd be late again. I dried my face and rushed to my desk, yanking out the magazine and flipping to the Flawless Faces section. "Okay, I suppose you're here to help me." I hustled a hand to a picture of a back-to-school model with perfect daytime makeup. "Let's do this." I swiped a finger across the page.

Lights flashed and swished, and color beams hit my eyes. Everything went blurry. Sounds gurgled away. Pressure pushed at my temples, and I slammed the pages shut. My vision sharpened into focus and I turned to face my mirror—highlighted cheeks, peach lips. Even my hair had been de-frizzed. "Wow!" I hugged the magazine hard to my chest. "Thank you!"

The yellow blurb on the cover lit up and now read, "Find Your One Best Look."

"That's okay," I said, understanding I'd just used one of the limited pieces of magazine magic. Still no biggie, since I could wish all the time.

I tossed my green earbuds around my neck, stuffed the magazine and my orange journal into my backpack, and ran downstairs. Outside, I slid into the front passenger seat of Dad's Prius and lowered the visor mirror for another once-over. Piper jumped into the backseat, clicking away on her phone.

Dad climbed in next, bringing with him the smell of cinnamon. He put a paper plate with a frosted roll on my lap. "Breakfast. Try not to get the car sticky."

"Thanks." I turned toward the window so Dad wouldn't notice the makeup.

"Dad," Piper said, concern in her voice. "You didn't eat one of those, did you? Your doctor says you have to eat healthy."

"No, Pipes." Dad sounded tired. "I had egg whites cooked in olive oil." He smiled at her in the rearview mirror and then flipped on the radio, messing with the controls. "I hope I can find NPR out here in the desert. They're broadcasting an interview with a leading researcher of quantum physics."

"Nice." I shifted to face Piper in the backseat. "Better?"

"Wow," Piper said in a breathy voice. "You look beautiful. How'd you manage that so fast?"

I shrugged and smiled.

She picked a piece of lint off her shorts and softly said, "Thanks for everything last night."

"Anytime."

Dad placed his hands at ten and two. "Second day of school," he said, pulling out of our driveway. "Every day you're less and less the new kid and more like everyone else."

Like everyone else? That would have been a step up from my last school, where, at best, I was the girl who could help with hard math homework. Nope. No more quiet girl and no more dork-motoring. This year I was going to be impressive.

CHAPTER 12

When we got to school, Piper headed toward the lower-division doorways and I went through the school's main entrance. Students wearing campaign buttons shoved flyers into the hands of anyone passing by.

"Get Spirited! Vote Rhena!"

"Ally for seventh-grade Captain!"

Loud chatter echoed through the hallways. T minus four days and counting until election Friday.

Mrs. Sinoway, my assigned counselor, walked out of her office. She tucked her cropped hair behind an ear. "Hello, Megan." She smelled like Banana Boat sunblock, the same coconut-mango scent Hannah would use when we'd hang out at the pool in Colorado. It always made my eyes itch.

"How was your first day yesterday?"

The itching started immediately. I rubbed at my face and a lash or something landed in my eye. I blinked, trying to squeeze it out.

"It was good." I stuck a finger in the corner of my eye and rubbed, which only added to the itch and made my eyes water.

"I'm sorry your student ambassador wasn't available to show you around yesterday," she said. "And unfortunately, I just got off the phone with her mother, and she's out sick again."

"That's okay." I scratched some more and wiped, expecting a watery line of mascara to appear on my knuckle. My finger came back wet but clean.

"We'll fix this. Don't fret." Mrs. Sinoway seemed overly worried.

I swiped under my eye a second time, and pity washed over her face. She thought I was crying!

"It's okay," I said. "Really. I just have something in my eye."

"Uh-huh." She scanned the hallway, seeming flustered and desperate.

Just then her eyes locked on a target. "Jackson, come here for a moment."

A boy turned toward us, and my knees buckled. It was mystery guy. The one I'd seen at the Humane Society. Here. At my new school! Everything went slow motion. He walked toward us, moving his head so his surfer-blond hair flicked across his eyebrows. And that dimple, the one that had made my legs wobble, appeared in his right cheek. Then he was standing next to me, a boy who Hannah would describe as H-A-W-T hot. He smoothed a hand over the Fueled by Ramen logo on his T-shirt, and his light brown eyes connected with mine, intense and piercing, like he could see inside my soul. My stomach fluttered.

I used to laugh when Hannah acted ridiculous around boys, giggling at jokes that weren't even funny, and twirling her hair over and over (and OVER) again. When I'd asked her why she acted like that, she'd shrug, or say she couldn't help it. Now I knew she really couldn't help it. Jackson hadn't even made a joke, and already a giggle leaked from my throat to my mouth.

I pressed my lips together. *Hello*, I said to myself, *you're smarter than this*. Rein it in. But my arm obeyed the laws of crush mode. It bent at the elbow, and my hand grabbed to twirl some strands of hair.

"Hi?" He smiled at me. I was already beaming back.

"Hey, Aunt Celia," he said to Mrs. Sinoway.

"Megan Meyers, I'd like you to meet my nephew, Jackson Litner," Mrs. Sinoway said. "Jackson, meet Megan."

Mmmm, he smelled like a stack of pancakes, and his voice was smooth, like soft-serve vanilla.

"Hi." My finger twirled away like I was on some kind of windup mission.

"My fellow cat wrangler, right?"

I giggled, holding in the snort. He remembered me! "Right." I dropped my gaze to my sandals.

"I expected to see you at first aid after the battle. No war wounds?"

I shook my head and swallowed. "Um, how's your arm?"

Mrs. Sinoway glanced between us. "Oh, you've met?"

"Yeah. Remember the cat chaos I mentioned?" Jackson pointed to his scratched arm, which gave me a chance to check out the cut of muscle right below his sleeve.

"Fantastic," Mrs. Sinoway said, smiling at Jackson. "Megan just moved from Colorado and needs a student ambassador. Her first class is science with Mr. Provost. Would you mind showing her the way?"

I didn't need a guide anymore—a fact I would keep to myself.

"Sure," he said. "I didn't realize you were an out-of-stater. How's it going so far?"

"Great. Other than the fact that moving is hard. I mean seriously, it's no Pythagorean Theorem, I can tell you that." Ugh, dorkjob alert. I cringed, but Jackson laughed.

"Nice one," he said, adjusting the black and green braided yarn bracelet on his wrist.

"That's pretty," I said. Pretty? Who tells a guy something he's wearing is pretty?

"Thanks." He looked down. "My little sister made it. It kind of itches since I've had it on for weeks now, but she made me swear not to take it off and so . . ." He shrugged, his words trailing off.

I should've said, "That's so sweet," or "What grade is she in?" or I could've even nodded, but my twirled hair now coiled tightly around my finger, cutting off circulation and pulling at my roots. I worked at casually untangling my self-inflicted knot and held down another awkward sound that lingered in my throat. My finger came free with a yank and I felt my face blaze.

Mrs. Sinoway cleared her throat and clasped her hands together. "Well, thank you for volunteering, Jackson."

"You bet." He grazed my arm. "You ready?"

"Right. Yes. Of course." I took a breath.

We walked down the hall, Jackson talking and me barely able to concentrate on anything he said. I did hear him mention that he did *not* volunteer at the Humane Society—he had been there Saturday to check into adopting a dog, but that was good, too. The cutest boy I'd ever seen in real life was a dog lover! Were my feet even touching the ground? I started to take a right, and Jackson placed a hand on my back. Electricity sang through my body.

"That way leads to the lower-division classrooms. This way's quicker." He redirected me, and I wondered how his hands would feel in mine, or what it'd be like if he walked me down every single hallway.

"So what were you listening to?" He pointed to my dangling earbuds.

"Oh, ah"—throat clear—"Meowklemore."

"Macklemore? Cool," he said. "Old-school."

I nodded.

"Do you like that new band, the Perceptions? Wait . . . that's not it. What are they called?"

"The Purrrfections."

"What?" Jackson asked. He tipped his head to look at me as we walked.

My face flushed. I hated how my nerves made me sound so goofy. "Perfections. The Perfections."

"Yeah. That's it." I kept nodding, not trusting myself to talk.

"So, nice shirt you wore yesterday. Woofstock. That's funny."

He'd noticed me yesterday?

My face must've looked shocked, because Jackson smiled and said, "I saw you in the halls and tried to catch up, but you disappeared too quickly."

"Uh, thanks," I said all breathy, and then I hurried with, "I mean for liking my shirt. Not for trying to catch me in the halls. Or. Umm." Swallow. "That was nice, too." Heat flooded my face. "You know."

"Yeah." He laughed. "So here we are." He gestured to the classroom door. "I zipped through the tour. So, ah, if you have any questions, let me know or we can talk later."

"Later would be great."

We said good-bye, and I entered the room. The teacher was filing books on a shelf, so I quickly texted Hannah on my way to a desk.

Me: I just met Mystery Guy!!! The one from Saturday!!!

Hannah: Did you get his name this time?

Me: Yep. Jackson Litner.

Hannah: Can't wait to Insta-stalk him ☺

I took a seat and the girl in front of me turned around. "Haleigh," she said, pointing a hand to herself. "And Zoe." She indicated the girl on my right. "We met yesterday."

I smiled. "Yeah. Hi."

"We like your look," Haleigh said.

"We do," Zoe said.

My look? Oh, right, the makeover. Then I remembered rubbing my eyes when I'd talked to Mrs. Sinoway. "Is my mascara smeared?"

"No. You look great," Haleigh said. "And your hair! It's amazing."

"Yeah." Zoe nodded. "What color do you call it?"

"Umm." Really? I ran my hand down a fistful of hair and looked between them. "Brown?"

"Come on," Haleigh said. "I'd say it's more caramel kissed. Am I right?"

Zoe shifted closer, like she needed to share a secret. "So, listen. We saw the whole zap lowdown in the cafeteria yesterday. You looked major stressed, but the snow was awesome. I'll bet you clinched the election for Ally, and Rhena is so mad!"

Haleigh scooted close and whispered, "Everyone's saying Rhena's super-worried you're going to help Ally win. And don't tell Rhena I'm talking to you, but that was bold. Nobody ever goes against her."

A shiver ran down my neck, but I was determined to keep things positive. "Thanks," I said. "I really wasn't trying to do anything against Rhena. And I don't think she's mad. She invited me to her house tonight."

Both girls blinked before Haleigh said, "For reals? Oh my God, you're so lucky!"

They bubbled on about how excited they were for me, and would I please report back on what the inside of Rhena's house looked like.

Things were working out. I had an invitation to meet friends, a cute boy had walked me to class, and I could have a no-fuss magical makeover anytime I wanted one.

"So, what are you planning next?" Zoe asked.

"Next?"

They both nodded. "Yeah. We heard you were doing something for the Spirit Week elections on Friday."

"Oh, that." My mouth went dry. "I . . . I don't know."

"You don't?" Haleigh put a hand to her lips.

"Something good," I quickly added. A tremble shook from deep in my gut, but I stopped it. I didn't have anything to stress about. I had the clock.

"Awesome! Tell us first, okay?" Zoe said. "And by the way, here's an insider tip on the hottie who just walked you to class. Jackson Litner. If you like him, you better stay on Rhena's good side."

"Oh?"

"Jackson and Rhena have grown up their whole lives together," Haleigh said. "They're really, really tight."

Got it. Another solid reason to avoid messing with the Rhena-plus-Ally equation—combustibles should be handled with caution. This meant a change of plans. I needed to do something fun on Friday *without* it affecting the election, so I could stay Switzerland with those two.

When the period ended, I ducked into the bathroom and leaned toward the mirror to check my magical makeover again. Was I being paranoid or was my eyeliner different? It seemed more angular than I remembered. And had the shadows gotten darker?

Stop, I told myself. Nervous Newton was the old me. Overanalyzing not allowed. I stepped back and took a breath.

Second period came and went. When the bell rang, I raced to Mrs. Matthews's classroom and grabbed a second-row seat, anxious to talk to Ally about backing out of doing an election event.

A mixture of smells hung in the air—fresh paint and eau de taco chips wafting from an opened bag of Doritos sitting on the edge of the teacher's desk. Now dressed in lime-green pants, Mrs. Matthews smiled with orange-stained teeth. "Hello, Megan." She handed a paper to me. "This is an application to our math team. Your transcript says you competed in Math Olympiads at your last school. I'd love for you to consider joining our team. We have a meeting at lunchtime today."

"Thanks." I took the paper and set it on my notebook, smiling. "I'll think about it."

"Please do. You haven't missed anything. We were supposed to have our first official meeting two weeks ago, but I was called away for jury duty, so we're just getting started now."

"Hello, Ally," Mrs. Matthews said, stepping out toward the hallway.

Ally greeted her and came to the desk beside me. She tossed her backpack on the ground. "Cute shirt."

"Thanks!"

She sat and looked around. "Is it just me or does it always smell in here?"

According to the magazine, ridiculous is better than boring, so I cleared my throat and said, "Yeah. Here's some math: orange teeth plus spicy smells equals Mrs. Matthews's favorite breakfast."

Ally laughed. "Doritos!"

"Oh. But I like her and all." I squirmed.

"Yeah," Ally said. "Me too. She's a good teacher. I mean, she takes her math too seriously, but she's nice."

"Right." I folded the paper from Mrs. Matthews and slipped it under my notebook. Note to self: math club was the old me.

"Listen, I didn't think it through when I zapped you yesterday," she said softly. "I was a jerk not to warn you about Rhena. I'm sorry."

I looked at her and knew she meant it. "It's okay. It all worked out."

"Right. That snow party was the best thing ever."

"Thanks." I cleared my throat. "Umm, about the election—"

"Yeah. Thank you so much for helping me with it. So many people here get bullied into taking Rhena's side, but not you." Ally smiled a big, honest smile, all gratitude and cheer. "I can't wait to see what you come up with for Friday. Let me know how I can help."

"Okay, haha." I couldn't bring myself to say that I really wanted out. I'd be making a Spirit Week election wish after all.

But that wish would have to wait for another day. Today, I had a plan to test magic with science.

CHAPTER 13

I rushed to fourth period—toward the wishing clock, magic, and the 11:11 plan I'd devised. *It's all good*, I told myself, not sure if my breath wobbled because I was excited or nervous. But the closer I got, the bolder I grew and the more I was sure this clock was a gift—the biggest break of middle school. My life was officially charmed!

I rounded the doorway into Mr. Kersey's room, where every single desktop was decked out with a pack of Juicy Fruit gum and a yellow flyer that read, "Chews Rhena for Spirit Captain!"

"Hey, granola," Rhena said.

Did she mean me?

Rhena sat at her desk, looking me up and down. "Hmm." She tapped a manicured figure to her chin. "Maybe I should find another nickname for you if that's the look you're going with."

Her friends giggled, and suddenly I felt like one of those "what not to wear" features, or like I was back to wearing yesterday's frizzed hair and fisherman shorts. I ran a hand over the back of my head. Hair still smooth. I glanced down. Green shirt and blue jean shorts. Okay? Everything seemed in place, so what was wrong?

Turner entered. "Hey, Megan." He stopped in the doorway beside me. "What's that about?" He leaned close and pressed his glasses up his nose.

"What?"

"Your makeup. You're a cat, right?" he said. "You have theater third period?"

"No?" A sinking feeling pressed on my chest.

"Ohhhh. It's a style. I get it. I never know these things. Like I felt sorry for Brandon with all the rips in his jeans. I thought he couldn't afford new clothes. But he told me distressed was in." Turner shrugged on the way to his desk.

Rhena's friends giggled again, the kind of giggles that reminded me of the judgy looks at my last school.

What was Turner talking about? A weird noise—an

attempt at a laugh, I think, maybe—escaped from my throat. I rushed toward a desk in the back, forcing a grin onto my face, acting like I was in on some joke, and trying to send vibes of "I'm chill, no worries."

I sat, fumbled out my phone, and turned the camera app to reverse.

Ahhhk!

My eyes were made up like some elaborate Halloween cat wannabe—thick eyeliner at exaggerated angles, and if that wasn't bad enough, I had spider-sized clumps of mascara on the ends of my lashes, like the makeup was piling on, heavier and darker by the minute.

Grams's warnings played in my head—those clockmakers are tricksters, and I was experiencing it firsthand with a makeover going off the rails. "Thanks a lot," I said under my breath, kicking my backpack where the magazine sat snug inside.

According to the *How to Survive Middle School* blog, I was supposed to act certain and secure no matter what, but who was I kidding? My confidence had fizzled, and I wanted the makeup off fast. I rubbed with my hands, swiping around my eyes. Heavy layers of color coated my fingertips. What a mess.

And to make matters worse, Rhena stood up, grabbed her backpack and purse, and walked toward me. Was she moving in for a close-up of my embarrassment?

"Maybe a little less liner and mascara next time," she said, sitting in the empty desk in front of me, her expression full of concern.

Du-uh, I thought, wanting to shrink and disappear.

"Fortunately for you, I always carry these." She reached into her purse and pulled out a travel pack of aloe makeup-removing wipes; then she plucked one out and handed it to me. "Here. And don't worry. I've done it before, too."

"Wow." I couldn't keep the surprise from my voice, but Rhena actually sounded sweet, like she had before she knew Ally had zapped me. I scoured my face, my skin tingling. "Thanks."

"No worries. It happens to the best of us." She smiled and handed over another wipe. "By the way, you know I'm just kidding when I say granola. And I totally thought your snow event was a blast."

"Thanks," I repeated. Why was she suddenly being nice to me? I thought of the quote from the magazine and wondered if calling me granola and joking was Rhena's way of being ridiculous instead of boring, and I was taking things too seriously. Mom had always handled awkward situations so easily.

"And your shorts are super-cute." She reached over

and mopped a flake of mascara from my face. "Besides the crazy makeover, you look pretty."

My shoulders softened down from my ears. "Thanks."

"So we're good?" she said.

"Sure." I swallowed. "Sure." Rhena had invited me to her house after all.

"Good." Her smile grew. "By the way, I saw you with Jackson Litner this morning."

"Uh-huh," I said.

"What's up with that?"

"He's my student ambassador." I shrugged, faking indifference. "Just showing me around."

The tardy bell rang. Stragglers took seats.

"Phones away now, people," Mr. Kersey said. "And Rhena, please face forward for class."

"Well, his parents and my parents play tennis together," she said to me. "We see each other like all the time. We're really, really close."

The way she was talking—all sweet and super-interested—made my head spin. I started to wonder if she was in reconnaissance mode. But it felt like she wanted to be friends, too. I was no good at these games.

"Yeah." I nodded. "I hear you guys are best friends."

A warm smile spread across her face. "Exactly. That's right." She sat tall. "So anyhow, we're good?"

"Yeah. Sure. Of course." Now would be a good time to bring up the study party. "About tonight—"

Mr. Kersey's voice boomed. "Open your books to page forty-nine."

Rhena shuffled to face the front, but not before handing me a pack of Juicy Fruit and saying, "You really should reconsider your options around here before it's too late."

CHAPTER 14

Wishing was the ticket to securing my new reputation, which meant I still needed answers on how exactly the magic worked. I reached into the front zipper pocket of my backpack and pulled out my Moleskine journal.

Dad had given me my first Moleskine years ago to chart and write out ideas for a science fair competition. Since then, I'd had Moleskines in many colors and sizes. This orange one would be where I'd sort out magic. The plan I'd drawn in it the night before included the four-step scientific method—ask questions, do background research, construct a hypothesis, and test with an experiment.

I set it on my desk and kept the journal closed until I was sure Rhena was into the lecture and wouldn't turn around and read my notes. Ten minutes passed before I smoothed open the pages and reviewed my list.

QUESTIONS:
Will sticking with specific wishes give me exactly what I ask for?
Can I dictate when a wish starts and ends?
How much magic can I get out of one wish?

I grabbed my pencil and added a new question:

How can I avoid tricks?

BACKGROUND RESEARCH:
Specific wish—asked for snow and got it
Nonspecific wish—asked for "some magic" and got a magical magazine

COSTS—magic has costs:
Magazine magic = headaches and nausea
Clock magic = none
Question: do I need to be specific to avoid costs? Snow wish was free, so are all "specific" wishes free?

I jotted another line, squeezing it in between my writing.

UPDATE: magazine costs = tricks (i.e., makeover).

My hypothesis had been blank, but now I wrote one in:

HYPOTHESIS: Specific wishes on the clock are safe, but magic from a nonspecific wish may be packed with pranks.

The experiment section was next, and that meant I'd have to use up today's wish for research. The wish would have to satisfy all my questions and yet be special enough to know it came from magic.

I'd laid out the perfect plan and reviewed it at least a hundred times the night before—I'd wish that a chocolate Lab and a wiener dog would run into the classroom at exactly 11:12 a.m. They'd each carry a bag of Skittles and then drop the Skittles at Mr. Kersey's feet. Next, they'd lie on their backs for a belly rub. Then, at 11:17 (my designated end time), they'd run a loop around the classroom and then out the door.

Now I just had to wait until the wishing minute.

Waiting is not my best quality, so I fidgeted with my phone, debating if I should ask Grams more questions. Even though she'd be mad that I messed with magic, nobody would know the answers better than Grams. I should have fessed up about receiving the package from the start, and now the makeup disaster and stress about the possibility of other tricks made me sure I needed to talk to her. She'd yell at me, and I'd beg forgiveness, and then I could question her for more details about the clock's magic.

I sunk low in my seat and sent her a text:

Me: Confession: I used magic and it did this weird makeover thingy, plus it's giving me headaches, but is that all? I need to talk to u!!

Grams's reply came quickly:

Grams: The Bellini brothers are patient and meticulous about their magic; they like to lull their victims into trust. You know what to do.

Me: But if I could just use magic for this week, I'd be set.

Mr. Kersey came down the aisle, passing out a paper titled "Test Review: Ancient Greece." I stuck my phone under my leg, took the handout, and faked like I was reading through the notes. As soon as he moved on I hid my phone under my desktop again and read Grams's reply.

Grams: What kind of friends do you think you'll have if you have to swindle them into liking you?

Before I had a chance to reply, she sent another text.

Grams: Sorry, Sugar. I'm taking a technology-free bike tour. Turning phone off now. I trust you'll figure everything out.

"Wait!" I typed, but I could see the message wasn't delivered. She'd already powered off.

Mr. Kersey displayed images on the Smart Board and lectured on point after point: Cretan life, poems of Homer, the Trojan War. I jotted two full pages of notes.

By 11:07, I knew more than I ever wanted to know about Greek civilization and pinned my gaze on the clock's ticking tail and hypnotic dancing eyes. I set my pencil down and waited, heart racing, hands shaking.

Then the time ticked to 11:11, and I whispered, "Pop. Click. Seconds tick. Wish at eleven-eleven, and watch it stick." I quickly scanned my list and returned to the first question: *Will sticking with specific wishes give me exactly what I ask for?* Jittery nerves jumbled my thoughts—dogs, Mr. Kersey, a belly rub. Grams said I knew what to do, and I did. Only thing, it was way different from what she wanted me to do.

"Megan," Mr. Kersey said gently. "This information will be helpful for the test."

I flushed and nodded, but when he continued on, I looked back at the clock. The second-hand whisker had already ticked to halfway around. Time was running out. My mind latched on to pieces of what I had planned on saying, and I panic-whispered, "Make Mr. Kersey bark like a dog."

Ahk, that wasn't the plan!

But nothing happened.

Why didn't anything happen?

The pop! I'd forgotten the pop. Yesterday, the lightning made the pop; today I'd have to make my own. Only twenty seconds left! Grams had always complained when I popped my knuckles, so I said the rhyme again, this time scanning my full list of questions and pressing the heel of my hand across my knuckles. *Pop, pop.* The time was almost up! I dorked out with panic, my whispered words tumbling out. "When the clock strikes eleven twelve make Mr. Kersey bark like a dog, hop on one foot, and rub his belly for five minutes and . . . and . . . and deliver Skittles. Lots and lots of Skittles!"

Rhena shifted in her seat. "What are you saying?"

I shook my head and pressed my lips together. She turned back around, and I'm not sure what else I might've added had the last seconds not ticked off. The whiskers moved to 11:12 and my arm hairs spiked like the fur of a spooked cat.

"Ruff. Ra ra. Ruff ruff ruff." Mr. Kersey scratched an ear.

The class stilled, all eyes on him.

He lifted a leg and hopped on one foot, snapping his jaw behind him like he was chasing a tail. Then he placed a hand on his stomach and rubbed. "Ruff, ruff ruff."

Everyone exploded in laughter. He barked and hopped and hopped and barked. My throat went dry and I froze, watching the spectacle.

Mr. Kersey kept barking, rubbing his belly, and chasing his tail.

Turner laughed. Shelby laughed. Yoona laughed. The guy who wore the Cardinals hat laughed. Everyone was laughing. Everyone except Rhena. She was turned around in her desk, trying to get a look at my list.

Hair on my neck and arms bristled and a rush of air left my mouth. I scooped up the journal and shoved it between my notebook pages.

"What's that about?" Rhena watched me closely.

Something clogged my throat, but I managed a cough and then said, "Nothing, haha."

"Really?" Rhena lifted an eyebrow before facing forward. The whiskers on the clock moved to 11:17, and Mr. Kersey's crazy behavior stopped.

"Good!" Mr. Kersey's eyes crinkled into a smile. "Now that I have your attention and know you're all awake, we can continue." He laughed at himself like nothing was wrong, like the barking was his idea and he'd intended to go berserk for a few minutes.

Had the magic done that to his mind?

Suddenly, there was a knock at the door. It swung open, and there stood that same guy from Backyard Blizzards. This time he was wearing a UPS uniform with a chest patch that read "Bruce." His green eyes glimmered under his cap, and he winked at me. "Delivery for Megan."

Blood drained from my face.

He disappeared from the doorway for a few seconds, and then reappeared with a red wheelbarrow stacked to teetering with . . . Skittles! He marched into the classroom, followed by five guys with identical red wheelbarrows, all towered high with bags and bags of colorful Skittles.

"Megan?" Mr. Kersey said.

"Ha-ha. Um." *Cough.* I cleared my throat. What could I say? And then: "It's . . . it's for the election? Brighten your day. Vote Ally."

"Cool!" The guy in the Cardinals hat jumped from his seat and scooped up two fistfuls of Skittles bags.

My hands and heart shook for the rest of class. The wishing clock would do anything I asked of it!

CHAPTER 15

At lunchtime, I hovered outside the glass cafeteria doors.

"I don't know how to thank you!" Ally said, running up and practically knocking me down in a hug. "The Skittles were brilliant! So creative! Thank you!"

"Yo, Ally!" the guy in the Cardinals hat said as he headed inside. He waved a hand packed with three bags of candy. "Nice!"

Walking behind him, Erin, Mia, and Noelle all had candy bags in their hands and pockets, too. Clearly, the whole school had heard about the wheelbarrows by now, because Skittles bags were in fists, pockets, and backpack zippers. They overflowed from purses and gym bags. On lunch trays and tables.

"Come on, you guys," Erin said, heading toward the line.

Ally took a few steps. "You coming?"

"Um. I'm going to talk to Mrs. Matthews first."

"Okay. I'll save you a seat." She ran inside.

The clock, the magic, and its tricks and treasures were exciting, but regardless of wanting to be impressive, I needed to catch my breath. Mrs. Matthews's invitation to the math team sounded like the perfect break, as long as I could keep it on the down-low.

Through the halls, I passed "Chews Rhena" flyers everywhere—on doorways, next to light switches, on the trophy case and over air vents. When I arrived outside Mrs. Matthews's room, her closed door had a single blue sign taped to it that read, "Math Social. Geniuses Welcome."

I looked around. No one was coming down the hall. Then I creaked open the door and froze in place—Mrs. Matthews wasn't there, but Jackson stood at the front of the room, laughing with Turner and a couple of athletic-looking guys. Had I come at the wrong time?

"Okay. This one's from Reddit. What do you get when you cross a mosquito with a mountain climber?" Jackson asked. He didn't wait for an answer. "Nothing.

You can't cross a vector and a scaler."

I snort-laughed, and Jackson caught me gawking in the doorway. "Megan!" he said. "You here for math team?"

"Umm." I looked at the handful of students sitting in desks. "Yeah, if that's okay."

"Come in," Jackson said. "Meet my algebros."

I walked over.

"This is Tank."

"What's up," Tank said. Even his muscles had muscles.

"And this is Wigglesworth."

"That's my last name," Wigglesworth said. "You can call me that. Or you can call me the Secret Weapon."

Jackson laughed. "Keep the ego in check, Wigglesworth." He shoved his shoulder and said, "And this is Turner."

I smiled. "Hey, Turner." He looked like a pocket calculator next to these guys.

"Hey, Megs."

"Megs?" Jackson said, looking between us.

"Oh yeah," Turner said, popping up his shirt collar. "Megan and I go way back. We have history together. Get it? *History*," Turner said. "Double entendre, 'cause we both have Kersey."

"We get it, Turner," Tank said with a groan.

"Here, sit here, Megan." Jackson pulled an empty desk closer to his.

I smiled. This was better than my wish.

A few more girls and guys came in. They introduced themselves: Ellie, Karen, Jacob, and Steve. Right away I felt at ease. I even added a joke. "What does a mermaid wear?" I said. "An algae-bra." My face burned—who mentions bras in front of a bunch of guys? But they laughed and we continued chatting, waiting for Mrs. Matthews to arrive.

"Hey, what's this?" Jackson leaned down beside me and picked up the red guitar pick from the floor.

"Oh," I said, feeling myself get shy again. "That's mine. It must've fallen from my pocket."

He handed it to me, and I cupped it like a fragile egg.

"So you play?" he asked.

"Well, my sister does. Used to."

"Used to?" Confusion covered his face. "I mean, I'm no good, but I can't put my guitar down."

A flash of Mom strumming her guitar played in my head, the ache from it spreading across my collarbones. I missed her. I missed hearing her. I missed talking about her.

"You okay?" Jackson asked, his face sincere.

I nodded. "Um. What kind of guitar do you have?"

"Fender jumbo acoustic. My parents won't let me go electric until I get more skills. Now spill. Why are you carrying around your sister's pick?"

I opened my palm and turned the pick over a few times before I glanced back up, his face still so genuine. "Well, my mom . . ." Just saying "my mom" felt rich in my mouth. "She played. So it's her pick, really." Swallow.

"That's cool." He tilted his head.

"She was a music teacher. And really good. And . . . and she died a year and a half ago." I held my breath.

"Geez. I'm sorry." And I could tell he was. He didn't try to look away or change the subject. He just listened. And I wasn't looking for sympathy, but it felt good saying her name to someone other than Grams.

The door clicked open and Mrs. Matthews walked in. "Hello! I'm glad to see you all here."

She discussed her plans for the club and passed out a permission form for our parents to sign. "We'll have a brief meeting after school tomorrow, so bring these back. I need volunteers to bring snacks for each of our competitions."

Everyone shouted out things they could make, or buy, or things their *mom* could bake.

"Okay, okay," Mrs. Matthews said. "One at a time.

I'll write a list, and anyone with an allergy, please speak up." Mrs. Matthews jotted the list on the board with the student's name and food item they shouted.

"What did you call out, Tank?" Mrs. Matthews said.

"CDPs. That's chocolate-dipped pretzels," Tank said. "Sometimes my mom makes them with nuts or sprinkles or whatever."

"You all right?" Jackson asked, bumping me with his leg.

I nodded, staring at a rip in my cuticle.

Mrs. Matthews wrote "chocolate pretzels" next to Tank's name. "Any nut allergies in here?" She looked at the group. I suppose everyone shook their head or said no, because she said, "Okay." Pause.

"Excuse me," Jackson said. "I'm going to volunteer my dad, because he makes an awesome Chex Mix."

"Great." Mrs. Matthews turned and wrote on the board.

"I love me some of your dad's Chex Mix," Wigglesworth said. "Especially when he uses Sriracha and honey."

"Dude," Tank said, "we could add some CDPs and that mix would be off the chain."

The mention of his dad, any dad, unfroze me, and I nodded a barely visible thank-you to Jackson. He smiled back, his dimple appearing.

"Um, my dad could make cinnamon rolls," I said. "They'll come from a can."

"Perfect." Mrs. Matthews wrote it on the board and called on the next student.

She completed the list and said, "Next up, I've prepared an exercise so I can analyze your problem-solving skills. We are going to break up into five stations and test your strengths in statistics and probabilities, geometry, algebra, expressions and equations, and number theory. You'll receive one math problem at each station and then rotate to the next. Your job is to complete the problem in the most elegant yet simple manner possible." She smiled at us. "Bonus points for creativity. Okay, let's get a cluster of desks moved to each corner of the room to represent a station, and we can set the final station in the middle."

We moved desks, and Mrs. Matthews taped a pre-printed sign at each cluster to label the stations. Then she dropped a stack of papers with a single math problem on the center desktop.

"Find a seat and let's begin. I'll be the timer." She held up her phone. "You'll spend no more than two minutes per section, and when my phone dings, please rotate. The limited time is so you'll push yourself to trust your instincts, and of course that'll save you enough time to make it to the cafeteria before lunch ends." She smiled again. "Remember to look at the problem and understand it first, then devise a plan to carry it out."

We began.

When our testing was over, Jackson leaned close to me and said, "Your mom sounded like a nice person."

I smiled at him and noticed three adorable freckles under his left eye. Then an odd rumble and a soft vibration started to build in my throat.

CHAPTER 16

After school, Piper sent me a text.

Piper: Sorry to ditch you. I reaaaaallly want to stay for yearbook club. Okay?

I typed back:

Me: Whatever.

Piper: Megan?

Me: It's fine.

I stuffed my phone into my backpack and headed to the orientation meeting at the Humane Society alone. The dogs in the outdoor play zone barked and wagged their tails. I smiled and swung open the glass front door. Mavis greeted me from behind her desk. "Hi, honey. Good to see you again."

"Thanks." I beamed. "Who is this?" I bent down and scratched the head of the sweet dog next to her.

"This is Marble," she said. "Wow. He doesn't warm up to just anyone. He only likes a select few people. And cats. Everyone else he ignores."

"Cats?"

"Don't ask me. The last owner must've had them."

Marble nuzzled me like we were old friends. "I'm guessing he's a retriever-collie-spaniel mix?"

"Yes!" Mavis said. "At least that's what the blood test showed. I adopted him from here."

I scratched under his chin and then petted the soft fur on his head.

"Wow. That's fantastic," Mavis said. "The way you can make that purring sound like a cat."

Huh?

"It's so real." She smiled.

Was I doing that?

"Now, Marble thanks you, but time for you to scoot. Orientation is through the blue doors on your left. There are a couple dozen new volunteers in there. Water bottles and cookies are set up on a table, so help yourself to a snack."

I shook off Mavis's odd comment and headed

inside, practically skipping until my bounce turned into a thud.

What was Yoona doing here? As in Yoona who hung out with Rhena and Shelby. This was supposed to be my drama-free zone, yet there she stood, leaning against the cookie table.

"Heeeey, Yoona?" I said.

"Hi!" Her greeting came out enthusiastic, louder than I'd ever heard her speak at school. Had I heard her speak at school?

She grabbed me in a hug.

My arms hung at my side.

"It's so awesome that you're doing this, too," she said. "Were you a volunteer in Colorado?"

"Uh-huh." I grabbed a few sugar cookies. She grabbed a handful, too, and in no time I learned that Yoona had four sisters and one turtle (no dog, but she was working on her parents). We liked the same music, and we both loved our grandmothers—she said hers lived with her family and baked chapssal donuts and hotteok every Saturday.

"Hotteok are Korean sweet pancakes and best hot off the griddle, even if they do burn your fingers a little. My grandma fills them with brown sugar and cinnamon. Mmmm, they're so good. You'll have to come over one weekend."

"Definitely." I wanted to ask if she was going to

Rhena's for the study party, but then that would've brought school into the conversation, and I really didn't want to talk about the Rhena-and-Ally drama or the election.

The director arrived and passed out our name badge lanyards and began the information session. She told us about the weekly Wednesday Night Walks, saying it was a volunteer opportunity to walk dogs late in the evening when the temperatures had cooled. Then she discussed special events, the foster program, walking paths, how we could help with the bath brigade, and safety and etiquette for introducing people to the animals. Afterward, she led the group of new volunteers on a tour. It ended near the front doors. "Everyone, find a volunteer partner. I'd like you to work in pairs."

Yoona grabbed my hand, and I smiled.

"Please see Mavis for your first assignment. She'll be your go-to person. Thank you all for caring."

We lined up beside Mavis's desk and waited our turn to sign up for a position, me hoping we'd get dog walking or bath brigade.

"I keep telling my dad these dogs need homes," Yoona said. "And I'd be the best owner ever. I'd feed and water and love. And I'd never get tired of the newness and forget about my dog. It sucks when people adopt puppies and then return them when they realize they're work. Or I hate when people want a dog, but then never play with them."

"Yeah. And you know what's worse?" I said as we inched forward. "Owners who leave their dog in the car, especially in the summer."

"I know, right. I mean, five minutes isn't bad, but people shouldn't go off and do their grocery shopping."

"Five minutes *is* bad. I've done the calculations," I said. "The temperature in a shut car rises by seven degrees in five minutes. And thirteen degrees in ten minutes. Around here, a hundred and ten in a car can turn into a hundred and forty degrees in half an hour."

"You did the calculations?" she asked.

"Yeah."

"Geez. I guess you're a genius." Yoona smiled for a moment, and then concern took over her face. "Listen, genius. I wish you'd be smarter about Rhena." She lowered her voice. "Seriously, Megan. You shouldn't go against her. She's freaking out about you helping Ally. And trust me. It's not worth it to cross Rhena." She paused before adding, "She'll do anything to be in charge of Spirit Week."

"Me?" I snort-laughed. "I'm not trying to go against her."

Yoona was sincerely trying to help me, but what

more could I say—that I wanted out of the middle of the Ally-Rhena spirit-storm? That I barely knew anyone and didn't have the juice to help Ally win? I mean, sure I had magic, but I didn't have votes.

"Please, Megan," Yoona said. "If you keep challenging Rhena, she's going to make sure you regret it."

"Hello, girls," Mavis said.

I snapped my attention Mavis's way, wanting to hug her for saving me from this conversation.

Mavis shuffled a pile of papers. "Don't be disappointed, but we need some volunteers on pooper-scooper duty, and then to spray down the outside play zone and refill water bowls."

"Great," I said, relieved to be headed off to our duties. Except Yoona had one more thing to say.

"Listen," she said in a low voice, like Rhena had spies at the Humane Society. "She's already salty about you. You don't want to see what happens when she's really ticked."

CHAPTER 17

At home, I cleaned up shredded bits of Dad's *Scientific American*. Archie had a tendency to tear things apart when he was left home alone all day. He lifted his eyebrows and tilted his head. It was all the apology I needed.

"It's okay, boy." I petted him. "This move is probably tough on you, too."

I found a shaded spot in the yard and tossed Archie's favorite red ball. He chased it and brought it back over and over until we were both dripping with sweat. I put ice in his water dish and then flopped onto the faded leather couch in the living room, snacking on blue corn tortilla chips and drinking a cold, orange Izze.

My backpack, laptop, and homework were scattered in a mess around me. I couldn't concentrate on any of it, because my phone kept dinging and dinging in that group text, everyone talking about tonight's study party at Rhena's house.

Ding! **Homewrk + Pizza. I can deal.**

Ding! **Want me 2 bring D.P. or root beer?**

Ding! **Cookies and diet coke?**

Ding! **Yassss! Please!!**

Ding! **See you guys 2nite!**

I didn't know who all was texting, but in a few hours, I hoped to have a bunch of new friends.

Piper burst into the living room and hit me over the head with a pillow. "Did you know that April third is International Pillow Fight Day?"

"Piper! You could've knocked over my laptop." I wasn't actually annoyed. Pillow fights were our thing—her way of saying, "I love you. We're sisters, even though I didn't want to volunteer at the Humane Society with you."

I grabbed a couch pillow and swung. Piper ducked, but I doubled back and hit her square in the head, making her hair fly in her face. She hit me, and I hit her, and she hit me again, and we battled for a few minutes until we fell to the floor laughing and catching our breath.

"Barett and I are going to have a pillow-fight party in April for the big holiday," Piper said. "But only if you'll be a part of it, since pillow fights are *our* thing."

"International Pillow Fighting Day? Did you make that up?"

"Oh no, it's real. It even says so on the internet."

"Like on Wikipedia?"

"Megan, it's real, and it's in April."

"Let's see." We scrambled up to the couch. I grabbed my laptop and typed in "International Pillow Fight Day." Sure enough, a website popped up, and it featured an article about a flashmob pillow fight held in Times Square last April. The website also had the next date for the event and listed hundreds of participating cities from all around the world: Barcelona, Spain; Budapest, Hungary; Melbourne, Australia; Phoenix, Arizona. There it was.

"See!" Piper said. She was always in the know.

"Okay, April. That's eight months away. I'll be there."

"And you'll help?"

"Sure. Of course—the Meyers sisters own pillow fights. We'll show everyone how to do it!" I'm not sure if it was from talking to Jackson about Mom, but I broke form and added, "And you know what else would be good—music. You could play your guitar at the pillow fight."

Piper looked as if I'd dropped a Saint Bernard in her lap. Her mouth hung open for a second, but she closed it and went somewhere deep in her thoughts. "That'd be fun," she said softly, staring at her hands, fingers moving like she was remembering some tune. She stayed like that for a moment longer, and I crossed my fingers under my lap.

"But you know I'm done with that, Megan." She fluttered her hand, waving away the idea like it was no big deal, but I saw the flash of missing in her eyes. "Plus, I need two hands to win a pillow fight." She hit me again.

"Hold up," I said, reading the headline on the computer screen. "Flashmob: Foundation of First Feathery Fight." I paused. "That's it!"

"What's it?"

"The pillow fight. It's perfect! I promised everyone at school I'd do something big on Friday. An all-school pillow fight would be . . ." Piper's face didn't seem nearly as excited as I'd expected. "Sorry. What am I thinking? That's your idea."

"Wait. That's okay," Piper said sweetly. "If you

promised everyone, you can have it."

"No." I shook my head. "No. That's your deal." I paused. "But I could have a flashmob!"

"Awesome," Piper said. "What'll we do?"

"Not sure yet." I put my hand to my chin. "I'll pick one to copy off YouTube and let you know."

"Fun!" Piper got up and headed to the kitchen, texting on her way. "I'm telling Barett right now."

I leaned back on a couch cushion, smiling. Flashmob Friday. That plus the snow would seal my reputation at school. Impressive would be officially checked off my list. Pressure as the new girl would end. I'd actually have a cool reputation. The rest of middle school would be a cakewalk. I'd even have my own page in the yearbook—"Awkward Girl Miraculously Transforms from Meek to Chic."

My phone lit up with a text from Yoona:

Yoona: Great seeing you today.

I replied with a smiley-face dog emoji.

Dad walked in and looked at my mess of papers. "I'm glad to see you're getting a jump on your studies." He laid down his briefcase and removed a box from a plastic bag stuffed with Chinese takeout.

I closed my laptop. "You're home early."

"I have to go back to work later for a department

meeting. But we can have a quick meal together." He wagged the box. "Look. Your favorite—lemon pepper chicken."

"Thanks," I said.

Dad took the bag into the dining room and laid out the boxes while Piper and I set the table with mismatched plates, chopsticks, and paper napkins. Yummy scents floated from the opened containers— lemon pepper chicken, fried rice, and beef with garlic black bean sauce. Then Dad dropped a pile of fortune cookies in the center of the table.

"You got low-sodium, right?" Piper asked. "No MSG?"

"That's right." Dad gave her a tired smile and shook his head.

We piled our plates with food. As we ate, Piper entertained us with talk about Barett, her three ambassadors, and her gazillion new friends. "And then I got zapped by my class rep and had to do a dare."

"What do you mean?" Dad set down his chopsticks. "I don't want you participating in dares. Dares are an invitation to break rules and get into precarious situations."

"Precarious situations? Oh, really, Dad. You're funny," she said in that à la Mom, bubbly way. "You have to lighten up."

He raised his eyebrows, but his face softened. "I'm serious."

"It's over anyhow. I just had to ask this boy, Tommy, for his phone number. He's so cute and it was super-embarrassing, but fun."

I dropped my chopsticks. "That's *all* you had to do?"

"Yeah." She shrugged. "Oh, and everyone keeps saying you brought in the snow for your zap dare, like just 'cause you're from Colorado, you're the snow fairy. That cracks me up. Anyhow, what did you really do?"

I looked at my rice. "The snow, of course, haha."

Piper seemed ready to press for an answer that didn't sound sarcastic, so I said, "Tell me about yearbook club." That got her talking nonstop about the scheduled meetings and plans.

"Sounds like you have a full calendar." Dad leaned back in his chair and smiled like he suddenly considered filling a social calendar equal to winning the Nobel Prize.

I cracked open a fortune cookie and crumbs scattered.

"Read it to us, Megan," Piper said.

I removed the thin slip of paper. "It says, 'Be who you are and say what you feel because those who mind don't matter and those who matter don't mind.'" I laughed. "That sounds just like something Grams would say. It's by Theodor Geisel." I looked to Dad to see if he knew that name.

"That's Dr. Seuss," Dad said.

"Well, thanks, Cat in the Hat." I stuffed the paper into my pocket. "But that's totally not a fortune."

Piper laughed. "Oh my gosh, Barett's going to love that quote!"

"You and Barett are becoming fast friends," Dad said. Then he focused on me. "I'm sure you'll have a bunch of friends in no time, too." He didn't sound sure, just uncomfortable.

I was actually doing all right, even if it was because I'd used a wish-granting clock to impress a bunch of people with the snow. I now had a lunch group, and math club was all me, no magic. After Flashmob Friday, I'd be set.

"Come on, Dad. Megan already has friends."

"I joined the math team," I said. "Our first competition is next month."

"That's terrific, Megan," Dad said.

"Is the girl who zapped you on your math team?" Piper asked.

"Ally? No. But she introduced me to a bunch of people at lunch."

Dad lifted his eyebrows. Relieved? Impressed?

I wanted to reassure him, so I added, "Everyone is super-nice. Erin is hysterical, and Noelle is so sweet and does amazing hennas, and Mia loves to read, I think she reads a book a day, and I'm getting to know this girl Yoona from my history class. She volunteers at the Humane Society, too, and . . ." I went on listing people, name-dropping as if I were talking about A-list celebs. It did the trick. Dad relaxed, seemingly satisfied that I was making my way. And I was—I did have friends. "I even have an invitation to a party tonight."

Dad's face turned to professor mode. "Whoa. We don't do parties on school nights."

"Come on, Pops," I said, trying to copy Piper's playful tone. "I know that. It's a *study party* for history. We have a big test coming up, and it's pretty awesome that this group from my class wants to help me out. Or I guess we'll help each other out. Anyhow, like I said, people are really nice here."

I sat up. Making a bunch of friends tonight was a big possibility. Right? That ironclad bond people make over greasy pizza and hard work.

Piper stood. "Oh, I think . . ." She leaned an ear toward the stairs. "Yup. My phone's ringing up in my room. May I be excused? Pleeease?"

Dad nodded, and she took off toward her bedroom.

"Something major might be unfolding right this

very minute in the oh-so-important world of fifth grade." I forced a chuckle. "Or it could be a yearbook emergency."

Dad ignored that. "You'll have fun at that study group." He sounded hopeful and like he was trying to assure me, which told me my upbeat tone hadn't fooled him into thinking I wasn't nervous.

I looked down at the crumbs on the table. "I know. I should probably get ready soon."

"How about we make a deal. I'll clean up tonight so you can get ready, and you and Piper can do the dishes tomorrow. Okay?"

"Purrrfect," I said, my tongue trilling the *r* without my control.

"What's that?"

"Nothing. Perfect. I said perfect." My voice came out shaky. "Thanks, um, excuse me." I pushed my chair away from the table and hustled up to my shared bathroom, shutting the door and peering in the mirror. Did I really just purr like a cat . . . again?

CHAPTER 18

I stared in the bathroom mirror and mouthed "perfect," over and over. "Perfect. Perfect." I'd made the same purr in the hallway at school. "The Perfections. The Perfections." Again, nothing.

Obviously, my subconscious was in hyperdrive about cats because of that clock. I shook my head. "Stop acting ridiculous, Megan." What I really needed to worry about was being impressive at Rhena's house. What would I talk about there?

I undressed and climbed into the shower. The label on the Pantene bottle read, "Lather, rinse, repeat." Nobody'd ever taught me how many times to repeat, and I didn't know why middle school made me suddenly start reading shampoo instructions. I scrubbed my hair twice (just to be sure), then dried and wrapped a towel around my body. In my bedroom, I yanked the door and shades closed, let the towel fall to the floor, and grabbed a pair of pink sport shorts from the dresser.

The magazine went berserk, twizzling and flapping pages.

I snatched up the towel, hugging it close to my naked body.

"What? What's wrong?"

Enchanted Teen fell from the desk, glossy pages sprawled open on the floor.

I stooped to pick it up, not quite trusting it and careful to hold on by the edges. It had landed open to an article titled "What Not to Wear to Live a Life with Flair." I shook my head and said, "What not to wear, does anyone care?"

Electric shocks ripped through my fingertips. "*Ouch!* Dang it." I tossed the magazine onto the bed. "Look, we need to work out an understanding. You wouldn't exist without my wish, so how about being a little nicer to me."

Nothing.

"I'm not using your trickster magic again," I said, digging through my shorts and tossing one pair after another in a pile next to the moving boxes on my floor, until suddenly the magazine flicked out a stream of sparks and purple glitter, urging me to choose the shorts in my hand.

"Okay. Holy geez, you're bossy." I slipped on undies, a pair of jean shorts, a bra, and my rose-colored peace-symbol T-shirt. Piper had once complimented it, so it must be at least somewhat stylish. I looked in the mirror—cute. Maybe the magazine could be helpful, as long as I didn't use it for magical makeovers. I carried it to the bathroom, where I brushed my shoulder-length hair, trying to calm the frizz factor. The pages opened to an article titled "Five Fabulous Hairdos."

"Nope," I said. "Not touching you."

"Hi." Piper slid through the door. "Who ya talking to?"

"Nothing. No one." I dropped a towel over the magazine. "I'm just getting ready for that study get-together."

"Awesome that you were invited." Piper opened a drawer and grabbed a ponytail holder. She wove it through her hair, making a cute messy-bun. "Want me to do your hair?"

"No, thanks. I think I can handle it."

"Okeydoke." She looked at me, sizing me up like a hairdresser would. "You know, your smooth hair looked awesome for school today, but you also have really cute natural curls. You should play up your wave. Are you sure I can't help?"

"Fine." I shrugged. "Thanks."

She kicked out a stool from between the sinks. "Here."

She gave me a side part and took mousse from our drawer, squirting foam into her hand and expertly working it through my wet hair. Then she opened a drawer and found the new blow-dryer and diffuser. "Nice! Where'd we get this?" She turned the T-10 in her hands.

I coughed and looked at my fingernails. "Um . . . I'm not exactly sure."

Piper placed the diffuser on the end of the T-10 and turned it on, scrunching my ends until the curls livened up.

"Thanks, Piper." I turned my head from side to side. "I'll let the rest dry on my walk over."

"You look great, and you're going to have fun, you know?" Piper looked at me in the way Mom used to when she was worried.

"Yeah, I'm just nervous." And with the purring and meowing, I had reasons to be nervous. Maybe motormouthing wasn't the dorkiest thing you could do in middle school.

Piper squeezed me in a hug and then skipped out of the bathroom. I grabbed my backpack and headed out the door.

On the walk to Rhena's, I was back to worrying about what to talk about once I arrived. Hannah had always been the one to keep conversations interesting when we did group things in Colorado. She was funny, and everyone loved her. Maybe I should be funny. *How to Survive Middle School* said so. I continued down the sidewalk, took out my phone, and Googled "funny things to say." Only one-liners popped up, but they all had to do with politics and other boring jokes, so I stuck my phone back into my pocket and practiced conversation openers instead. "Hi. Hey. How do you do"—ugh—this was tough.

The sun still blazed at six thirty when I arrived at the large iron gate blocking the entrance to Rhena's neighborhood.

Palm trees and flowers with bright pink blooms decorated the center island of the street. White oleander bushes lined the sidewalk where a smaller gate also had a keypad. Enormous houses were on the other side. I looked at my text message to be sure I hadn't missed receiving the gate code. Nope. I typed a message to Rhena.

Me: Hey! What's the code to your gate?

Her answer popped up within seconds.

Rhena: Who is this??

Um.
I typed, "Megan Meyers."

Rhena: I'm confused. Why do you need my gate code?

A sick feeling seeped into my stomach.

Me: For the history study group.

Minutes ticked by. I stood on the sidewalk waiting, sweating, melting. A gray cat stepped out of the bushes and rubbed his soft fur against my leg.

"Hey, cutie." I bent down and scratched its head.

Just then an SUV loaded with Team Rhena rolled up to the gate. Its sides had professionally printed car decals and window stickers that read, "Vote Rhena! Spirit Week!"

The mom driving punched digits on the keypad, and I angled my back toward the group, but not before I caught sight of Yoona squished shoulder to shoulder with the others.

I clicked my phone screen back on. Still no reply from Rhena.

I could have dashed inside when the gate opened, but the uneasy feeling continued growing; a feeling like I'd been sucker punched.

My phone finally vibrated.

Rhena: My bad. I have two Megans in my phone. I texted ur number when I meant to text the other Megan. Meghan with an H. That's

why u accidently got the message. Sorry 4 the trouble.

I reread the message, realizing I wasn't going to be walking through that gate. I wouldn't need any funny lines or conversation openers. I wasn't going to be part of that study group. "Disappointed" wasn't even a big enough word to describe me.

Another car rolled up. I kept staring at my phone screen in disbelief, waiting for an incoming text that would say, "But come on in."

It didn't.

"Megan! Hey, Megan," someone called from a car.

The driver's window finished unrolling. I saw Mrs. Sinoway first, and then the passenger. Jackson.

"Ahh, hey."

"Are you okay?" Mrs. Sinoway asked, looking at me with an odd expression.

"Sure, of course," I said, my tone ridiculously chirpy.

Mrs. Sinoway squinted.

Jackson leaned over his aunt. He gave me a strange look. Shocked, almost. But then he smiled. "Are you going to Rhena's for the study group?"

Keep it together. Don't let him see you're hurting. "Um, you have Kersey, too?" I managed.

"Yep. After lunch."

A car waiting behind them beeped. Jackson

glanced back. "You want to ride with us the rest of the way to Rhena's?"

"Oh, I . . . no. Thanks. I'm just on my way home." A huge lump choked my throat.

Mrs. Sinoway typed the gate code. Jackson glanced at my backpack. The gate slid open. "Are you sure?"

"I've got to run." Tears pricked the backs of my eyes. I turned and sped down the sidewalk.

Two days into a new school and I'd already been humiliated. Everyone was probably in Rhena's house, having a good laugh over seeing me waiting by the gate. Spirit Week was the worst thing that could've happened to me. Rhena was being so mean because of some dumb election, and I'd bet any money that she'd have her friends—her Rhenite clan—laughing at me again tomorrow.

On the walk home, I wiped my eyes and clenched my jaw. The magazine said it could deal with mean girls, and if I was willing to face another cost, I could take Rhena down.

CHAPTER 19

I threw open my front door and crashed into Dad, who was heading out.

"Whoa, sorry," he said, then did a double take and smiled. "Well, hey, Lion King. You're back early."

I dropped the heavy backpack from my shoulders, and my voice unleashed the anger meant for Rhena. "Lion King. What's that supposed to mean?"

Archie rounded the corner, took one look at me, and then tucked tail and ran up the stairs.

Huh? I turned back to Dad, crossing one arm over the other. "Well?"

"Oh?" Dad looked surprised. "I just thought . . . with the hair, you were trying . . . you wanted . . . you know . . ." His voice trailed off. "I'm sorry. I never know what to say to you girls." He looked down and jingled the change in his pocket. "Listen. I have to get back to the office. I'll see you in a few hours." He backed out the door.

Barett clomped down the stairs, carrying one of Piper's shirts.

"See ya, Piper," she called back toward the kitchen. "Thanks for the loaner." Barett headed toward the doorway. "See ya, Meg—" She stopped and blinked at me twice before speaking again. "What's with the hair?"

"Why?"

"It has a lot of voltage, if you know what I mean." She shrugged. "See ya."

I reached up and felt a tower of puff. Huh?

I ran to the bathroom next to the kitchen. "Ahhhhhhk!" I screamed when I got to the mirror. My hair had exploded to four times its normal volume—I looked like I was wearing a lion's mane.

Piper was at my side within seconds. "Are you all right? Whoa! I mean, wow. Your hair."

"Yeah. My hair. Thanks a lot, Piper, 'cause everybody from school just saw me looking like this." By everybody, I meant Jackson.

"Megan, that sucks! Do you think it was the T-10?"

I gulped. She was right. The T-10 and diffuser had come from the magazine, just like that horrible makeover.

"But it's kind of fun. And who cares. You should've stayed."

I hung my head and walked to the kitchen. Piper followed.

"That's not exactly why I'm home early." I pressed a glass to the icemaker, filling it with cubes and water, then I hopped up onto the kitchen counter and told Piper what had happened with the un-invitation.

"Are you kidding? That's awful!" Piper reached over and squeezed my hand. "She can't get away with this. What a witch!"

"I know, right? Rhena is so—"

"Rhena?" Piper released my hand. "She's my middle school big sister in yearbook club."

"Big sister?" Heat rose in my skin.

"I mean, that's what they call it in the club. Are you sure it was Rhena? She's really super-nice."

I stared at Piper. "Yes. I'm sure."

"But don't you think there could be a legit excuse, like maybe her parents limited the group size or there wasn't enough pizza or something?" She searched my face. "Grams would tell us to give her the benefit of the doubt."

"I don't think Grams would say that in this instance."

"I'm just saying Rhena's not like that. Maybe you got confused on the details?"

"Confused?" Wasn't Piper supposed to be on my side? "Whatever." I jumped off the counter and marched up the stairs while Piper called my name. I slammed my bedroom door and dialed Hannah. At least she'd take my side.

"What's going on in Boulder?" I said when she answered.

"Hey! Not much. What's up with you?"

It was embarrassing to admit getting uninvited, but I still wanted to talk to her about it and about all the stress I was feeling over pulling off a flashmob in T minus three days. "Well—"

"Oh, by the way, do you remember Brooke Sutherland?" Hannah asked. "And how we thought she was a big snot last year? We got it all wrong. She's actually sweet! I had lunch with her today."

I sank into the bed.

Hannah rattled on. "We should've hung out with her more last year. She's really funny."

"Yeah, that's great." What I really wanted to say was "How could you?"

"Oh, speaking of which. I have to run. Brooke and I planned to Skype tonight and I'm already a few minutes late."

"Don't go getting a new BFF." I faked a laugh, but Hannah had already hung up.

CHAPTER 20

In the morning, I added a few notes to my orange Moleskine journal under the costs category. The first line under "UPDATE" had "magazine costs = tricks (i.e., makeover)."

I wrote in the next line:

T-10 (from magazine) = hair disaster
??? = . . . Purring?

I dried my hair with a regular blow-dryer and diffuser. My phone dinged.

Yoona: We on for Wednesday Night Walks tonight? 🐶

Sure, Yoona had been in that car of Rhenites. She probably knew I got uninvited. But she couldn't be blamed for Rhena.

Me: Yep! Can't wait!

I pushed aside moving boxes, the ones still packed with books and Halloween stuff, and then I dug through my closet for something to wear to school. The magazine flipped and fluttered like a fish on sand.

"What?" I walked over and crossed my arms, refusing to pick it up.

It flipped again.

"No. I'm not interested in your next makeover or 'free' gift." I put air quotes around "free." "I'm sticking with the clock. Only the clock." I caught my reflection in the bedroom mirror, the zit on my chin still there but clearing up. "And you know what else. I should wish that Rhena's hair fritzes into a 'fro and pimples pile on her nose and chin."

The magazine did a backflip, but Marlo Bee's cover photo changed from a smile to a frown.

"What?" I said, looking at Marlo Bee's eyes. "You can't be mad. When I first opened this magazine, the card you gave me said, 'If you've got a dilemma, we've got your back.' Remember? Well, Rhena's a dilemma. What are you going to do about it?"

A cold chill zipped through the room and rushed up my spine. The magazine pushed open past the fashion week pages and the stuck pages and settled on an article titled "How to Deal with Mean Girls."

I carefully picked up *Enchanted Teen* by the edges and leaned in to read the small print. The line below the title had words running together in nonsensical gibberish. "BabbleGabbleCrinoseFlibbertigibbetFlapdoodleSingultusCacographyPalabra."

"Is this supposed to be a spell, like saying 'abracadabra'?" I reread the line. How could this possibly stop a mean girl?

I paused for a moment, reconsidering whether I actually wanted to get Rhena back. Nothing good had come from the magazine so far, and Rhena didn't feel worth the risk. Plus, revenge wasn't my style. "No thanks." I fanned the pages. "I don't trust you not to throw me under the bus again."

A thick card with sparks of glitter fell from the magazine and dropped to the floor. I picked it up. A perfume sample. The advertisement read, "Peppermint Wish, a Parfum de Cataire scent for girls who want to exude cool." Bold letters on the scented flaps read:

Open Here to Unleash the Magic.
Friends Are Sure to Follow.

"Like I said, no thanks. Probably more tricks." I shoved the perfume sample back between the pages and dropped the magazine on my desktop next to my backpack. I wouldn't touch it again. The clock was my only safe bet. It had given me the snow cost-free.

Enchanted Teen had been the problem causer. Right? I reconsidered the hypothesis I'd written in my orange journal—specific wishes on the clock are safe. Unspecific wishes cause problems. This had to be accurate. In fact, maybe specific and unspecific wishes in magic were like stable and unstable atoms—with stable atoms, all is well, but with unstable atoms, the energy is radioactive.

All I had to do to keep the magic in check was stick to clear and concise wishes on the clock, so that on Friday—T minus two days—I'd have stable magic from the clock to nail the perfect flashmob plan. I pushed the magazine to the far corner of my desk and decided not to touch it again.

I slid open the desk drawer, searching for bubble-gum—my backup plan in case my knuckles wouldn't pop at eleven-eleven. I scooped up two pieces of strawberry Hubba Bubba and stuffed them into my pocket.

Popping supplies, done. Clothing, hmmm. Ditching the full makeover was a no-brainer, and I'd keep my standard ponytail, but looking cute had felt nice, so I grabbed a pillow and headed to Piper's room.

Piper sat in front of her mirror with her laptop open to Style Rookie's blog. I would have tossed the pillow at her head, but she was clasping a sparkly clip in her hair.

"Hi." Piper glanced at the pillow I'd dropped. "I'm sorry. Especially about the un-invitation. That sucks."

I shrugged. "Cute clip."

"Thanks! It's the latest from Tarina Tarentino."

"I don't know who that is, but she looks good on you." I smiled. "So . . . hey, Pipes. Can I borrow a shirt?"

Piper practically sprinted the three steps it took to stand face-to-face with me. She put both of her hands on my shoulders, inhaled a deep yogic breath, and with all the drama of a soap star replied, "I've been waiting my whole life for you to ask me that question."

CHAPTER 21

Dad had enrolled Archie in Doggie Day Camp after the whole shredding of *Scientific American*. Even though that's Dad's favorite magazine, he'd taken it in stride and said, "It was such good reading Archie tore right through it." Then Dad had slapped his leg and laughed at his own joke, which was the part that had made me laugh, too.

In order to get Archie to camp and Dad to work on time, he had to drive Piper and me to school early. I put Archie in the front seat as per usual, but he squirmed out of my lap and jumped to the back.

"What's up with you?" He tried to tuck himself under Piper's feet and away from my reach. "So weird."

"You sure you brushed your teeth?" Piper said, her eyes twinkling.

"Ha-ha, Piper."

The school grounds were quiet when we pulled up front.

"Bye, Archie. Make lots of friends." I climbed out of the car. "Later, Dad." I closed the door.

As Dad drove off, I pulled my shoulders back and centered myself, ready to face the day. Even though things had sucked with Rhena and the study party last night, I had a lot to look forward to—magic, for starters. I could get the wish out of the way today, have fun at the Humane Society tonight, breathe easy on Thursday, and Friday would be the best flashmob in the history of flashmobs. Plus, my homework was done, I felt cute in Piper's clothes (low-rise white shorts, an ocean blue shirt, and a silver necklace), I had friends—Ally, Erin, Noelle, Mia, and Yoona—and I'd see Jackson again at math club.

"See you, Pi—" My foot skidded forward, my backpack went flying, and my hands hit the ground, saving me from landing in full splits. But my fingers squished between the same slippery pile I'd skidded in—a steamy mound of dog mess.

"GROSS!" I screamed, hopped up, and wiped my hand on a patch of dry grass, trying to scrape off as much as I could. The ick coated my sandal, too, and the smell was all kinds of horrible.

Piper grabbed my backpack and the stuff that had spilled out. "You okay?" she asked, picking up my notebook, calculator, and magazine.

Magazine! I hadn't packed that.

"Ugh! Gross!" I said again. I held my hands as far away from my sides as possible. "PIPER! Ew!"

"Come on," Piper said. "I'll carry your stuff to the restroom."

"Ewewewewew!"

We rushed to the nearest bathroom. Rhena's flyers were plastered all over the door. They featured a professional photo of Rhena smiling and holding a giant roll of Smarties and the slogan:

BE A SMARTIE!

VOTE RHENA FOR SPIRIT CAPTAIN!

If I weren't in such a hurry, I would've pointed out that Rhena had taped her posters on top of Ally's flyers and across other signs, too. Obnoxious!

I shoved open the door with my shoulder and power-scrubbed my hands at the sink. "So gross!" I repeated. "So gross." I wiped my sandal clean and squeezed a gallon of soap from the dispenser into my palms for another scrubbing.

Strung across the mirrors was more of Rhena's propaganda: "Chews Rhena Thornsmith for Spirit Fun!" Two wicker baskets tied with red and blue silk ribbons were sitting on the countertop. One was stacked with yellow packs of "Chews Rhena!" gum, and the other was filled with rolls of Smarties.

Piper leaned with the weight of both of our backpacks. "Uhhh, I hate to tell you, but that smell is not going away. Are you sure you got everything off your shoe?"

"Look." I bent my knee and showed her the bottom of my sandal. "This is disgusting." I turned back to the sink and rinsed my hands. This was supposed to be a great day.

I squeezed a third mountain of soap into my cupped palms, scrubbing and scrubbing, not paying attention to Piper. The next thing I knew our backpacks were on the floor and she was fanning the pages of the magazine.

"What are you doing?" I screamed.

"Victory," she said, snatching out the perfume sample. "I knew it. Magazines always have a bunch of these." She opened the perfume flap and—

"No!" I said, trying to block her with dripping

hands, but Piper reached around and rubbed the sample down my arm. "Mmmmmm. See? The smell is gone already." She smiled. "You're welcome."

She was right. The whole restroom brightened with the cool, minty scent.

"I should use some, too."

"No!" I snatched the card from her grasp and held it behind my back. "I . . . umm . . . I'll probably need it all."

"Okay, Miss Stingy." She smiled. "Well, here." She handed me a paper towel. "I've got to go."

"Thanks." As Piper bounced off humming a song, I reread the perfume card: "For girls who want to exude cool. Open here to unleash the magic. Friends are sure to follow."

My shoulders stiffened. The magazine was sitting on top of my backpack. The cover hadn't changed—I still had one more use of magic—so maybe nothing would happen. I hoped nothing would happen. My breathing calmed. Perhaps it was a regular perfume sample after all. I reopened it and rubbed it on my wrist and neck, then tossed the sample into the trash.

Just then the bathroom door swung open and in came the scent of tangerines, followed by the green-eyed delivery girl.

"Hello, hello!" she said in her double-shot

cappuccino frappy-happy way. "We meet again."

"I . . . I . . ." What had I done?

"Clipboard, check." She pulled a clipboard from her messenger bag. "See how easily I found this? I told you I was going to get more organized, and—*ka-pow*—I've done it." She patted the clipboard. "It's because of my new filing system. I put it under *M* for Megan. Wait, hmmm." She put a hand to her chin. "Maybe I should file it under *C* for clipboard. Or just *B* for board—"

I cut her off. "Okay, great. But, ummm . . . why are you here?"

"Ah, yes." She straightened her lens-free glasses and spent a moment reading her notes. "It says here the flap has been opened and—"

"What flap?"

She pointed to the perfume ad I'd tossed into the garbage. "And you used it. Now I need Piper's signature of receipt."

"Wait. Why Piper?"

"She opened the flap, right?"

"Yes, but *I* used the sample." I clenched my fist at my side. Nobody was going to drag my little sister into this. "Only me. Piper didn't use a drop."

"Okeydoke. Then I need your signature of receipt." She pushed the paperwork under my nose and produced the gold fountain pen.

"Wait, I—"

"It's really just a formality. You've already used the product. Please sign."

"But the sample came from the magazine, and that's from my original wish. Isn't the perfume included, like a package deal?"

"Nope. Not included. It's a tangible good, an add-on. Like ordering a latte but asking for caramel on top. You pay extra for that."

My shoulders dropped. More rules, and worse, more costs.

"Please sign. Quick quick. I have lots of deliveries today."

"What does it do?" I asked.

"Let's see." She pushed her glasses up her nose and looked at the clipboard. "It's pretty straightforward. Says here, you used the perfume and now friends will follow."

"And what's the catch? Am I going to start stinking once class starts?"

"Nope. Minty freshness all day long, lucky girl! Now let's get this show on the road."

She stared at me. I crossed my arms and stared back.

"Fun! I love staring contests. But I'm in a hurry, so either you can sign or Piper can sign."

I grabbed the pen and put my name by the X, noticing microscopic fine print. "What else does that say?"

"What else indeed." She snatched back the pen and looked at my signature. "Fantastico! You have lovely penmanship. It's a lost art, you know. And now for your bonus." She put the clipboard back inside her messenger bag and whipped out a crystal bottle labeled Parfum de Cataire, spritzing me down with a hazy mist. Then she breezed out the door.

CHAPTER 22

In the seventh-grade wing, the wall of lockers smelled like ham sandwiches, pencil shavings, and Fritos, but the enchanted perfume still wafted that bright mint scent to my nose.

I twisted my lock combination.

The door next to me clanged shut. A girl handed a book to her friend and smiled at me. "I love your necklace."

"Thanks." Overtalking or clamming up had been my middle school go-tos in Colorado. But no more. I reminded myself that *HSMS* had said to be positive and friendly, so I smiled at the girls and decided to keep it simple—say hi or how's it going—easy . . .

"Hi . . . ow . . . dy," fell from my mouth, followed by one of my snort-giggles. My blush came immediately.

But the girls didn't roll their eyes or give me a Brooke-Sutherland-Ronald-Miller look. Instead they smiled, and one said, "Are you new here?"

I nodded.

"If you need anything, just ask. I mean, we're locker neighbors, so you know where to find me."

"Wow, thanks."

They were really nice. Did the perfume do that?

They walked down the hall past Ally, who was headed my way with her friends. Stress tightened my throat. What if I snorted again? Or what if these girls were interested in me only because I was supposed to help Ally win Spirit Week?

Stop it, I told myself. The dog-poop drama and delivery girl had unhinged me, but these girls seemed genuinely nice. I had to quit overthinking or I'd come off like a total dorkjob. I grabbed books from my locker and glanced in Ally's direction again. She finished talking to Turner, squeezed his arm, and then headed my way, friends in tow.

I forced my shoulders to relax.

"Hey, Fun-meister!" Erin said.

A blush threatened under my skin.

"Mmmmm," Mia said, adjusting a stack of library

books in her arm. "Your perfume smells great. What is that?"

"Peppermint Wish." I took a whiff of my arm. "It is nice, right? I usually go for strawberry scents."

"Me too," Ally said. "Like I'm team strawberry ChapStick. Way better than cherry."

"Burt's Bees pomegranate," Erin said. "That's the real deal."

And just like that, I was in a conversation.

Realization hit—the magical perfume had said friends would follow, and here they were. This was easy! I stopped worrying about saying the right thing and just talked while the magic scent wafted from my arm. Everyone chatted and laughed until Erin said, "I heard Miss Dragon Fruit had a study party at her house yesterday."

My cheeks started to heat up, but I had a quick change of subjects at the ready. "Um, guess what? I've got Friday figured out. I'm going to organize a flashmob."

A flashmob really was the perfect thing for Spirit Week elections. It would be the hugest thing this school had ever seen, especially since I had magic. I could copy a singing and dancing number from YouTube, and then I could wish my flashmob to be ten times better. A hundred times! I could wish for a celebrity, a rock star, or even the president of the United States to do the flashmob with us if I wanted. Saguaro Prep's Spirit Week elections were going to be epic.

Suddenly I was beaming, and the group was smiling back, and Ally was saying, "A flashmob! I love it."

Everyone started talking at once and sounding more and more excited.

"Super-clever, Megan," Noelle said. "And Ally, you're going to win for sure."

"Yeah," Erin agreed. "And I've always wanted to be in a flashmob. I can't wait."

"Me too. I wish it were Friday now," Mia said.

Ally was nodding and smiling.

Everyone was happy. My world was perfect.

And then Rhena walked up.

"He-ey," she said. "What's going on here?"

None of her business. I didn't have to put up with Rhena and her games, especially since I had the perfume to keep her in check today.

Shelby stood on her right. Yoona shuffled close behind, darting apologetic looks my way and sending enough secret glances for me to get the hint: keep the Humane Society thingy on the down-low.

"Nothing's up." I crossed my arms and waited for the perfume to take action.

"Any update for your"—Rhena paused and did air quotes—"'big event' on Friday?"

Shelby arched an eyebrow. Yoona turned her gaze to the tile floor.

"It's going to be epic." I loved how my words came out confident. Even my smile felt relaxed. "You can count on it."

"But it's a secret," Ally said, placing her hands on her hips and winking at me. "The agreement was Friday, so no details for you guys until the Spirit Week elections."

Rhena smirked. "That's what I thought. A one-hit wonder."

"You've clearly got nothing," Shelby said.

Hold up. Why wasn't the perfume working on them? Not that I wanted Rhena's and Shelby's friendship, but it was weird that they weren't affected. Could they smell it?

"Excuse me," Erin said. "Whatever Megan does for Spirit Week, it's going to be for Team Ally. So it's not like we're going to give your group of legumes advance notice. You'll just have to hear about it when it's announced to the rest of the school."

I tensed as I listened to my allegiances get declared out loud. No more Switzerland.

Rhena raised a challenging eyebrow at me. "Really?"

I wished I had the guts to say, "Yes, really," but now my throat knotted.

Yoona looked at me, both worry and warning on her face. Then Ally looped an arm in mine and said, "Yep."

"Fine," Rhena said. "Let's see how that goes for you. See you at the Spirit Week kickoff pep rally." She turned to leave, but not before saying, "If I were you, I'd skip it and save myself the embarrassment."

Students passing in the hall glanced at us.

My legs felt noodly, but Noelle said, "Ignore her." She hooked her elbow in mine and patted my arm, her fingers dotted with henna hearts and rays. "Okay, move in, guys." Erin, Mia, Ally, Noelle, and I tightened our circle and spoke in hushed voices. "Back to the flashmob."

"Yeah," Mia said. "Let's do something fun, but can we please not do one of those singing and dancing numbers like on YouTube?"

"We'll definitely be original," Ally said. "Right, Megan?"

"Yeah. Mmmhmm. Of course," I said. "Original." There went my brilliant plan to copy.

"All right," Noelle said, scrunching her eyebrows. "I get what a flashmob is, and I'm game for whatever. But how exactly does it work?"

"Well . . ." I explained how we'd make it so the entire seventh-grade class could put on a surprise event for the rest of the school. Every seventh grader would show up at the same place at the same time on Friday.

We settled on noon in the cafeteria, and then Erin and Mia started talking about a flashmob video they'd seen.

Mia said, "There's this one where a guy proposes to his girlfriend by having her sit on the back of a truck bed. Someone in front slowly drives her down the street and the guy follows behind, singing to her and dancing."

"Yeah," Erin said. "And the truck is decked out with giant speakers playing music and it keeps slowly rolling along like she's on a parade float, and one by one the neighbors come out and they're in on it, dancing and singing with the guy, and everything is perfectly choreographed."

"Yep. Her parents were in on it, too," Mia said.

"Awwww," Ally said.

"Even a lady fixing the streetlight joins in," Erin said.

Ally, Erin, Mia, and Noelle were smiling and laughing. "Ours is going to be ten times better!" I said. It didn't matter that I didn't have an idea—I had the magic clock. "Our Spirit Week kickoff will be the best

Saguaro Prep has ever seen," I said. "After I'm done, you're going to wonder if I live a double life as a professional flashmob planner.

"In fact," I added, preparing a lie, "I want to keep it on the down-low, but I actually have a secret, not-ready-for-disclosure plan. And it's going to be major. My ide—" A cough exploded from my mouth before I could say "idea." Not a regular cough—more like a full-blown gack, like I was hacking on a fur ball.

Ally patted my back. "Are you okay?"

I gacked and yarped and gacked and yarped until I managed to say, "Purrrfect . . . ummm, I'm fine." I fumbled for my water bottle and chugged it down, wondering why the heck I sounded like a choking cat.

"So what are we doing?" Erin asked. "How can we help you prep?"

"Well . . ." My mind raced.

Mia pushed her glasses up her nose.

"Um . . . I—"

Just then the bell rang.

"You're not telling us?" asked Noelle.

"Ummm." I tucked my hair behind an ear. Parfum de Cataire wafted from my arm, reminding me I had magic—magic perfume and a magic clock—so I didn't need to lie or worry about anything. "I'm sorry." I swallowed. "I just . . . got excited. To be honest, I don't really know what the flashmob is going to be yet. We're definitely going to have a fun one, and I'm going to figure out the details before I involve you guys."

"All right, Miss Fun-meister," Ally said, smiling. "I'm sure it'll be epic, knowing you!"

"Epic!" Erin echoed. "Spirit Week elections and you'll make Ally the cherry in a room full of avocados!"

"Are you sure you don't mind doing all the planning on your own?" Ally asked.

I had magic. I didn't mind at all. "Nope. Just tell me what else I can do for your election and I'm there for you."

"You guys," Erin said. "The bell rang."

"See you later," I said, still coughing from that tickle in my throat.

"Later?" Ally said. "Aren't you coming with us?"

"Huh?"

"For the election speeches," Noelle said. "At the all-school assembly."

"Right! I forgot about the adjusted schedules."

"Come on. Sit with us," Ally said.

We headed down the hall toward the gym.

I coughed again. The tickle in my throat wouldn't go away, so when I spotted the water fountain outside the gym doors I said, "I'll find you guys inside." I jiggled my empty water bottle. "I need a refill."

Ally told me where they'd be sitting and said, "We'll save you a seat."

I hurried to the line at the water fountain, untwisting the lid of my bottle.

Suddenly, a sharp pain crunched through my big toe.

"Ow." I grimaced.

Rhena stepped off my foot and in line in front of me. "Whoops." She smiled. "I have a speech to make, so I'll need to go ahead of you."

Yoona drifted to the outside of the line and shot me an apologetic glance.

I bent my toes, testing the bones. Why didn't the perfume affect them? It was supposed to help me make friends.

"You smell nice," Yoona said, not chatty and confident like she had been at the Humane Society, but nervous, like speaking in front of Rhena was a big stretch.

"You smell like an old lady's herb garden," Shelby said.

"Exactly." Rhena laughed.

The perfume obviously wasn't making Rhena and Shelby like me. Grams did say the clockmakers had a tricky sense of humor. And the magic *never* did exactly what I asked for.

So if the perfume *didn't* work that way, it meant everyone else had been nice on their own. They'd laughed along with my snorts and were interested in me *before* the flashmob talk and *without* the perfume's help.

Even though Rhena and Shelby were mean-girling me, I couldn't help but feel a little happy.

Still, I'd signed for something. The hair on my neck bristled.

"You really think you'll be ready for Friday, huh?" Rhena said. "Well, here. Let me give you this helpful reminder." She whipped out a Sharpie from the side of her backpack, grabbed my hand, and scratched a big "2" across it in black ink, pressing harder than necessary.

"Two days till Friday," Shelby said, all singsongy. "Tick tock."

CHAPTER 23

I texted Hannah.

Me: SOS I REPEAT SOS!!!!! NEED FLASH-MOB IDEA PRONTO!!!

Me: T minus two days!!!!!!!

Me: ASAP!!!!

I rushed into the gym, stressing about how fast Friday would come and also worrying about what the perfume magic had in store.

Students sat crushed together on the bleachers. Blue and red banners hung from the ceiling, showing off the years when the Saguaro Mustangs had won different championships. A huge painted red horse covered the center of the glossy wooden floor. The faculty stood near entrances, talking and sipping from coffee mugs. Energy and chatter buzzed from all directions.

Principal Scoggins spoke into a microphone. "People, take a seat." His voice crackled from the speakers.

I looked to where my friends had said they'd be seated and saw Jackson with Tank and Wigglesworth, laughing and trying to organize their section to do the wave. So cute.

Ally was seated a few rows behind them and called my name. "Megan, Megan! Up here."

I hurried up several giant bleacher steps and squeezed in between Erin and Noelle.

"Stop searching for your friends," Principal Scoggins said, "and just take the first spot you see. Now." About a dozen stragglers plopped down wherever they were standing.

I searched the sea of faces for Piper, hoping she'd see me surrounded by friends so she'd know there was more to my middle school world than slipping in dog poop.

"Where did Turner sit?" Ally asked. "Is tech club doing sound and lights or should we save a seat for him?"

Mia and Erin shrugged.

"Helloooooooo, Mustangs!" Mr. Scoggins said into the microphone. "Welcome. We have a lot in store for you this morning. I know you're excited about our upcoming Spirit Week, so we'll get announcements out of the way quickly, then we'll move on to election speeches, followed by a brief presentation by our spirit club. We'll end with an act by our comedy duo, Mosquitos Suck."

The crowd roared.

"Okay. Okay. Let's get through these announcements."

Mr. Scoggins blazed through his list and then thanked the tech and engineering clubs for manning the music. This must've been their cue, because the sound of bugles and drums blasted from the speakers, and if Mom had taught me correctly, I was hearing "Ruffles and Flourishes."

Mr. Scoggins' voice grew animated, "As you all know, Spirit Week has been a longtime Saguaro Prep tradition, dating back to the founding of our school in 1978."

The crowd whooped and stomped their feet.

Like a conductor, Mr. Scoggins held a lifted hand toward the invisible tech club. When his arm swung down, another musical piece pumped out of the speakers. The crowd cheered, and Noelle leaned to me and said, "That's Saguaro Prep's school song."

It continued playing in the background while Mr. Scoggins delivered his speech. "Tradition holds that we kick off Spirit Week with our election on Friday. Events will continue through to the end of the following Friday."

The crowd cheered again.

"A representative from every grade will be elected; however, there will be only one Spirit Week Captain. The Spirit Week Captain gets to choose—"

"Dictate!" someone shouted from the crowd.

Mr. Scoggins laughed with the crowd. "Yes. It's true, the Spirit Captain gets to dictate what we wear, eat, and do for a full week as it pertains to spirit, so choose wisely." He raised his eyebrows above his glasses. "Voting will take place this Friday in the cafeteria. Please note, we will host an all-school lunch during fifth period to announce the winner."

More cheering and foot stomping shook the bleachers.

"As custom holds, specific themes may not be part of the campaign, but are revealed after the election."

This earned some groans from the crowd.

"No complaining," Mr. Scoggins said to the groaners. The song came to an end. "All you have to do is cast your vote wisely for a leader who you believe will foster school spirit through our three Cs: Creativity, Community, and Camaraderie."

Wigglesworth and Tank lifted fists in the air and shouted, "Triple C! Triple C!"

Jackson joined them. "Triple C! Triple C!"

Quickly, the crowd was chanting, "Triple C! Triple C!"

Mr. Scoggins let it go on for half a minute; then Coach Crosby blew her whistle.

Mr. Scoggins spoke again. "I love the enthusiasm, which provides the perfect segue to the candidate speeches. Entrants, you'll each get one minute to convince us why you're the best candidate to govern Spirit Week. Let's begin with the most important office, Spirit Captain. Candidates, please come forward."

Ally rose, climbed down a few bleacher steps, and crossed the wooden gym floor. Rhena stood on the other side of Mr. Scoggins.

"The seventh grade has put forth two candidates for Captain this year: Ally Menendez and Rhena Thornsmith. Going alphabetically, we'll hear from Miss Menendez first." Mr. Scoggins passed the microphone to Ally.

Our group clapped and cheered.

"Woot woot! Hey, fellow Mustangs!"

The crowd roared.

"So hey. The year's starting out awesome. Year-book club had a great turnout and spirit club is about to teach us some chants. Now all we have to do is make some memories."

The crowd clapped and gave another woot.

"As your Spirit Week Captain, I promise to make spirit my focus not just for next week but all year long. I'll support all the sports teams. In fact, don't forget we have a home football game on Saturday. Come out and show your Mustang pride and buy something at the bake sale."

Students in front of me, beside me, and behind me cheered and clapped.

"And I promise to have more school dances and liven things up around here. Thank you!" Our group stood, screaming Ally's name.

Rhena went next. She listed off campaign promises, receiving her share of applause, and added, "And Mustangs, I have an exciting announcement. Jackson Litner is joining my campaign ticket, so a vote for me is a vote for Jackson. We're running as a team—your Queen and King."

More cheers erupted.

Jackson stood up, smiling and seeming genuinely surprised by all the applause. My heart sank. Were they more than best friends?

"And one more thing to cover," she said. "Yesterday, in the seventh-grade quad, we made an announcement."

Now what?

"It really should've been an all-school announcement. You see, one of our new students was Ally's very first zappee. Her name is Megan Meyers—wave, Megan—"

Panic tornadoed through my body. Erin nudged me like the attention was a good thing, but I could feel this spiraling down a no-good track at a velocity that matched the speed of light, aka 299,792,458 meters per second.

Noelle pointed my way. Heads shifted.

"Did everyone like the snow?" Rhena asked.

Cheers. More applause.

I interlaced my fingers and squeezed.

"I thought you would. And of course, I was instrumental in helping Megan plan that little event. I'm calling it Saguaro Prep's First Annual Snow Day, and I plan to bring it to our school every year."

My eyebrows shot up. *She* planned it?

"What?" Noelle and Mia screamed.

"She's a lying lima bean!" Erin hollered.

Applause exploded around us. Ally shook her head

and reached to grab the mic back, but Rhena had control and pushed on.

"Megan had sort of a meltdown," Rhena said. "Being put on the spot and all, so of course I helped her. It's what any good leader does."

Seriously? She's taking credit *and* making me look lame? I stared at the faculty. *Stop her*, my brain screamed. Isn't her minute up?

Mr. Scoggins was busy directing late arrivals, and the row of teachers seemed to have tuned out, grading papers or looking at their phones.

"Most of you probably haven't met Megan yet, because she's pretty shy." Rhena nodded with an apologetic smile, making her voice all sweet while she delivered the next dose of venom. "Some even say she's mousy, so let's not put heavy expectations on her. I mean, she said she'd do something else on Friday, but unless I'm behind that, too, she'll probably choke."

My backpack vibrated against my legs with crazed energy. The magazine practically screamed for me to take it out, and this time I didn't hesitate. I leaned down and peeled back the zipper. *Enchanted Teen* jetted to the top.

Rhena went on, getting laughs from the crowd at my expense.

Enchanted Teen battered the side of my leg, frenetic

and wild. I grabbed it to my lap, and it sprung open, right to the "How to Deal with a Mean Girl" article. Rhena fit the bill—first with the un-invitation and now this public shaming.

Mr. Scoggins returned to the center of the gym floor, tapped his watch, and motioned for Rhena to return the microphone. She turned a shoulder on him. "And so when you vote, remember that I was the leader for the zap, I gave you the snow, I . . ."

"Okay?" I whispered to the magazine. "I don't know why I should trust you, but please work. Please stop her."

"Or you could vote for Ally." Rhena put her mouth close to the mic and fake-yawned. "I mean, you've met Ally, right?"

Here goes nothing. I slapped a hand to the article. Typeface from that strange gibberish tagline lifted from the page and hovered in the air. The words floated, swirled, and then zoomed in a flash, spinning around Rhena's head and then right inside her mouth, invisible to everybody except me.

"So remember, how you vote on Fff—flibbertigib-bet." Rhena paused. "Flibberty—" She looked confused, and she tapped the microphone like it was playing tricks on her. Then she tried again. "CrinoseFlibberti-gibbetFlapdoodleSingultusCacographyPalabra."

Students around me turned to one another, clearly wondering if they should laugh or wait for a punch line. I squeezed the edge of the magazine pages to keep my hands from trembling.

Rhena looked panicked.

Ally zoomed three steps to Rhena and snatched the microphone. "Okay, Rhena? That's a little odd. But let me add that *Megan's* snow day was fun. And Mustangs," Ally said to the assembly, "that was all Megan. Not Rhena. Not me. Just Megan. She's awesome, am I right?"

My face burned at the sound of applause.

"She's creative. They called her the Fun-meister at her last school!"

I stared down at my knuckles.

"In fact," Ally said, "this is kind of spur-of-the-moment, but with her level of creativity, I think Megan would make a great Spirit Week Co-Captain."

I gawked at Ally. What was she doing?

Ally smiled at me from across the room. "Megan, I hope you don't mind me putting you on the spot, but you said you wanted to be more involved, so what do you think?"

The noise in the gym made my ears ring. Erin patted my back and Noelle was smiling and nodding and nodding and nodding until I nodded back, mirroring her, not really processing what I was nodding about, and then Ally pumped her fist and said, "Yes! That's awesome! You hear that, folks? Vote Ally and Megan. A vote for us is a vote for Team Free Spirit!"

What?

Noelle, Mia, and Erin were on their feet, arms raised in the air. The students in front of me screamed and clapped. The kids beside me whistled. People on my left stomped their feet and cheered, and as the noise grew louder Ally paced to the other side of the gym floor, away from Mr. Scoggins. "Mustangs," she bellowed into the mic, "I can assure you Megan will not choke. In fact, wait till you see what Megan and I have planned for Election Day. We don't have all the particulars just yet, but if you thought the snow was fun, get ready, because next up, Flashmob Friday!"

More noise. More applause. A flustered Mr. Scoggins zigzagged after Ally and the microphone.

"So that's in two days, Mustangs. And for any seventh grader interested in joining in on the Free Spirit Flashmob, I'm setting up a closed group on my social media. Send me a message and I'll give you the details. All other grades, prepare to be surprised and delighted." Ally hurried her last words out. "Get ready. Friday is going to be legendary!"

Mr. Scoggins finally seized the microphone, but

nobody could hear him. The room had gone insane, students cheering, wooting, whistling, clapping.

"Come on," Erin screamed. "Let's move over here and sit with Tank's group."

Erin, Noelle, and Mia walked down a few bleacher steps. Somebody tapped my shoulder. I turned around and Yoona spoke close to my ear, her words rushing out. "Things would go smoother if Rhena wasn't so worried about you becoming too popular. Just tone it down a bit."

Then Shelby sidled in beside Yoona, shaking her head and speaking to me in a voice that traveled under the crazed applause. "Ally's just using you. You'll see."

Rhena still stood on the gym floor, shaking her head and holding her throat. Slowly, I closed the magazine, and when I did, Rhena let go of her neck.

The screaming crowd, the magic, Shelby's words—my head already hurt. I looked at the magazine in my lap. The yellow blurb on the cover read, "Expired Issue."

CHAPTER 24

When the assembly ended, I let Yoona and Shelby get some distance before I started walking toward history to cue up my wish. Hannah still hadn't replied to my text, so I tried again.

Me: Didn't you see my SOS. I need a Hannah-esque plan for a flashmob!!!

Hannah: Search YouTube?

Me: No can do. I need something original

Hannah: Okay. Kind of busy rt now . . .

Busy? Geez. I had only two days until Flashmob Friday. Ideally, I'd have liked to make a wish ASAP to get the stress out of the way. I decided that's precisely what I would do at 11:11. But this meant leaving the flashmob decision to the clock. Oh well. Fine. Probably better than fine based on how awesome the other wishes had turned out. All I had to do was launch the wish and have the drama behind me.

Far down the hall and in between the crush of students, I caught sight of a fuzzy pink feather bobbing and bouncing off the end of a pen that stuck out of someone's backpack. It swished. It swayed. It practically teased me to chase it.

It was like someone pressed a go button on me. I hunched my back and picked up the pace, shoulder-bumping anyone in my path.

The feather wove in between students, whooshing left and right, goading me forward.

I closed in.

The feather danced. It taunted. It dared.

I pounced, grabbing the girl by the shoulders and snatching the feather in between my teeth, plume in mouth, pen dangling to the side.

"What are you doing?" the girl screamed.

The girl being Rhena, of course.

People around us took backward steps.

My fingers released. Jaw unclamped. "Uhhh." I removed the feather from my mouth and silently offered it back. What was going on with me?

"Gross." Rhena wiped her arms as if a basset hound

had just slobbered all over her. "Keep it, weirdo." She hurried ahead of me.

With chin tucked, I tossed the pen into the garbage and followed behind. There I was, the other half of Team Free Spirit, spitting out bits of pink feather stuck in the corner of my mouth. But maybe I'd just finished paying the price for using unstable magazine magic at the assembly. My breathing relaxed. *Okay, that's over.* At least the cost was swift and behind me. Right? Still, a sense of looming disaster skulked under my skin.

Pull yourself together. I took another breath. *There's an important wish to be made.*

The clock's magic had never done me wrong, not really. Other than sending me an enchanted trickster magazine, that is. No matter. I just had to get that flashmob wish handled, and then I'd stop promising to do exciting things. There'd be no more zap dares, I'd be done proving myself, and the rest of middle school would be easy-peasy.

Rhena ducked into the history classroom ahead of me. I was just seconds behind her, but when I entered, one glance at Shelby and the other girls told me they'd already been briefed about the pen incident. Yoona kept her chin down and doodled.

A wish could fix this. It could fix everything. I turned to the clock. The cat eyes were frozen in a wide stare. Its tail didn't swish, and the whiskers weren't ticking or tocking! Its petrified smile mocked me, like it was punishing me for not believing sooner or for not being a good user of the magic.

"Mr. Kersey." My voice boomed, making half the students jump. "The clock's not working."

Rhena turned and narrowed her eyes, studying me and then the clock.

I didn't have time to worry about her.

"Oh . . . kay?" Mr. Kersey said. "I guess I'll have to get some more double-A batteries."

Was he serious—double-A batteries? How about pixie dust?

I stared back at the clock, urging gears to shift and tickers to tock. Nothing. Zilch. Nada. I sank into my seat. What would I do if it never worked again—switch schools, move to Bhutan, join the Amish?

Five minutes passed, and Mr. Kersey said, "All right, papers away. You have forty-five minutes to complete the test."

My head still ached from using the magazine at the assembly. It pounded. I would've traded all my science fair medals for a sip of mint tea.

The big "2" Rhena had written on top of my hand added to the doom. I was out of magazine magic and clock magic, and I had T minus two days until I needed to deliver on the biggest promise of my life.

CHAPTER 25

Forty-five minutes later, the bell rang. I tossed my completed exam on Mr. Kersey's desk and then rushed out the door. I was desperate to figure out how to call Grams and ask her how to get one more wish.

"There you are." Ally linked her arm in mine. "Lunch?"

"Um."

"Come on." Ally's cheeks were full of color and she was walking and talking fast, dragging me with her. "Assembly was so awesome! You didn't mind me asking you in front of everyone about being Co-Captain, right?"

She didn't notice my silence.

"Because when you said you wanted to be involved, I thought maybe you were giving me a hint that you wanted a bigger role. Especially with how active you were at your last school. And it seemed like perfect timing in assembly. I was all fired up once Rhena started lying." Ally glanced over at me. "Whoa. You look stressed. You do want this. Right?"

"Um. I just keep thinking about Friday." My voice went high and squeaky. "How about we move the flashmob to another time?" *Like never.* "That way we can give our total focus to the campaign?"

"Well . . . but the flashmob is the highlight of what we're promoting. Our creativity and the excitement we—" Ally jerked to a stop next to the emergency exit. "Did you hear that?" She leaned in. "There's a sound coming from the other side of these doors. Like a bunch of cats meowing."

"That's weird." I paused for a moment, before walking on. My mind was stuck on Friday. "Are you sure we don't want the flashmob to be part of Spirit Week—like the grand finale of next week?"

Ally caught back up to me, and we made our way to the cafeteria. "Spirit Week is already going to be so much fun, so we should definitely do the flashmob now. Like a way to show what's to come. Is that okay?"

She looked so excited and hopeful.

"Sure."

In the cafeteria, bowls of chili were paired with buttery squares of cornbread, steam rising from their golden centers. But for some reason, I grabbed chocolate milk and a tuna sandwich. We wove through groups of students until we arrived at the seventh-grade quad.

"Aww. Look, how cute," Ally said, setting down her tray and pointing toward a bank of windows. Yellow sunlight streamed through and a few cats sat on the ledges pressed against the glass.

"Do they normally hang out there?" A twinge of concern crept over me.

More cats jumped up and joined the others on the ledge. "Never," Ally said.

Mia, Erin, and Noelle arrived with Turner and a bunch of other girls and guys who filled in the bench seats.

Still standing, I glanced at the windows one more time.

They're just neighborhood cats hanging out at a school, I told myself. *People's pets. That's it.* They probably smelled the chili cooking. I had to stop the paranoia or I'd see cats in everything. I took a breath and scanned the crowd for Jackson, wondering if he'd be eating at Rhena's table.

"As your official student ambassador," said a cool-vanilla voice from behind me, "I'm here to advise you to never order the tuna surprise."

Noelle smiled at the person behind me.

My stomach fluttered and my face burned hot and fast. I grabbed my milk and shoved the thin straw into my mouth before turning around, like that could cover the glow on my cheeks.

"Jackson," I said, trying to be smooth but talking right into the straw. The milk bubbled and dribbled in a mess down my hands.

Jackson's knee-melting dimple appeared in his cheek. I fumbled for napkins, and as I leaned across the table my shirt rose and my shorts lowered, probably exposing the top of my butt. I yanked my shirt down and spun around. Whoever invented low-rise clearly never had to reach for anything. "Ummm," I said, letting the *mmmmmm* trail on until I gave up on finding words and plopped down at the table.

Jackson dropped his backpack to the ground. "Can I get in here?" he asked the group, pointing to the space next to me. "I mean, if you guys don't mind eating with the competition."

Tank walked up beside him. "Me too."

Erin scooched over and Tank and Jackson sat, Jackson squeezing in next to me, leaving just a femtometer between us—we're talking less than a microinch! Of course my arm hairs electrified.

Turner leaned toward Jackson. "So, King on Rhena's ticket, huh?"

Jackson shrugged. "Co-Captain," he corrected. "She's done a bunch of things for me. I sort of owe her."

Owe her? How could he even be friends with someone like Rhena?

"Plus, I have a motto," he said. "'Ask not what your school can do for you. Ask what you can do for your school.'"

"You mean what you can do *to* the school," Turner said. "Yo, if you win, please use a day to make everyone dress like Frisbee players."

Jackson laughed. "I don't even know what that would look like."

"Dude," Tank said, "that would be savage. You could make everyone dress for sports all week."

"Hey. None of that," Ally said with a laugh. "We're not supposed to talk about themes, and some of you guys are supposed to be my supporters."

"You know it," Turner said.

I licked my lips, still tasting the creaminess of the milk. Mmm, and when had a sandwich ever smelled so amazing?

Jackson turned to me. "I suppose we're running against each other."

I tore my gaze away from my plate and nodded. No interesting motto at the ready. "Guess so."

"Your Friday Flashmob sounds fun." Jackson twisted his yarn bracelet. "Fun-meister."

"I know, right," Turner said. "Everyone went nuts."

Jackson and Turner got into a conversation, and Ally leaned against me, whispering, "What are you doing?"

I stopped and stared down, realizing I'd been licking splashes of milk off my knuckles like a cat licking its paws. I slouched and dried my hands with the napkins still clutched in my fist. More cat stuff? I hadn't even wished today. I shook my head. This must be another unstable cost from using the magazine at today's assembly.

"Right?" Turner said to me.

I lifted my chin and nodded, not even bothering to figure out the question.

"Why didn't you tell me about the flashmob yesterday?" Jackson asked.

"I didn't really know then." I snorted. "The biggest decision I'd made by this time yesterday was about how long I could stay at the Humane Society."

Jackson smiled. "How's that going?"

"I love it. Tonight is the Wednesday Night Walks."

"Cool," Jackson said. "I've heard about that."

I smiled and purred. Purred! I stopped myself and my ears got hot. Jackson was still smiling and talking like he hadn't noticed. Had anyone noticed?

Ally was thumbing through Mia's latest book and asked her, "Did you finish *Metamorphosis*? I don't see it in your pile anymore."

"Yeah," Mia said. "Such a weird book. Spoiler alert. The guy turns into a bug."

I tuned back into Jackson. ". . . and talk about school clubs or whatever you want." He twisted his yarn bracelet again. "You're coming to math club today, right?"

I nodded.

"Megan, you humble genius!" Ally said, beaming. She set Mia's book down. "You didn't tell me Mrs. Matthews invited you onto the math team. Congratulations! You hear that, guys? We have brains and creativity on our campaign."

"Thanks." My math news never had that kind of effect on anyone other than my dad.

"How long will your meeting last?" she asked.

"Half an hour, tops," Jackson said.

"Awesome. We'll wait for you, Megan."

"Wait?"

"After school today, a bunch of us are going to

Mojo's. The Kierland location. Can you come?"

"Sure?" I looked at Noelle, my source for explanations.

"Mojo's serves froyo," Noelle said. "And Kierland is an outdoor mall. Lots of shops and restaurants and stuff."

"We'd planned for girls only, Jackson, but we can break code if you want to come," Ally said. "You should come, too, Turner, so Jackson's not the only guy."

"Wish I could," Turner said. "But I have Frisbee. One more win and I'm in the Frisbee-Golf Playoffs."

"I'm out, too," Jackson said. "Have your gender-biased event. I have lacrosse practice at four."

Ally laughed. "Suit yourself."

Jackson shifted back to me. "But maybe you and I could get together tomorrow."

I froze, staring at the flecks of gold in his eyes. Was he asking me out?

"I don't have practice on Thursdays," he said.

"Okay." My voice sounded mousy. I bit back the impulse to purr.

"After school, then? Can I text you?"

I must've nodded, because he handed me the last dry napkin and said, "I left my phone in my locker, but you could write your number here."

Party balloons floated in my head. Somehow a pen

landed in my grip, and with a shaky hand I jotted my number.

"Thanks." He stood up and folded the napkin and stuffed it into his pocket.

Just then Rhena swooped in, popping her gum casually like she wasn't walking into enemy territory. She hooked her arm in Jackson's elbow and said, "He-ey. Who's going to Kierland?"

"It sounds like everybody." Jackson smiled at our group.

"Not you, right? You have lacrosse?" Rhena squeezed his bicep and smiled possessively, like a dog marking its territory. "He's a midi, you know." Rhena tugged Jackson closer and blinked her big, shiny eyes. "Jackson, help me with my math homework, please." Her voice went sugary. "When our families got together last weekend, you said you'd give me private tutoring, remember?"

"Okay, sure," he said, his tone easy.

She looked at me and smiled like she wanted to make sure I got the message—Jackson was her turf.

Everyone returned to talking. Jackson stooped over to gather up his backpack, and as he did Rhena snatched the napkin from his pocket.

My phone number napkin!

She removed a wad of blue gum from her mouth,

squished it into the napkin, and smiled at me as she crumpled it into a tiny ball.

Alert! Alert! My brainwaves squeezed, trying to send Jackson an instant message: *My phone number is about to become lunchroom trash!*

Sure enough, Rhena tossed the napkin into the garbage can several feet away, and her shot landed perfectly on target.

Ally pointed to the windows. "Whoa, look at that! What's going on?"

Three or four dozen cats had gathered on the window ledges outside. A couple of custodians and the vice principal stood on the sidewalk, jaws moving, arms flapping. Several more cats crossed the grassy courtyard, and conversations in the cafeteria stopped. Kids moved toward the windows.

A hiss whooshed from my mouth, and just as quickly, my hand flew up to my parted lips.

Jackson straightened. "You all right?"

The meowing of cats grew loud enough to hear through the closed windows.

"Ummm." I blinked a few times. "I, um—"

"Ready?" Rhena dazzled a smile at Jackson.

"Yup." He flung his backpack to his shoulders. "See you guys."

They walked off, arms linked.

CHAPTER 26

I glanced at the doorway for the gazillionth time, watching out for cats and wondering where Jackson was. So far, five of us had shown up for math club: me, Turner, Tank, and the two girls I'd met last time, Ellie and Karen.

An easel with a three-foot pad stood at the front of the room. Ellie and Karen drew equations on the chalkboard, and Tank and Turner sat in the desks beside me, making paper airplanes.

"Good times in the cafeteria, today, huh?" Tank said, smiling and folding the triangle nose of his airplane.

Maybe is what I wanted to say, as in, "Maybe the

cats escaped from the Humane Society" or "Maybe an animal rescue is doing a publicity stunt" or any other "maybe" that could've led into an elaborate excuse even though my gut knew it wasn't true.

"Meow" was what popped out of my mouth.

Turner laughed. "Good one, Megan."

Rather than freaking out, I kept calm by rationalizing with science. According to the law of conservation of mass and energy, matter is neither created nor destroyed. Perhaps when you get something from the Magicverse, you give something from the regular world so there's an exchange of energy, or matter, or . . . I didn't know!

What had Grams said on day one about frivolous magic and lazy wishes? I sighed. There had been a lot of weirdness in the past three days—the makeover and hair, the purring and meowing, a legion of cats outside the cafeteria, and the fine print on the perfume contract I hadn't had time to read.

It was too much to organize in my head, so I unzipped my backpack and pulled out the orange journal, opened it to a clean page, and drew a line down the center to make two columns. At the top of one column I wrote "Frivolous Magic" and on the other I wrote "Costs."

I'd say the perfume was frivolous and was probably why the cats were hanging out at lunch. Funny.

And then *poof*, it was over, so frivolous magic must have a fast cause-effect price tag. I let out an exhale.

Also, making Mr. Kersey bark and getting all those Skittles was frivolous, too, not to mention playful, since I liked Mr. Kersey and didn't intend anything bad by the wish. That was probably why I did all those goofy cat things, sort of like how he was funny when he barked. This was making sense now. I jotted everything down.

Frivolous Magic:	Costs:
Makeover	Disaster
T-10	Lion do!
Perfume	Cats at lunch
Kersey barking	Meowing
Candy	Purrs, meows, feather mishap
???	Fur ball cough?

And then I wrote, "Cumulative???"

It felt like things were building. I wasn't sure about the cumulative nature of wishing, but I was starting to feel more and more relieved that I had the magic figured out. Until I remembered I'd meowed and purred *before* I'd made the Skittles and barking wish.

I reached into my backpack and carefully took out *Enchanted Teen*, hoping to find a perfume ad and maybe some answers. I flipped a few pages, knowing

I'd have to make this fast or suffer another headache, though I didn't know if that still applied, since the issue had expired.

Skimming through page after page, I passed clothing ads, makeup ads, and an article called "Seven Tips: How Smart Girls Speak Up!"; then I got to those stuck pages.

"Hey, Megan," Turner said. He and Tank were holding up their folded airplanes, one a Flying Fox and the other a Nakamura lock.

Dad didn't do coloring books with me when I was little, but he'd taught me paper airplane making better than an origami master could've.

"Which one is better?" Turner asked.

"They're both good." I focused back on the magazine, pinching the edges and careful not to touch anything just in case; then I started to peel the pages apart.

"That's a nonanswer. Don't play politics," Tank said.

I smiled and studied the airplanes more closely. "Okay, Tank, yours is nice and has the best look, but Turner's folds have the best design for thrust, lift, gravity, and drag."

"Ha," Turner said to Tank. "Told ya mine's more aerodynamic."

"Let's go again," Tank said. "Round two."

I finished peeling the magazine pages apart. The article headline said:

How to Get Away with Magic
Secrets of the Magicverse:
Rules, Wishing, and Enchantments

Whoa! I leaned in.

Congratulations! If you've been granted access to this page, you've successfully dabbled in the mysterious with a mixture of curiosity, smarts, and spunk. You may now read on for further instructions.

I steadied my hands to the edges of the page, wary of tricks.

The Magicverse (including but not limited to conjuring, augury, bewitching, wizardry, enchantment, and wishing) requires good stewardship, selflessness, and a lack of frivolity. Furthermore, the Magicverse strongly cautions against wishing for anything malicious or unmerited. These are considered spiteful wishes and/or cheater's wishes and are deemed offensive to the Magicverse. Such a wish, should you choose to proceed, will result in a punitive cost and payment in full will be demanded immediately. Please note, this cost will be quite expensive.

I sucked in a breath. My heart lurched to my throat. Assembly! Rhena's gibberish speech! What had I done?

"You okay?" Tank asked, giving me a concerned look.

I flung an arm over the article and started coughing.

Tank's eyebrows pinched together and I thought he'd say more, but then he refocused on the fold of his airplane's wing.

I quickly reread the article. "Payment in full will be demanded immediately." It had been several hours since the assembly, and that magic had been used in self-defense. And since self-defense isn't spiteful or malicious, my shoulders relaxed. Maybe I was safe. Thank goodness revenge wasn't my style and I'd never wished zits on Rhena. I read on.

Be a good steward of the magic.
It should go without saying, the Magicverse especially frowns upon laziness. The price is—

And as I was reading this line, the article faded and then disappeared!

"What?" I shook the magazine like I could shake the words back onto the page. "Come on." I flipped to other pages. All white.

Tank and Turner stared at me.

"Stupid magazine." I shrugged like it was no biggie and stuffed *Enchanted Teen* into my backpack.

What was the price?

I clearly didn't know the answer, but I was starting to realize wishes fell into categories: weather wishes, frivolous wishes, lazy wishes, and malicious wishes. I jotted extra columns in my journal and wondered what category my day-one wish fell under, the one when I asked for "some magic." Was it considered frivolous . . . or lazy? The answers were fuzzy at best, so I gave up and returned my orange journal to my backpack.

Wigglesworth dropped into a seat next to Tank, interrupting my worrying. "Hey. Where's Jackson?"

"I thought he was coming with you," Tank said.

I glanced back at the door. No cats and still no Jackson. "Maybe he had to talk to a teacher?" Or maybe there was something wrong with the space-time continuum.

"I saw him with Rhena," Turner said. "Probably talking campaign stuff."

The hair on my neck spiked.

When I checked the door for the googolplexth time, Mrs. Matthews and four more students arrived. But not Jackson.

Mrs. Matthews shuffled to the front of the room and stood by the easel. "Thank you again for joining Saguaro Prep's math club." Her smile fanned the small gathering. "As you know, our mission as Math Olympians is to foster the pursuit of individual excellence in problem solving by enhancing creativity and resourcefulness. These goals are similar to those found in the ancient Olympic games." She flipped open to the first page of the large pad and revealed a paper with the mission statement written on it. Mrs. Matthews grabbed a thick green marker and added:

Identify the problem
Devise a plan
Carry it out

"Why focus on creativity rather than just straightforward answers?" Ellie asked.

"Good and timely question," Mrs. Matthews said, smiling. She flipped to the next page. It had a blown-up copy of a blueprint with a picture of an eighteen-wheeler stuck under a bridge. Various mathematical calculations had been drawn in the margins of the blueprint.

Mrs. Matthews folded her hands together and said, "There once was a big rig truck that got wedged under a bridge in New York City. Traffic was blocked for miles. Mathematicians and engineers were brought to the scene to try to determine a calculation to make adjustments to the bridge, since the truck was so completely wedged it wouldn't move forward or backward. The experts studied measurements around the trestles and tried to come up with a modification that wouldn't damage structural integrity or support capacities. Then a child who came to see the spectacle said, 'Why don't you just let the air out of the truck's tires?'"

I laughed. So did Tank, and Wigglesworth, and Turner.

"Yep. I laughed, too, when I heard the story," Mrs. Matthews said. "Because I know I would've been trying to figure out that calculation to change the bridge, just like everyone else." She smiled. "It's important to understand math, and it's also important to understand that creative problem-solving techniques mean there's not just one but many paths to a correct answer. Sometimes you have to focus on the truck instead of the bridge."

She walked to her desk. "Today, I hope to help sharpen your thinking skills with a game. I need volunteers to help move the desks against the walls. Once we clear the space, we'll use the floor for a big game of math concentration."

"Yes!" Tank fist-pumped.

Turner and Wigglesworth high-fived.

"We only have twenty minutes remaining before many of you have to head over to your sports practices, so let's begin."

We placed giant cards facedown on the floor. Some cards had equations and others had answers. If we flipped over an equation card, we'd have to solve it with mental math and try to remember where the answer card was. I was so focused I glanced at the doorway only twice.

When our time ended, Mrs. Matthews thanked us, and I volunteered to stay behind and clean up.

"Megan," Mrs. Matthews said after everyone had left, "are you okay?"

"Oh, uh-huh. Yeah," I said. "Yup."

She softly said, "Sometimes the flaw is that one doesn't understand the problem."

"Didn't I do okay?"

"The math? Yes. You also had a perfect score on your strength-finders test from the other day."

"Okay?"

"I'm sorry. It's none of my business, Megan. But I just found today's assembly to be . . . interesting. It seems like you're under a lot of pressure for your first week here."

I nodded.

"Making your way as the new girl at school is a tough role."

She didn't know the half of it.

"I noticed you exclusively used algorithms to solve problems. And like I said, you got everything correct. But just know, it's okay to think outside the box and still arrive at a solution."

Were we still talking about math?

"If you need someone to talk to, I'm here."

"Um, okay, I'll keep that in mind. Thank you."

I finished stacking the game on a shelf and realigned desks. It was 3:32 when I finished, and I was late for meeting Ally and the others for Mojo's. "See you tomorrow," I said to Mrs. Matthews. I rushed out the door. . . .

And smacked into Jackson.

"Whoa, sorry!" we said at the same time.

I said, "It's oka—"

"Bye, Jackson," Rhena sang from down the hall. "Remember what we talked about." She gave me a look that told me there was a 98 percent chance she'd made that comment for my benefit.

Jackson's face flushed before he said, "See ya, Rhe."

What was his uneasy look about?

"Hey. Did I miss much?" he asked.

"Umm." I glanced toward Rhena swishing down the hall, then back to Jackson. "We played a game. And turned in our forms."

"Right. I've got that." He leaned against the wall. "I've got something for you, too." He set his backpack on the ground and pulled out a blue printed flyer with the title "Jazz Band" in bold lettering and under that "guitarist needed." "Here. I can't do this with my lacrosse schedule, but from what you said, it sounds like it'd be a good way to get your sister going again."

"Wow. Thanks!" Before I knew what I was doing I flung my arms around Jackson in a hug. This flyer was exactly the nudge Piper needed. "Thank you." I didn't know what else to say, so I added, "Gracias." Then I snort-laughed. Ugh. I let go of the hug before it got more awkward.

But Jackson laughed, and not in a mean way. "De nada," he said.

I laughed again. "Um." I carefully folded the flyer and glanced at the outdoor exit, where everyone was waiting for me. "Okay, well . . ."

"Yeah." Jackson shifted his weight. "You probably want to get going."

I nodded.

We parted ways in the hall. Jackson headed to talk to Mrs. Matthews and I headed toward the flagpole. A distinct purr vibrated in my throat.

CHAPTER 27

Based on my charting, I was 85 percent sure I'd just purred because I'd used magic at assembly. But what about the other 15 percent? I had no clear hypothesis for why the cat noises weren't over, and I'd just purred again for the umpteenth time!

On my way outside, I Googled "uncontrolled purring in humans." No valid results. I tried "can humans purr?" At AskaBiologist.org, I found that, yes, humans can dilate and constrict the glottis at the vocal cords to purr. That was good to know, but I'd never done it before. Was I subconsciously making this happen?

Cars and buses waited for students who were leaving after-school clubs. I texted Dad and Piper.

Me: I'm hanging with friends at Kierland today.

Then to Hannah:

Me: I'm going to froyo with friends. What's up w/ u? Any thoughts on the flashmob yet?

I took a swig from my water bottle and headed across a spread of dried grass, and then crunched through the gravel toward the flagpole.

Ally, Mia, Noelle, Erin, and a few girls from our lunch table waited on the rocks in the shade of a mesquite tree. I smiled at my new group of friends. This was going to be fun.

Then I saw Yoona and Shelby. And Rhena. What was Rhena doing here? Our eyes met and her Medusa glare turned my stomach to stone.

"Uh, hi?" I said. "What's going on?"

"Today sounded like a great day for Mojo's," Rhena said in her sugar-sweet voice.

Ally rolled her eyes. "What a super-random coincidence. And you thought meeting half an hour after school at the flagpole sounded like a good idea, too?"

"Free country," Rhena said. "You guys can always go somewhere else if you don't like it."

"Oh, we're going to Mojo's," Ally said. "We planned it first."

"Suit yourself," Rhena said.

I stood on the edge of the circle, squeezing and crinkling my thin plastic water bottle before I joined Erin in the back of the group.

"She's such a radish," Erin whispered. "And we're going to have to be careful what we tell Jackson in the future. He obviously told Rhena our plan."

"But Rhena was there," I said, feeling the need to defend him. "She heard the plan herself."

"Yeah, but there are a hundred places at Kierland. We only talked about Mojo's before she'd walked over to our table."

I hated how right she was.

"Are you guys ready?" Ally said. "We should—"

"We should get going," Rhena said, talking over her.

Rhena and the Rhenites walked only a few paces ahead of us, with low, whispery voices equal to any judgy look. Maybe that's why the hair on the back of my neck kept rising.

We left the school grounds and headed down neighborhood streets, passing adobe houses and sweet-smelling honeysuckle bushes. When we rounded a corner, Erin said, "Look." She pointed at two cats, a black one and a white one. They kept pace in the back of our group. "We're being followed."

My skin tingled.

"Smart kitties," Noelle said with a smile. "Are you following us for froyo?"

Ally dropped back to join Erin and me. "All those cats at school today and now this. Weird, huh?"

"I know. Right?" Mia said.

My head buzzed. Two more cats had joined the black and white ones. Dread slinked up my spine.

We rounded another corner.

"Look. Here come more." Erin's smile faded. "Creepy, huh?"

I turned as if to face a firing squad or the Bellini brothers themselves. Sure enough, eight cats swished their tails and practically smiled at me. "They're not actually following us, right?" My voice came out shaky.

"It is bizarre," Noelle said.

"They probably live on this street," I said, grasping for anything normal.

Rhena's group turned to investigate the commotion and everyone slowed to a stop, gawking. The cats slinked toward me. Some rubbed against my legs; others sat and looked up.

"That's cute," Yoona said.

"Are you dense, Yoona?" Rhena said. "You know I'm allergic to cats." She scratched at her arms. "It's not cute. It's weird with a capital *W*."

"Sketchy," Shelby said.

Rhena narrowed her eyes at me like a *CSI* detective. "And the cats aren't following *us*. They're only interested in *you*." She pointed her accusing finger toward my head. "Look. They're circling her." Her voice turned stuffy and she sniffled. "You're trying to win the election by making me too sick to campaign. Are you the one who brought the cats to our school?"

"No. Of course not." I tried to laugh it off. "Cats just love ME-ow."

"What?" Rhena took a backward step.

"Me, ha-ha. They love me." I swallowed.

The cats began purring and continued rubbing their soft fur against my legs.

"Awww," Mia said. "They really do like you."

Rhena backed away another few steps.

"I think it's sweet," Ally said.

I reached down and scratched a furry head, thinking about how I'd just meowed again. A shudder rippled through my skin—the meowing, the purring, licking my knuckles, the feather incident, the cats at school, and now this—all cat related, all building, and still happening. No *poof* and it's over! It left me wondering again about things being cumulative.

I thought of Einstein and his theory of relativity: $E = mc^2$. Except my equation was a little different:

$D = (C)c^2$. Doom = cat symptoms multiplied by the speed of light squared.

"What's wrong with you anyhow, Megan?" Rhena crossed her arms.

"Wow, Rhena. That's rude," Ally said, crouching down beside me to pet the cats. "Nothing's wrong with her. Megan volunteers with animals. Maybe the cats just know she's a good person."

"That could be true," Yoona said, fiddling with the hem of her shorts.

"What do you know, Yoona?" Rhena said.

Yoona hugged her arms over her stomach.

How to Survive Middle School had said to be cool and confident under pressure, so with a great deal of effort, I stood up and said, "Um, let's go." And with bogus confidence, I added, "They'll probably go home." I started walking. Ally, Mia, and Erin walked beside me. Rhena's group stayed ahead of us.

Chill, I told myself, glancing backward. The cats continued following, staying about ten feet back. Rhena whispered to Shelby.

"Lighten up, you guys," Ally said. "It's not like we're being stalked by zombies."

Erin, Noelle, and Mia laughed. The mood lightened, and the chatter moved on to zombie movies. I tried to act casual, but if I had clenched my jaw any tighter I would've broken my back teeth. Three more cats joined the trailing pack.

Ally leaned to me. "You don't have leftover tuna in your pocket, do you?" She tried to make it a joke, but she sounded weirded out.

"Ha-ha." I took an unsteady breath and got a whiff of the minty perfume on my wrist, reminding me that I'd signed on that scroll.

The perfumed card had said friends would follow, and of course the magic-makers were tricksters. It all made sense.

The cats were following me!

Car tires squealed. The intersection ahead zoomed with traffic. If one of my new feline friends got run over in the intersection, it'd be my fault. I turned around. A thirteenth cat, a black one, joined the entourage. It was too much—the unlucky number, a black cat. "Okay, sweeties. Go home." My voice trembled. "Scat."

The cats stopped walking. One by one they started yowling and meowing, and the chorus sounded pleading and insistent. At first my ears rang. Then the meows turned to words, and my blood ran cold.

Cat got your tongue? the cats cried.

What? I took a sharp look at the group.

"Awww, they're so cute," Mia said again, clearly not hearing what I'd just heard.

Cat got your tongue? the cats cried again.

"Why are they meowing at you?" Rhena's eyes could not have been wider.

I just stood there blinking. What could I say? The crying grew louder. And then before I could control it my shoulders lifted, my back hunched, and I screamed, "GO! Scat. Scat. Scat! Go go go go go!" I flailed my arms every which way.

The cats stopped meowing and obeyed, scurrying away. In moments, they were gone.

I snatched out a bottle of hand sanitizer from the top zipper of my backpack and squeezed drops over every part of my body where I'd dabbed the perfume on my wrists, on my arms, and on my neck. And since repeating was good enough for shampoo instructions, I figured it'd do for sanitizer, too. I squeezed out glob after glob and rubbed and rubbed until I realized Noelle and Mia were staring. Rhena's jaw hung. Shelby took backward steps. Ally closed her parted lips.

"Impressive," Erin said, breaking the silence. "Megan, the Cat Whisperer."

We continued down the sidewalk in silence, rocks crunching under our feet. Even Ally and Yoona avoided eye contact with me. I hung to the back of the group, stressing that I was on the verge of losing my new friends, especially if I kept acting like a freak show.

The magic kept going all kinds of wrong, and I still had to figure out what flashmob to wish for . . . even though the potential consequences were clearly CATastrophic. I shook my head at my dorkiness, but at least I could still laugh at myself.

I texted Hannah again.

Me: Ideas???

Mrs. Matthews's advice buzzed in my brain—it's important to develop multiple strategies for solving difficult equations. That's when I thought of the mathematical formula for creativity, $C = f_a(KIE)$.

CHAPTER 28

*T**winkle.** The bell chimed as Ally swung open the door to Mojo's. A blast of cool air hit my face, along with the smell of baking waffle cones. The floor was teal and white checkers, and the walls were lined with silver-handled frozen yogurt machines.

"Good stuff," Ally said, breaking the silence.

I nodded, but I was busy calculating $C = f_a(KIE)$.

Back in the 1970s, this professor, Dr. Ruth Noller, had come up with a mathematical formula for creativity: $C = f_a(KIE)$. Her formula says creativity (C) is a function (f) of knowledge (K), imagination (I), and evaluation (E). The small letter a is the most important part; it stands for a positive attitude.

Why not use the formula to come up with a flash-mob? *You can do this*, I told myself. That was my big pep talk. *You can do this*. I had the positive attitude. Now all I had to do was fill in the KIE.

Here are the details of what I could plug into Dr. Ruth Noller's formula:

(K) Knowledge. I'd seen enough flashmobs on You-Tube to know fun meant music, lots of people, plus high energy. Also, I couldn't copy. Got it.

(I) Imagination. One imagination is fine, but several combined could be the ticket. All I had to do was find a way to get everyone to collaborate. Then I could gather suggestions and go with the most popular idea for the flashmob. That way, everyone would be as invested in the plan as I was.

(E) Evaluation. After gathering ideas I'd evaluate the positives and negatives and pick one.

We filled our cups and paid, and between the two groups, we took every chair in the tiny place. Rhena sat at the table directly next to Ally and me—probably to be obnoxious. Nerves twisted my stomach tighter and tighter, and I kept looking out the window to see if any cats had followed us.

"Megan?" Rhena said.

"Huh?"

"Don't you like it?" She pointed her spoon at my half-melted yogurt. "Or do you and your cats prefer plain milk?"

"Ha-ha, Rhena." I wished I had the guts to challenge her meanness, but I just stirred my yogurt, staring at the number two that was still on my hand. Everyone else was almost done already.

"So tell us, Megan. What ideas do you have for the flashmob?" Rhena asked casually.

"Hey," Ally said. "No. We're not talking about that."

"What's the big secret?" Rhena shrugged. "You said it's for our class. We're members of the seventh grade, so it's not like we'd sabotage it."

"So you say," Ally said.

"Paranoid much?"

"Maybe we could all brainstorm together," I said, grateful for the perfect opening to get collaboration under way.

"You don't even have an idea," Shelby said.

"No, I do," I said, my voice high-pitched. "I was thinking . . ." *Think. Think. Think like a Math Olympian.* The odds of someone just blurting out an unprompted idea was probably like the odds of someone losing a limb in a chain-saw accident—1 in 4,464. But if I started the metaphorical idea ball rolling, the chances of someone else offering up a suggestion had to increase.

Ally's eyebrows lifted.

"Well." I cleared my throat. "I've seen all those flashmob dances on YouTube."

Shelby rolled her eyes. Rhena yawned.

Breathe, I told myself. *There are many paths to solving a problem.* "But instead of a dance," I hurried, "we could choreograph ahh . . ." *A what?* I thought. "Umm . . . a cartwheel routine?" The tone of my voice swung up with each punctuation, making what I said sound like a question. Math club was still on my mind, so I added, "Like three girls could cartwheel? Then nine people could go? And then twenty-seven? You know, like in increasing exponentials of three."

"Oh, I get it," Ally said. "I like."

"Sounds fun," Yoona said.

"Huh?" Shelby said.

"Three, then three times three is nine," I said. "Then nine times three is twenty-seven, and then twenty-seven times three is eighty-one, and so forth."

"Seriously?" Rhena frowned. "You want us to have a math flashmob?"

"I guess it would be rough when we got to two forty-three." My words dwindled to a mutter. What a mistake.

"Anything else?" Rhena asked.

"Maybe someone else wants to offer an idea?" I suggested.

"No," Ally said, smacking her hands together in one loud clap. "We're putting this to rest. The flash-mob was announced as part of *our* campaign, Team Free Spirit, and we're not talking about any more parts of the planning phase in front of you, Rhena. If it flops, it's our neck on the line, not yours."

There went my plan to collaborate.

"Yeah," Erin said. "Your pack of patchoulis needs to back off."

"Whatever." Rhena glanced at her phone. "Hey. My mom's here to drive me home. Who wants a ride?"

The Rhenites stood.

"Bye, you guys," Yoona said.

A few other Rhenites said good-bye. Shelby and Rhena left without a word. Soon others left, too.

Erin, Noelle, and Mia walked back to the dispensers for refills while I stared at my melted yogurt, feeling dumb about my exponential cartwheel idea.

"Hey," Ally said. "Moving's tough, huh?"

"Does it show that much?"

"You're doing great."

"Sorry about freaking out on the cats."

"Yeah. That was a little bizarre." She laughed and

wiped a napkin over her mouth. "So how's everything else going? At school, I mean."

"Good." I nodded. "Good."

Ally smiled. "Other than Rhena, Saguaro Prep's a decent place."

"Yeah. I've met a lot of nice people. You guys. And Jackson. And Turner. He's in my history class."

"Turner is great." Ally looked thoughtful, then smiled. "So quirky."

"Yeah," I agreed. "I don't have any classes with Jackson, but . . ." I looked down and moistened my lips.

"He's pretty cute, huh?"

I nodded.

"Crushing?"

I nodded again.

"So I moved here four years ago," Ally said. "My mom wanted us to live closer to my *abuela* after my parents divorced. The first month sucked."

"I'm sorry . . ."

"It sucked bad. I cried every day after school and before school and sometimes during school."

"About your parents?"

"Yeah. But I thought I was crying about school. I hated leaving all my friends and my neighborhood. And I dreaded lunchtime."

"Come on. You probably had a thousand friends

by the end of your first day."

"Not after the first day." She smiled. "But pretty quickly. Like you have all of us now." She spooned a Swedish fish into her mouth and between chews said, "Oh, and we're meeting at the bagel stand for lunch tomorrow. Can you come?"

"Yeah, thanks." Even after all the weirdness, Ally still wanted to hang out with me. This was so different from Colorado, where I would just tag along with Hannah and no one else really gave me a chance.

"Listen, I'm sorry about Rhena and the way she treats you and how she's negative about your flash-mob ideas. I think your idea was creative."

I nodded, wanting to ask—to beg—if we could call it off. But then what would everyone think of me?

"Rhena's such a pickle princess," Erin said, returning with the others and sitting down.

"Whoa, language," Noelle said.

Ally and Mia laughed, but then Mia adjusted her glasses and grew serious. "She really is mean."

"Right," Noelle said. "Remember when she shut Yoona out of their group for a few weeks last year and no one would sit with her?"

"That's ridiculous," Ally said with a scolding look. "She *thought* no one would sit with her. She could've sat with us. I invited her, but she said she didn't want to cause problems. That's why *she* chose to eat in the counselor's office instead."

"If you say so." Mia spooned up a bite of yogurt.

"I have no idea why people care what Rhena thinks," Ally said.

"I'm with Ally on this," Erin said.

"I don't know." Noelle traced a finger over her henna. "I wouldn't want Rhena's attention aimed at me."

"You guys!" Ally let out an exasperated breath and turned to me. "Never mind them. You stand your ground. Rhena's probably just freaking out since Jackson's crushing on you."

My heart hammered. "No he's not."

Mia nodded.

"Really?" I said, looking at my hands.

"Uhhh, yes, you gourd," Erin said. "Of course he is."

I couldn't hold down my smile.

Noelle smiled back. "We all saw him at lunch."

The door dinger chimed. Rhena stepped halfway inside and said, "Hey, Ally." She made her voice sound bored and monotone. "My mom's making me ask again if you'd like a ride since we're neighbors and all."

Ally shrugged. "All right. Sure." And then in a whisper to us, "I'll take the ride just 'cause I know it'll bug her." She tossed down her napkin and headed out the door.

Erin, Mia, Noelle, and I stayed to finish our yogurts. Then we said good-bye and headed in separate directions. The walk home was a scorcher. In addition to keeping a wary eye out for cats, I looked for any shaded paths I could find.

After twenty minutes, I got to my street. My nose twitched, and then I spotted two gray rabbits hopping around a saguaro cactus. It was like I could smell them before I saw them. Suddenly, I felt like I needed them. I had to have those rabbits! My shoulders lifted. My eyes locked on the bunnies, and before I knew it, the chase was on. "Rabbit! Rabbit!"

They circled a cactus. I kicked up gravel and circled with them. They dashed toward another yard, and I pumped my legs to keep up.

"What are you doing?" a lady called. "Stop. You there. Stop!" She flailed her hose in the air, cool water splashing me. I froze in place and peeled my laser focus away from my prey. My mouth formed a small silent *o*.

The lady sputtered words and held a hand to her heart. Her face expressed the very question in my head: *Have you lost your mind?*

"Young lady. You should not torment nature. Those

wild rabbits are part of our ecosystem."

"Yes, meow. I mean ma'am. I'm . . . I'm so sorry."

I ran the rest of the way home. The weirdness was getting worse.

Was I turning into a cat?

CHAPTER 29

My hands shook as I jiggled the key into the slot. "Piper? Dad? Anybody?" I hollered. I was alone. Even Archie was at that doggie camp. I raced to the bathroom mirror and inspected for whiskers and fur. Nothing, thank goodness.

I ran up the stairs, losing my flip-flops on the way. I dropped my backpack on the floor and rushed to the bathroom mirror to inspect my face again. Still nothing. I took a deep breath. I needed to talk to Grams. Her technology-free bike tour couldn't have come at a worst time. A growl rumbled from somewhere, either my stomach . . . or my throat!

I upended my backpack and dumped out my

Moleskine journal and the magazine. *Enchanted Teen* had to give me more information. It had to!

"Expired Issue" flashed on the cover, and the inside pages were all blank. The only page that had kept its print was the Marilyn Monroe quote I'd torn out and tacked up on my wall. I dropped onto the bed and Googled the name of the perfume sample I had used today, "Parfum de Cataire." Obviously "parfum" meant "perfume," but what was "cataire"? Nothing came up, so I typed "cataire" by itself. Google popped up with a result line that said: "Tip: Search for English results only." Under that was an image of a green plant and the word "catnip."

"Perfume of Catnip!" I said out loud. No wonder the cats had followed me!

My breath was unsteady. *Stop panicking and be smart*, I told myself. It was time to reassess the hypothesis. I opened my orange journal and scanned my notes. Seeing the stuff I'd written about specific and unspecific wishes made me start laughing. Not a happy laugh, but the kind of sound you might hear from a mad scientist who realizes she's gotten everything wrong.

Costs had been racking up over the past three days, and the formula was simple: the more magic I used—clock *or* magazine, specific *or* unspecific—the more costs I had to pay. Plain and simple.

My heart hammered. Grams would know what to do. Magic wasn't free, and I had no idea what the rest of the costs would be, but I was starting to think they had something to do with turning me into a cat!

Desperate times called for researcher thinking—Grams might not have her cell phone, but the hotels she stayed at during stops must have phones. I got online and searched the tour group Hannah had mentioned, Seniors in Provence. I scrolled down until I found a list of their Wednesday activities. The roster said: "Today includes thirty-one miles of riding—Joucas to Blavac to Pesquie to Mazan. Truffle picnic at Chateau Pesquie. Hotel at Chateau de Mazan." I clicked on the website link for the hotel and—ahhhhh, a phone number.

I dialed and it rang and rang and rang. Just when I thought no one would ever answer, someone picked up.

"Hello!" I sat up, pulling my knees to my chest and jetting out my words. "Hello. Do you speak English? I hope you speak English. I'm calling for a guest. Esmerelda Meyers. She's my grandmother. This is Megan. Meyers. May I please speak with her? It's urgent."

"It is very late," said a woman with a thick accent.

Right. I gulped. The nine-hour time difference

meant it was almost two in the morning.

"Please. *Lo siento* . . . or . . ." I paused. "I'm sorry. I don't speak French. This is important." I squeezed an arm around my shins.

"You are her granddaughter?"

"Yes."

She was silent for a moment. "*Alors*. Please hold."

Some time passed, and then I heard Grams's tired voice. "Hello?"

"Grams. It's Megan."

"Megan, honey! What's wrong?"

"Ummm." My words stuck. I pulled at a green thread on my ruffled pillowcase and gulped.

"Out with it. I'm getting older by the minute."

I rushed out the full update on the catnip, meows, et cetera, ending with a high-pitched "I think I'm turning into a cat!"

Grams was chuckling. Chuckling! And under her breath she said, "Catnip. Giuseppe Bellini, you are funny."

"Hello! What do I do?"

"For starters, calm down," Grams said. "There's no point in panicking. You said no whiskers, no fur, so there's no outward sign that you're becoming a cat, right? My guess is that you're just taking on catisms."

"Catisms! I can't go around middle school meowing!"

"True."

"When will I be finished paying?"

"When, indeed." She laughed. She actually laughed!

"Grams!"

"Listen, sugar. You invited this problem in, so now the cat noises are with you until you figure out how to send them away."

I bolted up to sitting. "How am I supposed to do that? I don't even know why I'm still paying. I've only wished for frivolous stuff. Or . . ." I paused. "This is about my original wish. Isn't it?"

"Perhaps."

"Do you think asking for some magic is lazy, Grams?"

"When you said it, what did you really want? What was the truth behind that desire?"

I stared at my ceiling and shook my head.

"Well?"

"I guess I wanted to be popular."

"Pshaw," Grams said. "That's surface stuff. What's at the core of what you want the most?"

"Well." I thought for a moment of how easy it had been talking to Ally's friends when I believed the perfume made me sound interesting. "I guess the truth is that I struggle with what to say or with tripping over my words or clamming up or saying a bunch of stuff that's not even true just to impress people."

"Okay, now we're getting somewhere. You want the courage to speak up authentically. Good. Think hard," she said, urgency in her voice. "What else aren't you telling me?"

"I . . . I think I understood the cats today. I just don't know what it means."

"Keep talking."

"Everybody else heard meows. But I heard the cats say, 'Cat got your tongue?'"

"Interesting," Grams said.

The panic of understanding sent my tone high-pitched. "Is the cost my voice?"

I wanted Grams to say no, of course not. But she stayed quiet before softly saying, "What do you think?"

I knew what I thought. But I also wanted to be wrong. I wanted a loophole. "How do you know about the clockmakers and stuff?"

Grams sighed. "Let's just say Giuseppe Bellini was sweet on me back in the day."

"You dated the clockmaker!"

"For a short while. He had his good traits. But he wasn't for me. Grandpa was friends with him, too, so when Gramps and I got married, Giuseppe gave us one of the eleven cat clocks he and his brother had crafted."

"And he told you all the rules."

"Not exactly. His brother, Remy Bellini, was sweet on me, too. He's the one who etched the rhyme on the back of the clocks and fessed up the secret of how to use the magic properly. Remy couldn't remove the magic Giuseppe had attached to the clock, but as a favor to me, Remy cast his own spell that would provide an energy source to help influence good choices."

So that's why Marlo Bee scowled when I said things she didn't like.

"And more important to note, Remy's spell added an exit strategy," Grams said. "That's what you need to figure out now. You have to find your way out."

"Do you still talk to the Bellinis?" I asked. "Can you call them to stop all this?"

"Sweetie. They leveled the spell long before you were born. That's done. Once you launched your wish, it was removed from their hands. I can't help you and they can't help you. Everything relies on your efforts."

"How do I fix this?"

"How, indeed," Grams said with a giggle.

"You're laughing at me?"

"I'm sorry, Megan, the whole cat-got-your-tongue part is funny. And you've got to admit, you've had trouble speaking up for a while now. This might be the best thing for you. I'm not able to fix what you've done with your wishes, but I will say this, if you give away your voice to others, you might as well give it to a cat."

"But Grams—"

"Your choice, sugar. Speak up, or else the meowing takes over. Simple as that. Now, it's the middle of the night here, so I am going to have to go back to bed. I love you. *Bonne nuit.*" *Click.* And with that she was gone.

I grabbed my empty magazine from the floor, the cover still glossy and the bright blurb still declaring it an expired issue. But I spoke to it anyway. "How am I going to gain confidence, prepare a flashmob, *and* give up magic all in less than two days?"

"Expired Issue" flashed on and off at me.

I wished I had the Math Olympiad team in my room right now, because I had a big problem and needed a new, non-magic path to a solution.

Time for creativity.

CHAPTER 30

"**Y**ou ready to go?" Dad asked after dinner.

"What?" I looked up from my plate of grilled chicken, my mind busy thinking through my conversation with Grams.

"The Humane Society. You wanted me to drop you off for Wednesday Night Walks."

"Oh, right." I set my fork down. "Piper, you coming?"

"I can't," she said. "My class has been reading *Savvy* and I want to catch up. It's about a girl, and everyone in her family gets a special power when they turn thirteen. I wish that would happen to me."

"Be careful what you wish for," I said.

Piper shrugged. "Sorry I can't go."

"Your loss." I'm not going to lie—it felt like Piper

was blowing me off again.

"I'm grabbing my briefcase and then the mail," Dad said. "I'll meet you at the car."

Dad cleared his plate and I picked up mine.

"What's that for?" Piper pointed at the number two that Rhena had written on my hand.

"Two more days until my flashmob."

"Oh, right! The assembly!" She looked at me. "Are you all good with that?"

I twisted my mouth. "We'll see."

"Umm. Will Rhena be at the flashmob?"

"I guess. But since you brought her up, I don't think you should have her as your yearbook buddy."

"Why?"

"Because she does sneaky, mean stuff to me, and if she can do it to me, she can do it to you. I don't want you to get hurt."

"Mean stuff like what?"

I reminded her of the un-invitation and pointed out that assembly was Rhena's attempt to embarrass me.

"She did act pretty strange at assembly," Piper said. "But everyone's saying that's because she got food poisoning or something. I mean, that has to be true, because of all the gibberish. Right? I'm sure she wasn't trying to be mean about you, she was just messed up then."

I sighed. "Piper, you're so naïve. There was no food poisoning. Just trust me."

Piper sighed, too. "I'm telling you, she's really nice. She's taken time to get to know the name of every fifth grader at yearbook. She brought us all cupcakes the other day. And when there was a spider in the room and everyone screamed, Barett wanted to squish it, but Rhena stopped her and grabbed the teacher's Tupperware container, scooped it up, and carried it outside—just like you would do, Megan. I swear you guys are so much alike, you'd like her if you just got to know her. She's really nice. You have to be misunderstanding her."

I thought about Hannah saying how we'd misjudged Brooke last year, but I wasn't ready to accept it. "I don't know." I stuck my plate in the sink and scrubbed the "2" off my hand, wishing I could wash away the flashmob promise, too.

"Don't be mad," Piper said. "Okay?"

"Fine." I rinsed off the final suds. "Will you put water in Archie's—"

"Sorry," Piper said, her phone ringing. "It's Barett." Then into her phone she said, "Hello," and walked out of the kitchen.

After I refilled Archie's water bowl, I headed to the front door. "Come on, Arch. Want to go for a ride?"

Archie stayed under the desk and wouldn't look my way.

"Archie? You love going in the car."

He ran out from his hiding spot and around the corner away from me.

Fine. I shut the front door and met Dad, who was standing by the car and shuffling through the mail.

"Ready," I said. We climbed inside. "Archie is staying with Piper."

I had no mental energy to figure out what was wrong with Archie, because I was back to thinking through Dr. Ruth Noller's creativity formula, $C = f_a(KIE)$.

With Hannah's help, I'd get the flashmob figured out. She always had fun ideas. I pulled out my phone. *Sigh*. Still no reply.

Dad stuffed the mail into the side pocket of the car door. I stared ahead at yellow streetlights blinking on down the road, thinking through the formula.

Here are the new details for what I could plug into Dr. Ruth Noller's formula.

(K) Knowledge. I had magic, but the Magicverse would possibly take my voice if I used it again.

(I) Imagination. Collaborating with Hannah would be as good as brainstorming with the Mojo's group.

(E) Evaluation. Gather ideas, evaluate, and pick one.

"Seat belt," Dad said as he turned on the head-lights. He backed out of our driveway, and I clicked my seat belt into place. We drove on, Dad spending the whole ride asking me about school, science, and math as per usual, nothing about mean girls or magic. And definitely nothing about weird catisms. At a red light, he reached into his blazer pocket, took out a pack of cherry Life Savers, and popped one into his mouth. "Want one?"

I took the roll. Mom's favorite candy.

The light changed and Dad pulled forward.

"So you really like Mrs. Matthews, huh?" Dad said, breathing out a whiff of wild cherry.

"Yeah." I took in a breath and held it, and with my eyes closed and that sweet candy scent I could almost imagine Mom in the car. It had been nice talking about Mom to Jackson. Maybe the time was finally right to try to bring her up to Dad. I opened my eyes, cleared my throat, and picked the easiest approach. "Dad, tell me the story about how you and Mom found Archie."

I loved this story. My parents had told it a million times—how they found Archie, a stray, when Mom was pregnant with me. She was ultra-sick throughout the pregnancy, but when Archie snuggled next to her, she suddenly felt fine. So Dad said they had to keep him. Mom and Dad would smile every time they told me about finding Archie, the miracle dog—and they'd say I loved animals even before I was born.

We'd almost arrived, but there was still time for Dad to say something about Mom. He always smiled whenever he told that story. Would he smile now?

His face was a mask. The turn signal clicked in the silence. Then he pulled into the Humane Society lot, shifted the car to park, and stared at his hands.

"Not tonight," he said.

I sighed, but I wasn't ready to give up. I took the blue jazz band flyer from my pocket and slid it over to him. "This would be good for Piper," I said softly. "But only if it came from you. She wants your approval or just to know it's okay."

He looked at the form for a moment before stuffing it into the center console. "She knows she doesn't need my permission. If Piper doesn't want to play music, it's not for me to push her."

"Don't you see?" I tried to sound gentle. "She doesn't want to upset you."

"Why would that upset me?"

"She worries if she plays music, it'll make you sad about Mom." I swallowed and added, "She worries you might have another heart attack. Why do you think she's so hyper-focused on what you eat?"

"That's malarkey."

"No, it's not. She watches every crumb you swallow."

"I've been managing my diet just fine."

"You know that. But she doesn't."

He straightened his tie, a tie Mom would've made him take off the minute he got home from work. "We're done discussing this."

We hadn't discussed anything.

"You probably need to get going," he said, staring out the window at the doors to the Humane Society.

The space between Dad and me filled with awkward silence. It had never been awkward when Mom was around. Back then, Piper and I'd do our homework after school while Mom prepared her lesson plans. Then when Dad got home, all work stopped and Mom would make Dad change from his tweed jacket and bow tie into sweats and a T-shirt. He'd transform from stiff to relaxed.

She'd helped me, too, like that time I lost in the science fair and burst into tears in front of my whole school and completely humiliated myself. I ran to the car to cry and be alone, but Mom climbed into the backseat beside me and said, "Honey, just like celebrations, losses are meant to be shared."

Better than her hand-holding, Mom's laughter had been the best thing about our family. It had filled our house, whether we were baking, watching movies, or just teasing Dad. She loved challenging him with science, like saying since he knew so much about physics, shouldn't he be better than her at changing flat tires—he wasn't. And he'd come back with the fact that his knowledge of chemistry was why he was the best baker in the family—he was. She'd say, "Prove it!" And we'd all hope he'd whip up a crème brûlée.

We could always count on Mom's good spirits. Whenever the Monopoly board came out, Dad and I would get into goofy arguments about who got to be the banker and if we should charge compounding interest rates and balloon payments, and then Mom and Piper would laugh and ask if we could please just have one game without higher math.

Dad's voice broke into my thoughts. "I'll pick you up in a few hours."

I climbed out of the car.

"Megan," Dad said, unrolling his window. "Maybe we could do this together next week. You know if I wasn't a college professor I'd be a professional dog walker, right?"

I smiled at his effort. "Sure, Dad."

"Oh, and this came in the mail for you."

Dad held up a brand-new copy of *Enchanted Teen*!

CHAPTER 31

I snatched *Enchanted Teen* from Dad and flung it through the window and into the backseat.

Dad ducked. "Whoa. Take it easy."

I wiped my hands down my shorts. "Sorry. I'll get it at home." I didn't want Dad touching it, and I didn't want that magazine anywhere near me, and especially not here. A green light glowed in the backseat where the bottom corner of *Enchanted Teen* lit up with "Five Fun-Filled Uses of Magic." I didn't like how tempting it felt.

Dad drove off, and with shaky hands, I pushed open the glass door into the Humane Society. There in one of the blue lobby chairs sat Jackson, his hair wet on the sides like he'd recently showered. His gaze was down, and he fiddled with his yarn bracelet.

Could Ally be right about him liking me?

"Hi," I said, my voice wobbly. "I thought you weren't a volunteer."

Jackson stood up and twisted his bracelet one more time. "I'm not, regularly." He smiled. "I just thought when you mentioned the Wednesday Night Walks that it'd be fun, and we could help."

"We?"

Jackson glanced toward the restroom door, and with perfect timing, it swung open and Rhena stepped out. "Hey, Megan."

A hiss threatened in the back of my throat. What was she up to now? And here, of all places!

Marble raced around the corner, passed me, and ran straight into Rhena's arms.

She dropped to her knees. "Hi, Marbs." She rubbed his face. "I've missed you."

Missed you?

Mavis came around the corner with her purse and leash in hand. "Hello, Rhena! So good to see you. It's been ages."

Rhena stood and hugged Mavis, holding on for a second longer than I'd expect.

"Hello, Megan. Jackson." Mavis smiled at us. "I wish

I could stay, but it's time for me to get some dinner."

Rhena took the leash from Mavis and hooked it onto Marble's collar. "I'll walk you guys to your car."

My jaw must've been hanging like a cartoon character as they left, because Jackson said, "Rhena volunteered here all last year, but her mom refuses to drive her anymore, something about it conflicting with tennis lessons. She made a special exception for tonight."

It felt like universes were colliding. How could someone like Rhena be a volunteer?

A few moments later, Rhena returned, her smile buoyant. She was about to say something when the door swung open again and her expression twisted.

A tall woman in high heels and a cream silk shirt hurried through the door, bringing in a rush of flowery perfume.

"Mom? Why are you back already?"

"Is that how you behave? Not 'Mom, it's nice to see you.' Or 'Mom, say hi to my friends.' But 'Mom, why are you here?'" She crossed her arms, tapping a red-lacquered nail to her forearm, and then turned toward Jackson and me. "Hello, Jackson."

"Hi, Mrs. Thornsmith," he said carefully.

Rhena's mom gave me a dismissive glance before focusing back on Rhena. "I know I said I'd give you an hour and a half, but let's make it forty-five minutes, tops. I don't like how your allergies make your skin splotchy. Did you take your allergy pill?"

"Yes, Mom."

"Good." She made a face. "Honestly, Rhena. You shouldn't be wasting time here when you have so many important things to do—homework, the treadmill, and your hair." She gave Rhena's hair a once-over, and her mouth twisted down. "Perhaps we could swing by the salon and get some of those split ends cut off. Your election is in two days, no?"

"I'll get everything done, Mom. I promise. Please."

Yoona came through the entrance while Rhena's mom was talking.

"Rhena, let's not sound whiny. It's undignified." Mrs. Thornsmith looked at her sparkly watch and then turned on her high heels. "Forty-five minutes." And with that, she whooshed past Yoona and out the door.

Rhena stared at the squares of tile flooring.

"Sorry, Rhe," Jackson said sweetly.

"Forget it. Let's go find some pups that need walking." She lifted her chin. "Hey, Yoona."

Yoona stood like a block of stone, eyes wide. "Everything okay?" she asked.

"Yeah," Rhena said. "You know how my mom can

be." Then to me she added, "Well, you don't. But now you have a pretty good idea."

My muscles stayed tense.

It's a proven fact that 93 percent of communication is nonverbal. My tight face and crossed arms must've told Rhena I didn't want any part of a group activity.

"Listen, Megan," she said softly. "I just want to hang with the dogs right now. Can we leave everything about Saguaro Prep out of here tonight?"

Yoona lifted her eyebrows.

"Megan?" Jackson said.

"Okay." I nodded. I'd do it for the dogs.

We picked up leashes and signed out four dogs, a German shorthaired pointer, a boxer, a Lab mix, and a border collie. Then we went to the back where there were several walking paths, an open space, and a play zone.

Most of the other volunteers were on the walking paths. "Let's do the play zone," Jackson said. "It's empty." He grabbed a few orange cones and some cardboard boxes and set up an obstacle course.

First, we walk-raced the dogs around the course. Jackson won. Then we did it walking backward, and he won again.

"One more time," I said. "Let's see who wins, but

this time we have to do the course skipping the whole time."

Rhena laughed. "Yeah. Skipping and singing happy birthday."

Yoona added, "Skipping, singing happy birthday, and pinching our noses shut."

We all laughed and agreed.

It wasn't long before Jackson, Rhena, Yoona, and I were laughing together about other things and actually having a good time. Could this be the Rhena who Piper was getting to know? The Rhena Yoona hung out with? The Rhena Jackson had been friends with his whole life? I'd been stuck on believing Rhena didn't care about anything except herself, but she was sweet with the animals, and they loved her back. It made me think of what Hannah had said on the phone: "Last year we thought Brooke was a snot. We got it all wrong." I knew I hadn't gotten it *all* wrong with Brooke or Rhena—they'd done some mean stuff. But there had to be an in-between. Maybe Rhena deserved another chance.

CHAPTER 32

On Thursday morning, I woke to the dread of knowing I had T minus one day to deliver a megadose of creativity. I powered up my phone. Still nothing from Hannah. Sigh.

I'd gone to bed with wet hair, which meant it had probably dried in a super-tangled mess. I reached a hand to my head, and my fingers snagged on a knot. Half asleep, I climbed out of bed and nearly tripped on a pile of pillows and blankets on the floor—Piper must have set up camp in my room in the middle of the night.

I lumbered to the bathroom in search of a brush and flipped on the lights. There, on my granite countertop next to my brush, was a brand-new ceramic-plated Chi flatiron and a gold bottle of straightening serum.

I picked up the flatiron with my hands shaking like I'd downed a triple-shot latté. Under the brand label Chi was the script:

FOR A TOUCH OF MAGIC

"No, no, no, no, nooooo!"

Above the mirror, a lightbulb buzzed and my nerves charged. I snapped my head left and right, searching for the green-eyed delivery girl.

"Where are you?" My voice sounded wild, feral even. Then I spoke to the flatiron. "Listen up. I put the kibosh on wishing, so what are you doing here?"

The menacing object felt like a viper in my hands.

"Oh, I get it, all right, 'for a touch of magic.' But I didn't make another wish and I didn't accept any add-ons from that stupid magazine, and I didn't ask for the September edition, either. I haven't even opened it. So go away. I'm not paying any more costs."

The citrus scent hit my nose first, and then the bathroom door slid open. "Who are you talking to?" Piper said, peeling back the skin of an orange.

I jumped, waving the flatiron like a weapon before I let it clatter to the counter. "Don't do that."

"What's up with you?" Piper's tone told me that she wasn't only asking why I'd spooked up to the ceiling; it also had to do with my do.

I turned to see my reflection. "Ahhhkk!" My hair looked like it had been styled by a blender.

"Um . . . so Dad and I got the Chi for you at the mall yesterday."

"Oh." I took another glance at the flatiron, nodding fast. "Right. Thank you." I stuck a brush into my pile of tangled hair and gave it a tug.

"We got a new outfit for you, too. I'm going to lay it out on your bed, so no peeking till I'm done."

"Thanks." I smiled, took a breath, and softly said, "Hey, Pipes. Another bad dream?"

"Yeah. But I didn't want to wake you."

"You can, you know. Anytime."

"I know." She dumped her orange peels into the trash, grabbed a Nordstrom bag from her doorway, and crossed from the bathroom to my room.

I tugged at more knots, and after spending several moments wrestling a brush around my head, I found a bottle of detangler and sprayed its watermelon mist over my hair. Finally, the brush ran through. I pulled my hair into its standard wet ponytail and put the Chi in the drawer for another day.

Piper came back in. "Do you want French toast?" Buttery scents from the kitchen floated to my room.

"Two, please."

"All right. I'm going down now to check out what Dad's eating."

The door clicked shut and I almost let out another morning yelp, because *Enchanted Teen* was sitting on my desk instead of in the backseat of Dad's car where I'd left it. A cold chill washed over the room. "You shouldn't be here," I said, before picking it up and slamming it inside the desk drawer.

The outfit Piper had laid out was a flowery, high-waisted miniskirt with a navy tank and navy flip-flops. She'd also left me a pair of small silver earrings. I dressed and then applied a single layer of eye shadow and some light lip gloss. Not bad. Not as great as a magazine model, but perfectly me.

I dragged Piper's pillow and blanket to her room. There in her trash was the blue jazz band flyer, crumpled in a ball. I sighed. At least Dad had tried.

Archie's tail poked out from under Piper's bed. "There you are," I said, crouching low. "What's wrong, Arch?" I reached for him and he scooted close and licked my hand. "Why did you sleep in here?" He panted and licked my hand for a moment before backing farther under the bed.

Ugh. Even my dog.

I needed Hannah, not only for help with the flashmob, but also to feel less alone. She could put a positive spin on anything. Like the time when we'd ridden our bikes by the soccer field in Boulder, and I slipped in gravel and ate dirt in front of the entire

Force team. Hannah had said, "You don't do anything halfway, Megan. That fall was a ten out of ten." It had made me laugh.

I walked back into my room dialing.

"Hi, Megs!" Hannah said.

"What's up, H?"

"Everything! Guess what. Brooke and I are going to wear neckties to school today."

"Nice," I said. "I'm wondering if you have—"

"Neckties!" she repeated. "Isn't that great! Like from our dads."

"Okay, so—"

"We want to see if we can make it a thing. Isn't that hysterical?"

I sighed.

"Maybe you could get everyone there to wear neckties, too," she said.

"For the flashmob?"

"I don't know. Hmmm. Oh, I almost forgot to tell you. Remember how you always said you were going to have the balloon guy on Pearl Street make a pink crown for me, and then you were going to dare me to wear it all day since you know I can't resist a challenge?"

"Sure, but—"

"Well, I did it! Can you believe it? The balloon guy made it ridiculously tall and I had to wear it walking up and down Pearl and of course we ran into Ronald

Miller and Jerry Plinker, and everyone from school. And—"

"Hannah!" I hollered. "Can you stop already?"

"I'm just saying I can't believe we didn't do stuff with Brooke last year."

"We didn't do stuff with Brooke because she sucked. Remember?"

"Oh. Geez," Hannah said, "I'm sorry, Megs." And she sounded sorry, until she added the "but": "But people can change."

I wanted to growl.

"I'm really sorry. I didn't know that still bothered you."

Of course it still bothered me!

"Hey." Piper came bouncing into my room. "Oh, sorry." She stopped bouncing.

I waved her in to stay. "Hannah, I've got to go. Piper needs me." I pressed END and threw my phone down on my bed.

Piper stared at my face. "What's going on?"

Where to begin? My dog was ignoring me. My best friend had a new best friend. A new edition of *Enchanted Teen* was buried in my desk drawer and probably wanted out. I had to come up with the most impressive event in the history of Saguaro Prep tomorrow. I'd spent the past week acting like a cat. And if I messed with magic again, I'd spend the rest of middle school meowing! I was sick of trying to figure everything out by myself.

"Piper." I grabbed her hands. "Can you keep a secret?"

"Absolutely," she said, "but you're squeezing my fingers too hard."

"Sorry." I let go and we sat on my bed, me hugging a pillow to my chest to stop the anxiety from spilling over.

"What's wrong?"

"Well . . . there's this cat clock in my history class. And the weird thing, it looks like one Grams used to have. And there's this rhyme."

"Uh-huh?"

"And . . . and . . ." Suddenly I stopped myself. I didn't want to break my word to Grams. And more important, I didn't want to get Piper in trouble with the Magicverse. She needed to stay safely away or she'd be meowing, too. A tear stung the corner of my eye.

"Okay. So there's a clock and a rhyme and what?" she asked softly, her face full of worry.

"And, umm." I had to tell her something else. "I mentioned the clock to Hannah." I swallowed. "I told Hannah I thought it was good luck, but you know how she's such a skeptic, and so she said it was dumb and I called her a Negative Newton." All true, but that had been yesterday's conversation and we'd already moved on.

"Oh, Megan. I'm sorry. You guys will work it out though. Plus, Hannah's wrong. The clock sounds cool. I can't wait to see it."

"No, don't! I mean never mind. It's all dumb."

"It doesn't sound dumb."

Dad whistled for Archie. "Breakfast!" he called.

I jumped up. "You better open your door. Archie's in your room."

"Okay. But if you want to talk later . . ."

"I know." I squeezed her hand one more time. "And Piper, you can always wake me. You don't have to sleep on my floor or deal with a bad dream alone."

"Thanks."

Piper left and I brushed my teeth, loaded my backpack, and was about to stick my phone in my pocket when a text popped onto my screen.

Yoona: HS w/ Rhena and Jackson was fun!

Me: Super fun!

Yoona: I hope u don't mind I gave Jackson ur number.

Me: !!! ☺

Right away, another text popped up from someone with an Arizona number. Jackson, maybe? It said:

Starbucks after school?

Me: Who is this, haha?

Jackson. ☺

I typed, "Sure," hesitating only to figure out how many exclamation points to use. I settled on one and pressed send.

Piper poked her head into my doorway. "Dad says it's time to load up and your breakfast is—hey, why the goofy look?"

I smiled and the phone vibrated again.

Jackson: I'll meet u at ur locker after last period.

I held in a squeal. "Thanks for the outfit, Pipes."

"Of course." As she tucked her hair behind her ears, a stain on her hand caught my eye.

"You've got a smudge on your hand or something."

She held it out. "Nope. That's not just something. That's a number one. You know. One more day till the flashmob." She smiled. "In support of you."

CHAPTER 33

The number of Spirit Week flyers had quadrupled overnight and the hallways looked like they'd thrown up confetti. After third period, Ally said, "Remember. Bagel stand today. The cinnamon raison is to die for."

"Sounds great. See ya."

When I got to fourth period, Mr. Kersey was sitting at his desk, reading on an iPad and taking sips from his icy can of lemonade. The cat clock remained frozen. Good. Who needed that kind of temptation?

A group of Rhenites were gathered by the Smart Board. Rhena beamed at me like we were besties. "Hi," she said all singsongy. "Come chat with us."

I took a deep breath. We'd had fun the night before. Bonded. But I still wasn't sure I could trust her on school grounds.

Rhena spritzed her wrist with cotton candy perfume, then dropped the bottle inside her pink purse. "Mojo's was fun." She was smiling, but as I walked closer, I could see the smile wasn't the same as last night's. This smile was wooden like the cat clock, and lacking an energy source.

I forced my own smile into place, my spine tense. Something was up.

Rhena sidled up to me and hooked my elbow in hers, her face feigning concern. "So . . . are you okay?"

"Me?" I knew I was about to open Pandora's box, but I asked anyhow, "Why?"

She patted my arm. The Rhenites lowered their eyes. Rhena whispered, "Ally told us how you're crushing on Jackson. The whole school knows."

My face heated up.

"It's okay. Most girls crush on him. You probably thought he might like you back, because of how nice he is. He does the whole showing-you-around thing, and that extra attention can be confusing."

I just stood there, wordless. Why would Ally tell Rhena, of all people?

"At least the rumor is out there, so someone like me can help you."

My brain raced to catch up. "Help me?"

"That's right. Since it's Thankless Thursday."

I looked from Rhenite to Rhenite. *Thankless Thursday?* Yoona kept her head buried in her notebook, doodling, but Shelby and the others seemed genuinely sorry for me.

"Whenever a girl who is—well, let's just admit it"— Rhena paused and patted my arm—"out of Jackson's league starts crushing on him, he uses Thursday to let them down gently. He's so nice. He'll probably invite you to Jamba Juice or Starbucks for the big talk."

I felt like the stupidest version of myself. Not like a science-fair-winning Math Olympian, but a dumb girl who had a dumb crush on a boy who was way out of her league. My shoulders sagged. Why hadn't Ally warned me?

The bell rang. I glanced around, hoping Mr. Kersey would tell everyone to take a seat, but he wasn't in the room. Most of the class headed to their desks, but Shelby and Rhena stayed in front of me, blocking my path.

"Oh, did he already ask you to do something after school?" Shelby asked.

No way was I going to admit it. "N—*ghaaak*." My

voice caught like I had a hairball stuck in my throat. I coughed and cleared my throat, trying again with a lie. "Well, sort o—*ghhaaaaaaaak.*"

Rhena took a backward step. "Eww, if you're sick you better not be contagious."

Slow down, I told myself. *Breathe. Say you're doing a whole group thing, not just something with Jackson.* "It's a grou—*ghaak ghaak ghaak.*"

"What the heck?" Rhena narrowed her eyes.

Shelby's eyebrows disappeared into her bangs. "It's a yes or no, Megan."

The honest answer slid out easily. "Yes." I put my chin down and walked to an open desk and sat down in front of Turner. My hypothesis turned into fact. I couldn't lie without doing something catish!

"Excuse me. Pardon me," Mr. Kersey said, dragging a ladder through the classroom door. He waved a couple of batteries with his free hand. "See, Megan? I've got it all taken care of."

Oh, geez, I thought, sinking in my seat. His timing couldn't have been more categorically awful. Temptation wormed under my skin, and I sat there considering one final wish for the flashmob.

"Rhena, will you kindly hold the ladder for me?" Mr. Kersey asked.

He hiked up the ladder and handed down the clock

to Rhena. She was holding *my* magic clock. Would she feel something special even though it wasn't 11:11?

"Just pop in the new batteries, please."

She flipped it over, and as she worked in the batteries, the expression on her face turned puzzled. Her mouth moved like she was reading something.

I stood up.

"Megan, please have a seat. We've got this." Mr. Kersey leaned toward Rhena. "Hand it back up to me now."

Rhena arched an eyebrow.

A shiver traveled over my skin.

"Hello." Mr. Kersey snapped his fingers. "Hand it back, please."

Rhena passed it up to him and I shook the paranoia from my head. No way. No how. Grams's story was unique. Rhena wouldn't know how to use it.

My phone buzzed with a message from Piper.

Piper: We're all rooting for you. Can't wait till Flashmob Friday. Go Team Free Spirit!!! #TFS

She attached a photo showing dozens of hands pressed close together, all with "#TFS" written on them. The text was meant to be encouraging, but it only added to the pressure.

The magical clock. There it hung, back on the wall.

Ticking. Tocking. Tempting. And there was Rhena, watching me watch the clock, the lure of wishing like a ball of yarn waiting for me to chase it. T minus twenty-five hours until I was supposed to do a flashmob.

Mr. Kersey lectured on Rome. He said something like "triumvirate" and I tuned out. The cat's ticking whiskers and the sweet smell of cotton candy lulled me into believing just one more wish wouldn't hurt. If I could just check off the flashmob wish, there would be a 99 percent chance I'd impress Ally, Jackson, my little sister, and the whole school. All I had to do was make one small wish.

At eleven o'clock, Turner whispered, "Megan. Hey, Megan? Do you have a pen?"

I passed a pen backward, keeping my eyes tethered to the cat.

"Megan?" Turner's voice drifted to me at 11:05. My arms felt heavy like I was under a spell. I didn't budge. His voice faded while the ticktocking beat in my ears. The enchanted eyes moved in a hypnotic dance with the tail.

"Turner." Mr. Kersey's deep voice floated past.

I waited for that magic minute, stretching my fingers and testing the heel of my palm over an index finger. *Pop pop*. Rhena shifted and looked at me again, before looking out the windows. She was watching me.

Eleven ten. I tensed. Every cell in my body vibrated. Then the clock struck 11:11. *I shouldn't wish; my catisms could get worse.* Self-control teeter-tottered. I clasped my hands tight. The seconds raced. *Do I risk it?*

Tick, tick, tick.

Do I?

Tick, tick, tick. Rhena's mouth was moving and I almost panicked, but there was no lightning. No popping. No way she knew how to make the magic work.

At 11:12, I let out my held breath. Rhena stared at me and me at her. I broke first and laid my head on the desk. My stomach filled with a mixture of gratitude and disappointment. No wish. But at what price? Exhausted, I closed my eyes.

"Hello . . . HELLO?" Shelby said. "Bell rang."

"Huh?" I lifted my head. I must have dozed off. Class was over.

Everyone filed out of the room.

I gathered my stuff and entered the hall, looking for Ally. Mia headed toward me, carrying a tower of books.

"Hey, Mia. Let me help." I took part of her stack.

"Thanks. I have to get these returned to the library. *Girls in the Stacks* has a new blog post, and now I have a giant wish list."

We turned the corner to the library and dropped one book at a time through the slot.

"Can I ask you something?" I said, dropping in the last book.

"Sure."

"Do people here call Thursday 'Thankless Thursday'?"

She pushed her glasses up her nose. "Sure. That's a thing. Why?"

"Oh." My insides sagged. "Never mind."

"Okay, I'm going to hurry and see if they have my books. See you in the cafeteria if I finish on time." Mia rushed off.

Forget the cafeteria. I was going to call my dad and tell him I was sick and needed to go home. I couldn't face Jackson today.

I took out my phone and dialed.

"Hello, Megan," Dad said.

I intended to say, "Hi, Dad. I'm feeling sick." What I said was "Hi, Dad. *Meeooow.*"

"What?" he said. "Megan, are you okay?"

"Um. Never mind."

I stuffed my phone into my pocket and headed down the hall to find Ally. Why didn't she warn me about Thankless Thursday? And for that matter, why was she telling everyone about my crush on Jackson?

Unless that was just another one of Rhena's lies. Should I ask Ally, or would I end up blowing up our friendship like I'd just done with Hannah?

Everything I'd read on *How to Survive Middle School* advised avoiding confrontations. But Grams's words about being authentic came rushing at me.

I found Ally at her locker, her eyes red-rimmed.

"Whoa. Are you okay?" I asked.

She grabbed my arm. "Come with me?"

We ducked into the nearest girls' bathroom.

"I can't believe it," Ally said, fuming and checking the stalls before coming back to me. "Rhena is a first-class witch."

Ally must've already heard that Rhena was talking about us. "I know. Right."

"She . . ." Ally sniffled and took a moment to gather herself.

"I know."

"You do? Well, don't repeat it, because rumors spread like wildfires at Saguaro Prep, and even though it's not true, people love to gossip, and it's so embarrassing."

"Wait. What are you talking about?"

"I got called to the office and told I have to meet with Mr. Provost at lunch. Rhena told him I copied her answers during the science quiz last week. Like

I would ever cheat, and especially off Rhena's work." She puffed out a breath and shook her head. "She's such a liar."

"I can't believe she'd do that . . . well, I can. But seriously."

"I know. And if my *abuela* finds out I've been accused of cheating, she'll be so ashamed. The rumor alone will crush her."

"Does Mr. Provost believe Rhena?"

"He has to take the accusation seriously, so now I have to use my lunch defending my answers to him. Anyhow, I'm really sorry I can't eat with you. Come on." We left the bathroom and walked toward the cafeteria. "I'll help you find Noelle and everyone. You can eat with them."

No way was I going inside the cafeteria and risk running into Jackson. I'd hide in the bathroom or outside if I had to but I wouldn't worry Ally with the details. "Look. You get going. I'll find Noelle and them on my own."

"Huh?" Ally stopped walking, her face a knot of confusion.

"I said I'll find Noelle and them on my own."

"No you didn't. You just meowed a sentence."

"What? No . . . I . . ."

"You just said, 'Meow'll meow meow meow.'"

"Oh." I looked at the floor. *Right. I lose my voice every time I try to lie.*

"Hey," Ally said, "thanks for trying to make me laugh. I'm going to run before I'm late to my interrogation. Wish me luck." She headed toward the science room.

"Good luck." I angled toward the cafeteria until she disappeared from sight, then I veered toward the outdoor exit, where Jackson was filling his water bottle.

CHAPTER 34

"**H**ey," Jackson said, before I had a chance to turn away and pretend I didn't see him.

"Hi." I couldn't make eye contact without feeling like the world's biggest dorkjob. How did I lull myself into believing he could possibly like me? I pushed open the door that led to the outdoor patio.

"Wait." He put the cap on his water bottle. "Have lunch with me. There's a great shaded spot by the Palo Verde trees with misters and all."

"I, no, it's just that . . ." Oh gosh, I couldn't start making up a lie or I'd meow or gack. He followed me outside and I stopped walking.

"What? Come on." He smiled, his freckles looking cute to the tenth.

I folded my arms over my stomach. "Look. You don't have to keep being nice to me. Your ambassador duties are over."

"Huh?"

"We don't need to go to Starbucks or whatever. I get it." I stared at his shoulder.

"Get what?" Jackson asked. "That I like you?"

I looked up. "Uhh . . . that you don't," I said, surprising myself for being so honest.

"I don't know what would give you that idea." Jackson stepped closer and waited for me to meet his gaze.

It made my stomach wavy.

"I'd still like to go to Starbucks," he said. "And have lunch with you. Okay?"

"Okay." I couldn't hold back my smile.

"Good. Come on, I'll split my turkey sandwich with you."

We started walking.

"Mustard or mayo?" I asked.

"Definitely mustard."

"Phew! I'm not sure I could keep hanging out with you if you were a mayo guy."

"Never."

I felt like the second element on the periodic table. Helium. And I was so floaty walking with Jackson that when we got to the Palo Verde trees, I didn't notice

Rhena until she was right on us.

"Hi, you guys," she said sweetly.

The float in my feet turned to bricks, and I stopped walking.

"Sit with us." Rhena pointed across the courtyard, where Shelby was fluffing out a floral tablecloth.

What a turnip, I thought, channeling Erin.

"Awesome," Jackson said, failing to receive my "NO" brainwave message.

"Wednesday Night Walks was fun," he said. "We should all do that again."

"Absolutely," Rhena said, like she hadn't just tried to crush my soul an hour ago.

Jackson's phone dinged. "Shoot." And then, "I'm sorry. Coach Crosby needs me and says it's urgent." He fumbled to open his backpack. "Let me get my sandwich. I'm still giving you half."

"It's fine, Jackson," Rhena said, looping her elbow in mine. "I have plenty to share with Megan."

"Okay, cool." Jackson flung his backpack on a shoulder. "See you later."

My head spun with how fast this had unraveled, Jackson jogging off toward the gym, and Rhena leading me toward her group.

Two Palo Verde trees shaded our picnic area, their pale green bark looking as sick and unnatural as I felt surrounded by Rhenites, buzzing around their queen.

Shelby smoothed out wrinkles from the tablecloth. Yoona smiled at me and set down napkins at each spot while another Rhenite placed bottles of iced tea in front of each napkin. Two Rhenites distributed chopsticks, and then Rhena unzipped a pink cooler and put down a bowl of green edamame and three trays of sushi. Yellowtail, California rolls, and delicious pink salmon nigiri.

Mmmmm. It wouldn't hurt if I stayed for just a few minutes.

My nose twitched. And suddenly I snapped up two pieces of yellowtail straight off the rice strips. I sucked them down with a big *sluuuuurrrrrp* and grabbed for more.

Everybody stopped what they were doing.

"Uhhh." I licked my lips and peeled my gaze off the next piece of fish clutched in my fingers. "This is really good?" I said, mortification echoing in my high-pitched voice.

"We have soy sauce," Rhena said. "And chopsticks."

My face burned. I placed the fish back on its rice strip and slinked down onto the bench seat. My speedy exit plan was kaput. I fiddled with a set of chopsticks and nibbled on some rice. The group chatted and I slumped back and listened as they bashed on people.

"Did you see what so-and-so wore today?" and "Blah blah blah is a loser." Shelby looked at me, and I forced out a laugh to fit in. It made me feel grimy. Ashamed. My "meek to chic" goal at this new school was turning into "meek to creep."

Then Shelby brought up Friday's flashmob. "You're going to need to figure out how to ditch Ally."

"Yes," Rhena said. "Or you could sabotage it completely."

My spine stiffened. "Why would I do that?"

She looked at me like I'd spelled "cat" wrong. "Don't you get it? Why should you help Ally win? She's using you to get votes, and she's talking behind your back, so instead of being a victim, you could pull off a great blindside by *not* having a flashmob. Then you'd have the last laugh."

"Yeah. Du-uh," Shelby said.

"You're new and just building your reputation, like it or not." Rhena crossed her arms. "If you want to be attached to Ally's group, then you should run along and find her now. I hear she's in the science lab." Rhena smiled at her crew. "Or you could sabotage the flashmob like I suggested."

Unbelievable.

"Good. That settles it, then," Rhena said, as if my speechlessness was a silent agreement. She popped edamame into her mouth. "See, girls? Megan's with us."

First a cat took my voice. And now I was letting Rhena put words in my mouth.

"No," I said, my voice barely audible. "That's not what I'm saying."

Nobody was listening. I had been quiet too long and the conversation had moved on.

I shifted and Mom's guitar pick poked my leg from inside my pocket like even it wanted me to speak up. I needed to get away from this group. And Piper needed to stay away from Rhena, too. Sure, Rhena might be kind to animals, but she clearly wasn't decent with humans.

Piper had been fooled, because Rhena was a good faker. I would be fooled, too, if I'd seen Rhena only like she was last night. But if Piper could hear Rhena now, she'd understand why I wanted her to stay away. I fiddled with my phone. The gossip blabbered on, and I pressed record on my video app, casually holding the phone at an angle. I'd show this to Piper later.

It was as if Rhena was cued to be her perfectly horrible self. With a big, malicious smile in place, she bragged to the group about how she'd lied to Mr. Provost and told him Ally cheated off her.

"What?" I said, startling even myself.

"Of course I made up that little tale, Megan.

Cheaters never win Spirit Captain."

Speak up! screamed inside my head. But *HSMS* screamed, too, and it said, *Do not get into confrontations!* I squirmed. I avoided. I diverted. "Umm, how'd everybody do on Kersey's test, 'cause I . . ."

I let my words trail off. Nobody was even paying attention to me. Rhena had moved on to the next bashing topic. I pushed the stop button on my phone. How could I let Piper listen to this now? Sure, I had proof that Rhena was the mean girl I'd said she was, but it also showed that I was a horrible friend, since I didn't speak up for Ally when I knew she'd been set up in a lie.

Somehow, I muddled through the rest of lunch. When my phone vibrated with a text from Hannah asking if we were okay, I ignored it.

As soon as the bell rang, I went to find Ally by the science classrooms.

The rims of her eyes were puffy and red. "Mr. Provost says he's fine with my test," Ally said. "But I know he has doubts."

"But you knew the answers, right?"

"Well, I guessed on a few of the multiple-choice questions and got them right, so that looks suspicious."

"Were there essay questions and fill-in-the-blanks?"
She nodded.

"You nailed those, right?"

"Yeah. Mostly."

"What's he going to do?"

"Oh, he gave me a speech about Saguaro Prep's code of conduct and integrity expectations. Basically, he said he was accepting my test, but I know I'll be under suspicion forever. And who's going to vote for me for Spirit Captain if people think I'm a cheater?" Her voice rose. "Do you see everything Rhena accomplished with her lie? Mr. Provost now questions my integrity, if the rumor gets out I could lose the election, and if my *abuela* hears about it, she'll freak."

I wanted to tell Ally what I'd heard, but getting in the middle of stuff between Ally and Rhena was what started all my messes in the first place. Plus, I'd have to admit to eating lunch with Rhena. Would Ally be mad at me for that? The warning bell rang, alerting us that we had one minute left to get to class. I'd never been so happy to hear a school bell before.

"Shoot. I better run." I hugged my books to my chest and raced down the hall. When I rounded the corner, I bumped smack into Mr. Provost.

"Oh, I . . . I . . ." I could tell him. It was like destiny.

"Megan, is it?" Mr. Provost said. "Are you okay?"

"I . . ." *Tell him!*

"Can I help you with directions?"

Avoid confrontations, I told myself. He wouldn't believe me. It'd be my word against Rhena's, unless I showed him the recording. But if I did that, then instead of being thought of as a dorkjob at this school, I'd get a new reputation: the snitch. Saguaro Prep's tattletale.

I hugged my books to my chest and raced down the hall before the hiss itching inside my throat escaped from my mouth.

CHAPTER 35

"**H**i." Jackson walked up to the lockers and leaned against the one next to mine. "Ready?"

"Yep." I coughed, swallowing down a hairball-sized gulp.

I ignored another text from Hannah and stuffed my phone into my pocket, and we headed out. The hallway shook with the end-of-day noises—chatter, slamming lockers, shuffling feet.

Now that the date was officially here, what would we talk about? I rubbed Mom's guitar pick, wishing she had given me some boy advice before she died. Jackson must've felt awkward, too, because we both studied our shoes as if there'd be a quiz on them later.

We left the school grounds, passing the same adobe houses and sweet-smelling honeysuckle bushes I'd passed the other day. When we rounded the corner where I'd seen the cats, I couldn't help but check left and right. I hadn't used the perfume again, but still.

"So," we finally said at once. Then we laughed and got quiet.

We rounded the end of the sidewalk and I tried again. "How was—" while he said, "Did you—" Again we laughed, and this time I said, "You first."

"Want to play a game called Rapid Fire?" he asked.

"Okay. How do you play?"

"It's kind of like Truth or Dare, but there are no dares, it's all truth. I shoot off a question and then you give the first answer that comes to your head. No explanations required. After you answer, you get to fire a question my way. We rapid-fire questions back and forth as quickly as possible. That's it."

"All right." I took a breath. *Just don't ask anything embarrassing.*

"All-time favorite song?" he asked.

"'Handlebars.'"

"Nice." Jackson nodded.

"Favorite video game?" I asked.

"*Guitar Hero*," he answered. "Favorite thing about Colorado?"

"Snow. Favorite thing to do in Arizona?" The butterflies in my stomach calmed.

"Water-ski on Saguaro Lake."

The game was genius! It kept us talking the entire walk. Just fun stuff and nothing uncomfortable like "Who do you think will win Spirit Captain" or "What are you going to do for the flashmob" or "How do you feel about knowing that Ally's been accused of cheating and you're doing nothing to fix the situation?"

Ten minutes later, we arrived at the corner of Scottsdale Road and Greenway and made our way to the Starbucks. Overhead misters pumped out fogs of moisture. Large pots of yellow and white flowers decorated patio tables covered by huge green umbrellas.

The sun had turned my back sticky, and drips of sweat trickled down my neck.

"Do you mind if we grab an inside seat?"

"Sounds great."

Jackson opened the glass door for me, and along with the air-conditioning, the word "date" fluttered over me. We entered and plopped our backpacks next to a couple of brown leather chairs facing the patio with wall-length windows. Then we stepped in the back of the line to order our icy drinks.

The rich scent of coffee and baked goods filled the air. As I cooled off, my jitters returned. *Will we order together? If so, how does paying work?*

When it was our turn, I jumped ahead of Jackson and faced the girl in the green apron, whose name tag said Natty. "One tall iced soy caramel macchiato, please. That's all." I rattled off the order quickly, took a crumpled five from my pocket, and slid it across the counter. Then I prayed she'd received my telepathic message, which went, *Hello. Natty. Please maintain eye focus with me. Do not, I repeat, do not look at that cute boy behind me and ask embarrassing questions like "Will this be together?"*

Thankfully, Natty clicked her cash register and called out the order to the barista.

Without a backward glance, I took my change and stepped aside to wait at the next counter for my drink. The barista blended my concoction while Jackson ordered. I stole sideways glances and wished I could read his mind.

"Soy caramel macchiato for Megan," the barista announced. "Caramel macchiato for Jackson." I liked the way she slid Jackson's drink right next to mine, his topped with white whipped cream and crisscrossing caramel. Jackson picked up both cups and handed one to me.

"Thanks," I said.

We grabbed straws and sat on the soft leather cushions of chairs angled toward the windows. Jackson ripped the paper from the top of his straw and blew the remaining paper at me, something Piper or Mom would have done. I tore the top paper from my straw and blew back, knocking him straight between the eyes.

"Great shot, commando." Jackson laughed.

"A move right out of *Call of Duty*," I said.

"Ahh, you have good video game taste, too. Nice."

His dimple. Those freckles. Even his eyelashes were perfect. I held his gaze for another moment and then glanced out the window before it got awkward again.

A set of sparkly, Hubba Bubba pink shoes caught my eye in the movement of people outside.

"Hey, I think that's my . . ." I leaned toward the window, a small smile on my face.

"Yeah, that is my . . ."

Then a girl stood up from underneath one of the green umbrellas—Rhena.

A clammy feeling flashed over my skin. "They can't be meeting up."

"What?" Jackson asked.

"Hold on. I'm not sure." People hurried down the sidewalk, going left and right under the hazy mist, blocking my view.

Who else would own a pair of custom Chucks just like that?

Rhena headed toward the girl.

"Hey, there's Rhena," Jackson said. "Weird. I told

her we'd be here today when I asked her and Yoona for your number."

"But is that . . ." I stood up and pressed my forehead against the window, angling for a better look. Jackson joined me. The crowd on the sidewalk parted, and there was a sparkly clip and honey-blond ponytail. "Oh my gosh. That's my little sister! With Rhena!"

"Yeah?" Jackson said, probably wondering at my freaked-out tone. "Are you okay?"

I couldn't keep it together, no matter how cute he was. "Piper is with her." My words came out fiery.

Rhena and Piper headed down the sidewalk. I swept my backpack over my shoulder, slammed my cup into the trash bin, and bolted out the door.

I was already halfway down the sidewalk before Jackson caught up, huffing to catch his breath. "Megan, what's going on?"

"She . . ." I pressed my lips together. "They . . ." I shook my head. "Ugh. I just can't believe this!" I picked up my speed.

Rhena and Piper passed several storefronts and then took a left, walking into Marble Slab Creamery.

I hustled to the ice cream parlor and threw open the door. "Piper?" I spit out her name and popped my hands to my hips.

"Megan!" Her face flushed.

"Oh, hey, Jackson. Megan," Rhena said all

singsongy. She scooched closer to Piper and smiled. "Piper and I have been talking about what a hard time you've been having with this move; that you and your best friend back in Colorado are fighting."

I glared at my sister. "You're talking about me to her?" The words squeezed from my tight throat.

"Megan. I want her to know about you and you about her so you guys can be friends," Piper said, her face begging me to trust that she had everything worked out. "And Rhena promises everything I say stays between us. She's not going to talk about you to anyone."

"She's talking about me now." I flung a hand toward Jackson, who was studying his shoes and probably thinking I was the lamest person ever.

"Piper says you're a bit obsessed with a cat clock, too."

"I didn't say obsessed," Piper said, looking at Rhena.

"And I'm thinking," Rhena said, "it's that cat clock in Kersey's room, right?"

I couldn't say a lie, so I shook my head.

"Hmm," Rhena said. "Are you sure? Because after school I showed it to Piper." Rhena smiled at my sister.

Piper didn't see the malice dancing in Rhena's eyes. She looked at me in her hopeful way. "You're right, Megan. I do think that clock is cool."

"And," Rhena said, "she says your grandma has a clock just like it and used to *wish* on it." Rhena paused. "At eleven-eleven." Pause. "With some fancy rhyme?"

A cold chill drained through my face and neck.

"It's too bad Piper can't remember the rhyme," Rhena said sweetly. "Do you remember it?"

Every hair on the back of my neck spiked.

Rhena narrowed her gaze. "Because I was thinking your Grams's rhyme might be the same one I saw etched on the back of the clock when Kersey took it down to change the batteries yesterday?"

"Megan," Piper asked, "what's wrong?"

A satisfied smile smeared across Rhena's face. "Anyhoo, we need to get back to our yearbook planning now, soooo . . ." She gave me a look that said I was dismissed. "Oh, and Piper." She rested a hand on Piper's arm. "Didn't you say you wanted to talk about the big pillow fight we're having in April?"

I flinched.

"Hold on, Megan." Piper stood and grabbed my arm. "Of course it's *our* pillow fight. I just thought Rhena could help. We need lots of people."

"Sure. That's right," Rhena said, sweet as ever, the perfect actress. "Stay. We'll all plan it together."

How could Piper have invited Rhena to be part of our thing?

"See?" Piper said. "She wants you here, and if you

guys just get to know each other—"

I shook off Piper's grip and pushed open the door to leave Marble Slab.

"Wait, Megan," Piper said.

I whipped around to face her just long enough to scream, "Leave. Me. Alone!" Then I blazed a path down the sidewalk, Jackson rushing to my side. When I rounded a corner, I nearly knocked over a small child with my swinging backpack.

I stopped. "I'm sorry," I said to the little boy. He clutched his mother's leg. "I'm sorry."

"That's okay," the mother said kindly before scooping the boy into her arms and walking on.

Jackson rested a hand on my shoulder.

"Here," he said softly. "Let me carry that for you." He took my backpack. "Megan, what's going on?"

My cheeks were wet, and I was probably a vision of loveliness—all drippy nose and mascara trails.

"Are you okay?"

I wiped my face and blubbered, "We were going to plan a pillow fight."

"Yeah?"

"We, as in me and Piper," I said, because he wasn't getting it. "Not Rhena. Definitely not Rhena. What are they even doing together?" I looked at him accusingly.

"Um," he shifted. "I don't—"

"I texted her today." I sniffed.

"Rhena?"

"No! Piper." I let out an exasperated sigh and started walking, slower this time. "And I told her I had plans after school. She could've told me she had plans, too. But she didn't. Not telling me is just as bad as lying. Right?"

"Um—"

"Why would she talk about me? I've already asked her not to hang out with Rhena. I'm the one who's there for Piper in the middle of the night," I said, kicking a pebble. "Not Rhena. I don't know why Piper even wants to be around her." I sounded stupid and jealous and full of drama. But the words continued to fall from my mouth.

"My life is out of control, Jackson. Moving here. I'm losing my sister. And I don't even know how you could be friends with someone like Rhena." My hiccup turned into a slurpy sniffle. "And I promised to wow you all with an amazing flashmob to help Ally win the election, when the truth is I've got zip, and I probably shouldn't be telling you this since you're the competition." I shook my head in disbelief. "My biggest flashmob idea so far has been to have an exponential cartwheel-off." I scoffed. "Can you imagine? How nerdy is that? That's about as exciting as having a hundred people call off the numbers of pi."

"That could be fun," Jackson said softly.

I blubbered a laugh and rubbed away tears. "That announcement in assembly about how the flashmob's going to be legendary. Well, what's the opposite of legendary?" I shook my head. "By this time tomorrow I'll have ruined the Spirit Week election for Ally and everybody's going to hate me."

"Nobody's going to hate you. Here, stop walking for a sec." Jackson offered me a Starbucks napkin. The sweet look on his face made me want to cry all over again.

I took the napkin and turned my face away, wiping snot and tears.

"It doesn't matter that we're running against each other in the election," he said. "The flashmob is for our whole class, and I'll help you brainstorm or whatever you need or we can forget it completely." Jackson handed a fresh napkin to me. "You need to know people already like you—our math group, the lunch group, a bunch of people. It doesn't matter if you throw a whopping Megan-palooza or not. Really. You can forget the flashmob if it stresses you out. You don't need to do anything."

"Forget it? You don't have a clue. You've lived here forever and already have a boatload of friends. More than a boat—a cruise ship." I sighed. "You don't understand the pressure. I can't just not do anything."

Suddenly, the familiarity of being urged to forget the flashmob hit me hard. It clobbered me. Jackson was on Team Rhena. They'd been friends forever. He'd skipped math club to meet with her, probably to discuss their own blindside. Lunch was probably a setup, too.

"Did Rhena tell you to tell me that?" Hair bristled on the back of my neck. "That's why you asked me out?" My voice rose. "To try to convince me *not* to have the flashmob so you and Rhena can win the election?"

"No?" he said, but his face flashed a flicker of guilt, that same flicker I'd seen in the hallway. "I'm just saying—"

"Right," I said. "Forget it. This was a bad idea, and I have to go."

"Can I walk you?"

"No." I grabbed my backpack from him. "How dumb do you think I am?"

"Megan?"

"Remember what we talked about, Jackson," I said mimicking Rhena's voice from the other day. They'd probably planned this whole let's-fool-Megan scheme together.

CHAPTER 36

I stormed circles around my bedroom, kicking my trash can and then the moving box of books. I felt sorry for myself and even sorrier for Ally—because of me she'd lose the election. And worse, Rhena would probably theme Spirit Week in ways to make me miserable: Millionaire Monday, only the wealthy can play. Tahitian Tuesday, wear a bikini to school. Weirdo Wednesday, dress like Megan. Ugh!

I had a mini tantrum, shoving my chair under my desk, stomping over my pile of laundry, and kicking the next thing in my path, the box with the Lincoln mask. Suddenly the "I" in the creativity formula sparked. C = f_a(KIE): Creativity is a function of attitude multiplied by Knowledge, Imagination, and Evaluation.

I stooped over and picked up the Lincoln mask and could've kissed it right then and there. Pieces of a plan started to gel and an idea for the flashmob came to me, something that could be funny and timely—one part flashmob and one part Spirit Week election.

Would everyone think it was dumb?

I squeezed the mask, thinking about what Mrs. Matthews had said at math club—understand the problem, devise a plan, and carry it out.

I had an idea, but doubt crushed my chest. People might think it was dumb. But according to the formula, the f_a, the function of attitude, was up to me, and I liked it. A lot. It wasn't a perfect algorithm for a mind-blowing flashmob, but it was a creative solution. And before I talked myself out of it, I set the mask on my bed and used my phone to open the social media forum Ally had set up for the seventh-grade class. I typed "#TeamFreeSpirit." I took a photo of the mask and posted it with the same hashtag and plastered it on all my social media sources, adding: "Noon. Cafeteria. Show up wearing a president mask—Nixon, Clinton, Lincoln, whoever! Vote Ally 4 Spirit Week Captain!"

Then I copied and pasted the post in a text to Ally.

My phone rang right away.

"Megan," Ally said, "I love the idea. It's brilliant!"

"I know, right? It's an election, so I thought presidents. Anyhow, in the morning we could meet early and plan some kind of chant for our group and we could march into the cafeteria with our masks on, all saying something together and then scream out 'Vote for Ally!'"

"The thing is . . ."

Uh-oh. She sounded flustered, not excited.

"I don't have a president mask. And I don't mean to sound negative, because it is a funny idea and so perfect for an election. But I doubt most people own Obama or Nixon masks or any other president for that matter."

How could I be so lame?

"I mean," she continued, "I'm sure a few people do, but for those of us who don't, it's kind of a hard thing to get ahold of before lunchtime tomorrow."

"Right," I said softly, hanging my head. Of course she was right. I should have talked to her before sending the post. $C = f_a(KIE)$. I forgot the "E" as in Evaluate.

"Oh man," Ally said, sounding panicked. "I have my computer opened right now. Look at how many likes the post is getting. What should we do?"

"I don't know," I said, feeling defeated. "I'm sorry. I shouldn't have promised a flashmob. Now I've probably ruined the election for you."

Ally didn't say anything for a moment. Then she said, "It's okay. If I can't win an election without a flashmob, then I don't deserve it. And you didn't ruin anything. It was me. I shouldn't have gotten so braggy at assembly." Did she sniffle? "My mouth gets me in trouble sometimes."

She was being so nice when I'd just destroyed our chances of winning. I wished I could do something to fix this.

The horrible weight of messing up things for Ally pressed on me. Rhena would win. Again. The thought spun anger through my veins.

I was tired of Rhena winning. She won with lunch, with my sister, with Jackson. And now she knew enough about the clock to be dangerous. I couldn't let her win the election, too. There was only one way to stop her—I'd have to make sure we had the best, most magical flashmob possible.

"Hold on, Ally," I said. "I've got this figured out." I pushed down the warning crawling up my spine. "I have a way to get as many masks as we need delivered outside the cafeteria before lunchtime."

"You do?" she asked. "How?"

"I can't really explain, but trust me. I have it handled."

"Seriously?"

"Mmmhmm."

"Wow! Okay . . . thank you!"

"Don't worry when you don't see the masks first thing in the morning," I said. "But trust me. They'll be right outside the cafeteria door before lunchtime. In fact, they'll be there at eleven twelve on the dot."

I didn't consider what could happen to me. All I knew was that Rhena wasn't going to win again. I'd risk one more wish to make sure of it.

CHAPTER 37

On Friday morning, I got up at T minus five hours—that gave me plenty of time to take Archie on an early walk and another opportunity to practice saying my wish fifty more times. When the clock struck 11:11, I would say, "At eleven twelve a.m., please have Bruce deliver enough US president masks to Saguaro Prep's cafeteria so that every single seventh grader can wear one."

After the walk, I poured myself a glass of orange juice, grabbed a brown paper bag, and returned to my room. Archie tried to go to Piper's room, but I forced him to come with me. He went under my bed.

A moment after I shut my door there was a knock. "Megan, can I come in and talk to you?" Piper said.

"No." I locked the door and also the Jack-and-Jill side of the bathroom.

Then I stared at that crumpled fortune cookie paper from the other night. The one that said, "Be who you are and say what you feel because those who mind don't matter and those who matter don't mind."

Dr. Seuss obviously never went to middle school.

I snatched the Marilyn quote off my wall and shoved it into my backpack—a little extra motivation in case I started to chicken out.

"Please, Megan," she said, knocking again.

I thought about flinging open the door and showing Piper the video of Rhena. But then she'd see me as lame. Spineless. Doing nothing to stand up for Ally. "Just go."

Thinking about Piper talking about me to Rhena made me angry all over again. And now Rhena knew about the rhyme. It was only a matter of time until she figured out she needed to make a pop and she'd be on the road to wishing. And then no one at Saguaro Prep would be safe!

My phone had texts waiting. The first from Yoona:

Yoona: No matter what happens today, good luck.

I replied "Thanks" with a smiley face and dog emoji. Next, a text from Hannah:

Hannah: Good luck w/ ur flashmob. I want to hear all about it.

At least she remembered.

Then a text from Ally flashed on the screen.

Ally: SO excited about the flashmob!!!

A tidal wave of jittery nerves rippled through my gut.

Me: Me too ☺

I slid open my desk drawer, magazine still hidden inside. I carefully placed it in the brown paper bag and tucked it into my backpack.

Ally: This'll go down as the best Spirit Week kickoff ever!!!

Yep, I thought . . . *as long as the magic works, Rhena doesn't mess with the clock, and I don't grow a tail.*

After second period, my phone vibrated with an incoming call. Probably Piper. I reached into my pocket and clicked decline.

"Hey," Jackson said.

His voice startled me. Embarrassment flooded my veins. But so did anger, because now I knew what he was about.

"What?" I shut my locker and glanced left and right for an escape route.

My phone vibrated again. Decline.

"I tried catching up with you before both first and second period this morning." Jackson moved closer, and the kindness in his voice squeezed my ribs. He tried to make eye contact. "How are you?"

"Managing" was what I tried to say. "I'm fine" was what I wished I'd said. "Meow" is what came out. Ugh.

"Huh?" Jackson said.

"Hey, guys." Rhena sidled in next to Jackson.

"Later," I said.

Jackson looked flattened. "Megan?"

"Let her go," I heard Rhena say. "I hear she's got a thing for Turner, anyhow."

The math room smelled like the egg burrito sitting on Mrs. Matthews's desk. As I took my seat, a boy in the front row said, "Flashmob at noon, right, Megan?"

Pressure churned my gut. "Yep."

Outside, the rain drizzled. There was no choice but to risk one more wish at 11:11.

Too bad I couldn't wish away the past. If I could, I'd rewind this week and zip my lips after the snow day. I'd never claim to be the Fun-meister or promise a flashmob. I'd skip the assembly. I wouldn't tell Piper anything about the clock. And I'd wish to undo all the drama I'd created. At least Ally and her group would be my friends after all this was over. They had been nice from the start.

"Hey, Megan." Ally walked into the room, face pinched.

Why was she looking at me like that?

"Having lunch with Rhena again, today?" She flew past the open seat next to me and chose a last-row desk.

I turned around. "No, I'm not—"

"I can't believe I told you about Rhena and science yesterday, and then you danced off and had lunch with that group of fakes."

Explain.

"You could've eaten with Noelle, or Erin, or anybody else," she said.

My phone vibrated. *Piper needs to chill.* Again, I hit decline without looking.

"Oh, do you need to get that? It could be Rhena. I hear your goal is to sabotage the flashmob, too."

"That's not true!"

"Really? Because I hear you've just been pretending to be my friend all week to set me up for the fall." Ally stuck a book in front of her face. The rain came harder. Thunder cracked in the distance.

"Ally—" A text vibrated my phone. This time I looked. Dad—

Dad: Call me ASAP. It's about Grams.

CHAPTER 38

A *SAP?* Worry vacuumed the air from my chest.

"Who would like to pass these out for me?" Mrs. Matthews asked the class.

"Excuse me," I said. "May I go to the restroom?"

She seemed ready to say no, but something about my face must've changed her mind. "Please take the hall pass."

I grabbed the yellow wooden pass hanging near the door and rushed down the empty hallway. I ducked into the bathroom, dialing Dad's number, Mom's guitar pick already clutched in my hand.

He answered on the first ring.

"Dad?" I asked nervously.

"Megan, honey." Dad sniffed.

I waited, heart in throat.

"It's your grandmother. She . . . she's been in an accident. She broke her leg and they have to operate."

"But she's going to be okay, right?"

"Of course, of course." Dad's voice sounded strained. "They just have to be cautious. It's a pretty severe break, and at her age they have to be careful about an embolism."

"Embolism! That's a blood clot, right?" Tears stung my eyes. "It could travel to her lungs or brain and kill her!"

"I'm sure there's nothing to worry about. Your grandmother is a strong woman. They are just being cautious."

He didn't sound confident. "Look, a nurse called from the hospital in Drôme, France, and when they put your grandmother on the line she insisted on talking to you. I tried calming her down, but the more she asked for you the more agitated she got. The nurse thinks if you spoke with her, it would help calm her down and lower her blood pressure before surgery. Talking with you seems to be her single focus. Are you able to go to your school's office and get permission to make the call immediately?"

"Yes. Of course. Text me the number, and I'll call right now."

Dad's phone line clicked. "Hold on. That could be

319

them on the other line."

I waited in the silence, turning the pick with my thumb.

"Megan?" Dad said when he returned. "I'm sorry."

"What! What happened?"

"The doctors had to rush her to surgery."

"Why?"

"I'm not sure." His voice wobbled. "My French isn't that great. The nurse said an English-speaking doctor would call me as soon as possible."

"She's going to be fine, right?" I forced myself to take a breath.

"Honestly, we don't know."

"Please, just text me the number. I'll call now. Maybe they're just getting her ready."

Dad's other line clicked again. "I'm sorry. That's the hospital." *Click.*

"Dad?"

He'd hung up.

I leaned against the gray bathroom wall and sunk down to the floor, propping my head against my bent knees. Tears streamed down my cheeks. What could I do? I wrapped my arms around my shins and stayed that way until my nose got too stuffy to breathe. Finally, I got up and blew my nose, threw cold water on my face, dried up with a paper towel, and returned to the math room.

I zoned out for the rest of class, the storm my sullen backdrop. A crack of thunder made me tune back in. A classmate tapped my shoulder on her way out and said, "Can't wait for the flashmob."

Class was over, and most of the students had already left, Ally included.

My eyes felt swollen and puffy, but I couldn't worry or even care about how I might look. I'd be wishing soon, and I needed to get my thoughts together. Mrs. Matthews tried to speak to me, but I rushed down the hall and around the corner to fourth period—to the clock. When I walked into history, the classroom had been rearranged. The Smart Board had been moved to the center, instead of at its normal angled position. And it completely blocked any possible view of the cat clock.

"Why is that there?" My voice screeched.

Mr. Kersey stepped forward. "I thought it'd be nice to change things up a bit."

I grabbed my phone from my pocket and clicked to my clock app. Maybe wishing in this room at the right time would still work.

"Megan," Mr. Kersey said. "Megan."

I looked up. His eyebrows rose, and he crossed his arms over his chest.

"Yes?" I looked back at my phone, enlarged the clock, and switched to digital mode with a seconds reader.

"Excuse me. Megan? I asked you to power that thing off."

"What?" My head shot up.

"No phones during class time."

Thunder popped outside. My hope fizzled away.

"All the way off."

I pressed the off button and watched my phone power down.

Mr. Kersey handed out a worksheet and told us we could use our notes to find the answers. I squirmed and fidgeted. The rain beat against the outside of the windows. *Crunch.* The broken gray tip of my pencil rolled off the desk. I slogged to the pencil sharpener, feeling utter doom. But when I leaned in to use the sharpener, I realized that if I angled my head I could see the cat clock! It was 11:04.

My adrenaline surged. I returned to my seat. Rhena was watching me, but I didn't care. I tried to count seconds in my head. *Okay. It's probably 11:09 or 11:10.* I crunched my pencil lead and returned to the sharpener, Rhena following my every step.

Only 11:07.

Mr. Kersey gave me an odd look. I sat back down, tapping my foot to the imagined beat of a clock. *I've got to time this just right.* I crunched my pencil lead a third time, walked to the sharpener, and checked the clock.

"Megan?" Mr. Kersey said.

Eleven ten.

"Last time, sir. I promise."

Rhena got up and walked over to a bookshelf on the opposite side of the Smart Board. She leaned in to see the clock, too.

The second hand was halfway to the wishing minute.

"Are you done?" Mr. Kersey asked.

"Almost." I dropped my pencil, squatted, grabbed it, slowly tied my shoelace. Rhena pulled a dictionary from the shelf, opening it without checking the page. Our eyes met for a brief moment and then mine went back to the clock. Seconds dragged, until the time struck 11:11. My knuckles were ready, but it didn't matter, since the thunder outside made the crack and pop. The classroom lights flickered and students jumped.

"Whoa!" Mr. Kersey said.

Rhena didn't move. Her eyes were closed, lips moving.

The thunder continued rumbling. It cracked, popped, and sizzled. Lightning flashed, filling the classroom with a burst of white, and with the next snap of thunder I whispered, "Pop. Click. Seconds tick. Wish at eleven-eleven, and watch it stick." I threw out one wish—the single, most important plea of my life: *Please, please, please let my grandma get better.*

CHAPTER 39

The bell rang.

I powered up my phone.

Dad: GRAMS IS DOING GREAT!!!

I exhaled. The cat clock ticktocked like it was no big deal. "Thank you," I said before hurrying into the hallway.

I had to find Ally and apologize for promising a flashmob, since I hadn't delivered the masks after all; and I had to let her know about Rhena bragging about the cheating accusation. Maybe it'd be too little too late, but I had to try to explain.

Mrs. Matthews walked toward me in the busy hall-way, searching my face. "Megan, are you feeling all right?" I stopped, and she rested orange-stained fingers on my shoulder. "Can I help you with anything?"

"Meow." I grabbed my throat. "Meow." It had really happened! I knew the risk, and it had really happened. Wishing costs *were* cumulative. Plus, the whole exchange in energy—you get something from the Magicverse, you have to give something in return. My last wish was a big one, and now my voice was gone completely.

"Okay then?" Motherly concern spread across Mrs. Matthews's face. "You know where you can find me."

My phone was still clutched in my hand from texting Dad. I had texted real words, not meows, so at least there was that.

Students rushed past, amped and saying stuff about how they were on their way to the cafeteria for the flashmob. "You're the best, Megan!"

I pressed my back against the wall and typed a message to Ally:

Me: I'm sorry about the masks. I really meant to have some.

Me: I'm sorry that you felt betrayed when I had lunch w/rhena.

Me: It probably feels I like I don't care about the mess she caused u w/ mr. provost but I do.

Maybe apologizing through a text was lame, but I kept hitting send.

Me: Also—I KNOW you didn't cheat. Obvi.

Me: Can we meet in the cafeteria? I'll let everyone know the flashmob fiasco is my fault.

My shoulders dropped. I didn't know how I'd let everyone know it was my fault without a voice, but I'd mime it out if I had to.

The hallway traffic had thinned. Down by the water fountain, Rhena and the Rhenites were circled up, probably gossiping about someone.

The time had come for me to deal with Rhena. Even if I had to write down every word. I cracked my neck, hooked my thumbs in my backpack straps, and marched toward them.

"Hey, Megan," one of the Rhenites said.

The way they all smiled made me cringe. Now what?

"I got my teacher to let me out of class before the bell rang," Shelby said, "in case you came through with masks. But you didn't. I guess you're on Team Rhena after all."

"You are?" Yoona asked, walking up at that moment.

"Yep. She didn't deliver squat." Shelby stepped aside and made room for us in the circle. "Nice job sabotaging the flashmob."

I shook my head no. "Me . . . Meo."

"Yep, you," Rhena said, patting my back. "What'd you do? Tell Ally you had it all handled so you could lull her into failure? Good one."

"I know, right?" a Rhenite added. "I mean, you sort of had us all fooled into believing you were really going to help Ally."

My head spun. Was that how it looked?

"At least we know Rhena will win the election now," Shelby said. "You made Ally look like such a joke."

"Oh, I'm going to win. It's guaranteed. Right, Megan?" Rhena winked at me. The Rhenites, minus Yoona, smiled.

"MMm." I felt like a muzzled dog. "Mmmm."

Nobody cared that I was trying to speak. "MMMmm."

In the past, I wanted to blend in and hoped nobody would ask my opinion. Now I realized how stupid that had been—how could someone know if they liked the real me if all I did was agree? All week long, I'd given my power away by trying to impress, trying to please, or trying to be someone I wasn't. The frustration of being struck silent with so much to say made me desperate for the chance speak up now.

"Shouldn't we hurry to the cafeteria to vote?" Shelby asked.

"No need to rush." Rhena stretched and yawned. "That loser won't have any votes."

I looked around the circle more closely to see if that comment made anyone else cringe—a few girls shifted uncomfortably. They might be Rhena's friends, but some of them liked Ally, too. Still, no one said anything until Yoona, in a teeny-tiny voice, asked, "Are you okay, Megan?"

I opened my mouth. "Meow."

Yoona's eyebrows went up. Rhena and Shelby didn't care what I said or that I meowed. They were too busy throwing shade on the next person.

". . . such a loser," Shelby said.

"And did you see how bad Brit's face broke out?" Rhena said.

"She really needs to try Proactiv," said a Rhenite.

"We should call her Zit instead of Brit," Shelby said.

Listening to the gossip had made me part of it. Just like when nobody spoke up for me at my last school when Ronald and Brooke had made me feel smaller than a microbe.

I dropped my chin. *Come on, voice. I get it now.* I'd wasted too much time sitting silent and letting Rhena speak for me.

Please. I squeezed my eyes shut. *Please, if I can just talk, I promise to speak up and never give my voice to anyone else again.*

I tried. "Meow." A kitten sound. "Meow." Nobody gave me a glance. I put my hands on my hips, and as loud as I could I said, "MEOW!"

Conversation stopped.

"Meow." I didn't care if I looked dumb. "Meoooow!" I had something important to say and I wasn't willing to give up. "Meooooooow!"

"Megan?" Yoona said. "Do you want to sit down for a minute?"

A circle of shocked faces stared at me. Heat lit up my neck and cheeks. But I shook my head no. "Meow. Meow. Meoooow." My voice sounded high-pitched and scorched. My mouth was dry, but again I tried. "Meeoooow." And then finally, fantastically, I heard myself say, "Rhena." It was a word! A real word! "Could I talk to you for a minute?"

"Uh, Megan. You're being weird," Rhena said. "I'm not sure if this is how things worked at your last school—the freaky-cat announcement—but it's not how things work here." Her face was smug. "And FYI, you don't have to ask permission to speak. Go ahead."

Blood galloped to my heart, but unless I had a full coronary attack, I wasn't going to be too scared to talk. "I mean can we speak one-on-one?" I didn't want to call out Rhena in front of her squad.

"No."

"It's private," I said.

"Say what you have to say here."

I swallowed and looked at the group. Most of them had been at the sushi lunch. They knew what had happened. Someone had to agree with me. I searched for a friendly face in the crowd, but the girls either stared holes through the floor or crossed their arms and smirked.

"We really should get to the cafeteria," Yoona said, her face begging me to bench this conversation.

"Stop," Rhena said forcefully. "Let's hear what Megan has to say."

"Umm . . ." *Now or never.* "Don't you think lying about Ally cheating off you has gone on long enough?"

Everyone got quiet. Only Yoona gave a slight nod.

Then Rhena laughed. "You're joking, right?"

"No, I'm not. You could tell Mr. Provost that you made a mistake, or you were pranking and you didn't think it would go this far. There's still time to work this out."

"I think you're misunderstanding, because one, she cheated, and two, I don't care about Ally and her problems."

"But it's not true. She didn't try to cheat off you."

"That's your opinion."

"My opinion? It's the truth. You said so yourself." I

looked around the group for confirmation but got zip. "Really? You're all going to act like you have nothing to say? Come on! Speak up."

Crickets.

Rhena held the group's collective voice captive. It made me all the more determined to never be silent again.

"I don't know what you *think* you heard," Rhena said, "but it's my word against yours." She leaned over and took a sip from the water fountain. "And you should probably keep your mouth shut."

Keeping my mouth shut was no longer part of the plan. But I didn't know what to say next.

"All right, girls. To the cafeteria," Rhena said.

The weight of giving up started settling on my shoulders.

"Megan," Yoona said, "if you want, I could—"

"Will you stop all that talking, Yoona?" Rhena said. "Your voice is grating on my nerves."

Yoona looked crushed, and it reminded me that Hannah had always stood by my side. Even when I snorted. Even when I lied.

"I like hearing what you have to say, Yoona," I said. "And Rhena." I shook my head. "Get over your need to make everyone feel lame. You might think that makes you appear superior." Pause. "But trust me, it doesn't."

The bewildered group waited for a cue from Rhena.

"You need to watch your—" Rhena started.

But I cut her off. "Why is stabbing people in the back your specialty? Or is lying your specialty? I mean, you're definitely good at it."

Shelby gasped.

"Here." I whipped out my phone. "Let me show you what you sound like when you brag about what a super-convincing liar you are." I opened the video app with the recording of Rhena and pressed play, holding it forward for them to see. There was Rhena in bragging mode, laughing about her lie to Mr. Provost.

Nobody gasped. Nobody was surprised by what they'd heard, but some heads bowed. Maybe they felt ashamed, too.

"Look how pathetic we *all* were," I said.

"So what." Rhena smirked.

I stopped the video and shook my head. "Rhena, you're pretty. You're smart. Sometimes you're even fun. You don't have to be like this."

Rhena's mouth twitched like maybe I'd gotten through to her. But the moment quickly passed, and she narrowed her eyes, dismissing me with a "Whatever."

But I wasn't done. "It's no longer my word against yours." I waved my phone. "Either you can tell Mr. Provost the truth, or I will. By the end of the day." I crossed my arms over my chest, burying my shaking hands. Even with the jitters, speaking up felt way better than hiding.

Rhena blinked for a moment, clearly not used to being crossed.

I took that chance to walk the other way. "I'm going to find Ally."

When I got halfway down the hallway, Rhena's voice erupted in a screech. "You're going to be sorry."

My heart slammed in my chest—shaking nerves, adrenaline, and satisfaction combined. Once I was finally out of view, I slid down on a bench to catch my breath. Rhena was checked off my to-do list, but all my problems weren't even close to solved. I still had to face the cafeteria and own up to my mistakes. While I sat there letting my heartbeat calm, I dialed Dad. No answer.

A nearby locker clanged shut.

I texted Ally again.

Me: Cafeteria in five?

Footsteps came toward me, and then someone tapped a large Nike against the edge of my Converse.

CHAPTER 40

"**M**egan?" Jackson's voice lacked its usual confidence. "Do you mind?" He pointed at the space next to me.

I nodded.

He sat on the bench, set a guitar case at his feet, and seemed to be searching for words.

Why? There was nothing more to gain. The flashmob had already flopped.

Mrs. Matthews's words echoed in my brain: *Sometimes the flaw is that you don't understand the problem.*

Had I been summing up Jackson with the wrong set of variables? And then the truth about him hit me—he'd appreciated my Woofstock shirt, he'd liked my nerdy jokes, he'd seen my lion hairstyle and my face not only makeup-free, but also full of snot and tears. The campaigning was over, yet here he was, still interested in talking to me. It was time I spoke up to him, too.

I cleared my throat. "I need to ask you something."

"Okay."

"Did Rhena tell you to work on me to get me to throw the flashmob?"

Jackson's gaze dipped to his shoes and my stomach buckled.

He let out a sigh before meeting my eyes. "Of course she did. That's Rhena's way, and it's too bad, because there are some decent things about Rhena. But I hate when she acts like that."

"Wow," I said, dropping my chin. I wanted to hide my disappointment, but I was committed to being real. "Bummer."

"Hold up. It's not like that. She asked me to ruin it, but I told her no."

"You did?"

"And I stand by what I told you," he said. "You don't need to have a flashmob or pull off anything special to have people like you. I like you."

He searched my eyes.

"Thanks," I said. This was the second time he'd said he liked me. "I'm sorry about last night and for being so weird at my locker this morning."

"It's all good."

"It's not. Look. I've been sort of ridiculous and I'm sorry, because I like you, too." I couldn't believe I'd just said that out loud, but I didn't turn away when the blush burned my face.

Jackson scooted close, reached over, and tucked a piece of my hair behind my ear. "Mmmhmm. Tell me more."

My breath caught. "Well, I've been wanting to tell you all week how I like that you wear the bracelet from your little sister. That's super-sweet. And I want to hear more about her." My words picked up speed. "And my sister's pretty awesome and I gave you a bad impression of her yesterday, but that's all on me. And I'd love to come to your lacrosse game sometime and you could tell me what a midi does. And maybe we could do another Wednesday Night Walks. And—" I took a breath and realized I was rambling. "Uhhh. Sorry. Word vomit."

Jackson laughed. "No. It's great. And about my mask. I wish I had a president mask."

"I know." I looked down. "That's my mess-up, too."

"But I have this." Jackson reached into his backpack and pulled out a Scooby-Doo mask, slipping it on his head. "What do you think? Scooby would make a great president."

I laughed.

Just then someone rounded the corner with a light-saber. "Awesome, this day is," said a voice under a Yoda mask.

I looked at Jackson, confused.

"Oh, you don't know?" he said.

"Know what?"

"Come on." He picked up his guitar case and ushered me through the empty hall toward the cafeteria. Halfway there, the boys' restroom door swung open. Three superheroes and someone wearing an astronaut helmet walked out and gave me a thumbs-up.

"Wait, what?" I said.

"President masks are in short supply," Jackson said. "But nobody wanted to be left out or count on getting one of the extras you were going to bring, so practically the whole seventh grade texted saying to bring a mask—any mask—and everybody dug through their old Halloween stuff. It's pretty funny."

We arrived at the cafeteria entrance, and two people wearing Grim Reaper costumes stepped out of the double doors and stopped in front of us. "Megan!" They pulled off their matching masks—Turner and Ally.

"We were just looking for you," Ally said. "I love this! It's the most spirited thing I've ever seen our school do."

"Yup," Turner said. "The cafeteria is a veritable Halloween in September. Definitely my speed."

"Veritable." Ally smiled. "Anyhow, Megan, you did it."

"I didn't," I insisted. "I didn't deliver any masks. I'm sorry. It wasn't a sabotage on purpose or anything, but I can't take credit for all this." I waved a hand to the costumes streaming into the cafeteria.

"Sure you can," Ally said. "The snowball effect. You said to show up in masks, and that's what's happening. It's so fun." She smiled at Turner. "Luckily Turner brought an extra costume."

"We can switch classes and pretend to be each other," Turner said.

"Nice," I said.

Ally laughed. "Megan, I'm sorry about everything. Putting you in the middle of my stuff with Rhena must've been a lot of pressure."

"Yep," I agreed. "Like substituting nitro groups for three hydrogen atoms."

Turner and Jackson cracked up.

"What?" Ally asked. "Is that a chemistry joke?"

"Yep," Turner said. "A dynamite one! Get it, because three hydrogen atoms?"

Ally shook her head and smiled before continuing. "I'm sorry. To be honest, I was jealous about you guys hanging out at the Humane Society and then lunch." Her mouth twisted. "I just didn't want her to steal you away. So lame of me. You should be able to eat lunch with whoever you want. I just want us to be friends, too. Okay?"

"It's a deal," I said.

Hannah should be able to be friends with whoever she wanted to also. I took out my phone. "Just a sec, guys."

Me: Sorry, H. Talk after school?

She replied immediately.

Hannah: Sorry 2. Yes!!! Love you!

"Hey!" Three people walked out of the cafeteria and lifted off their Ninja Turtle masks—Noelle, Mia, and Erin. "It's time."

Ally grabbed my hand and pulled me toward the doorway. "Come on. You and I are first."

"First?"

"Your exponential flashmob. We're doing your cartwheel idea, but in twos because with threes it got to be too many people." She nodded like this was perfectly normal. "Just keep cartwheeling across the cafeteria floor until you make it to the other side. Okay?"

"Uhhhh?"

"Come on. It's going to be fun. Turner got his tech

and engineering friends to doctor up the cafeteria's lights and sound system. And the big cartwheeling groups are being handled by the spirit club and band. When they finish, we'll all start dancing. Okay?"

My head spun. A crowd? Eyes on me?

"Hurry. Give Jackson your backpack and slip on your mask," Mia said.

Jackson touched my arm, restarting my pulse. "See you in there." He headed inside.

"Okay?" Everything was moving quickly. I put on my Lincoln mask.

Ally grabbed my hand again, pulling me to just outside the closed cafeteria doors. "We'll count down, open the doors, and when they get to the chorus we'll cartwheel through to the other side."

My entire body vibrated, not the purring kind but the shaking in my shoes kind. "Oh . . . kay?"

Turner spoke into his phone. "Yep," he said to the person on the other end. "Cue the lights and music. Be ready to bust out the sound system after the Minions." Then he counted down: "Five, four, three, two, one."

Erin and Mia swung open the cafeteria doors and the crowd stepped aside.

The lights went dim, and I couldn't see anything for a second; then two lights popped on, one above Jackson and the other above . . . Piper!

Piper and Jackson were holding guitars. The gym

was silent until their strumming began. My brain took a second to catch up.

Piper was playing music. For me. For my flashmob.

Instead of owning the room the way she usually did, she looked tiny. Small. The strain showed in the stiffness of her back. The strumming was off, and then she glanced at me and hit a wrong note. And then another. My heart tightened. Piper stopped.

I held my breath.

She turned to Jackson and gave him a nod that must have meant to begin again. The strumming restarted, and this time it was perfect. Or it was perfect to me, because Piper was being brave, finding her voice in music even with mistakes and all. And she had taken the risk for me.

My heart welled up.

The truth about my little sister hit me. Piper's life wasn't just bubbles and rainbows. She pretended everything was okay, when really she spent her days worrying over Dad and her nights struggling with guilt and bad dreams about Mom. Our eyes connected again, and she smiled at me the way she used to smile on those long-ago Saturday mornings, and her song took off.

"You okay?" Ally asked.

My eyes blurred and a snort came out. "I'm perfect," I answered.

The music flowed, the beats energetic. Then the

center lights popped on in time with their chorus. The middle of the cafeteria floor had been cleared and a crush of students in masks pressed together and against walls making a horseshoe around the cleared space.

"Go!" Ally said.

In we went, Ally and me cartwheeling to applause, adrenaline thrumming through my ears. We cartwheeled to the other side. I didn't even know I'd been laughing the whole way until we landed our final cartwheel. Then Tank and Wigglesworth stepped from the crowd, each strumming a ukulele. They joined Piper and Jackson, and now the four instruments played and the music picked up tempo. Lights blasted at the entrance and heads shifted to the next group of masked cartwheelers—Mia, Erin, Turner, and Noelle. They turned as a synchronized set of four, and Ally and I couldn't help but laugh at Turner in his Grim Reaper mask with his clumsy cartwheels. When they landed beside us, four students with horns stepped from the crowd and joined the musicians, making an eight-member band. Eight students in Minion masks detonated from the crowd, backflipping across the floor like Olympic gymnasts.

"The Minions are the cheerleaders!" Ally screamed.

The crowd roared and Turner whipped his phone from his Velcroed pocket. "Now," he said. Right on cue, music exploded from the cafeteria speakers, and I could only guess it was sixteen instruments popping out galvanized beats, and sixteen people went next, then thirty-two blasted out of the left side of the room and cartwheeled across the floor. The music boomed in full tilt, and everyone started dancing and jumping. I caught sight of Rhena and Shelby, propped against a wall, arms crossed, scowling. Then Jackson grabbed my hand and pulled me to the center of the room with Turner and Ally, who screamed, "Dance party!"

The faculty let the dance party go on for a full fifteen minutes. Even Mrs. Matthews and Mr. Scoggins hit the floor with a few moves that must've been popular back in the day. Then Coach Crosby blew her whistle and announced it was time to vote.

Spider-Men, a few Bart Simpsons, several zombies, pumpkinheads, Marios, Zorros, Star Wars characters, and clowns made up the seventh-grade voting lines. Voting was monitored by teachers and faculty.

We cast our ballots and grabbed some of the free election day food from baskets that had been set up with water bottles and plastic-wrapped hoagie sandwiches.

The cafeteria tables had been stacked or pushed against the walls to clear an open space in the center, so we sat on the floor. I caught sight of Piper by the sandwiches and waved. She returned the wave, grabbed a sandwich, and ran back to the lower-division side. I placed a hand over the pocket where I had Mom's guitar pick. Mom would have been proud to have seen how today went down.

Turner was three rows over, high-fiving Wigglesworth and Tank. I sat squished between Ally and Jackson.

Ally leaned close to me and whispered, "I never realized that Turner's so cute." She took a swig of water. "And he's always himself."

"Always," I said, and we laughed.

Toward the end of lunch, the faculty tallied up the votes. Mr. Scoggins waited in the center of the room as Coach Crosby and Mrs. Sinoway crossed the floor with the results envelopes. The coach blew her whistle and the room quieted.

"Thank you to all who ran for Spirit Week," Mr. Scoggins said. Mrs. Butler stood beside him. "If you did not win, please offer your enthusiasm and support in another club or volunteering capacity. It's people like you who make our school great. And now for the results."

Instead of sitting on the floor like everyone else, the Rhenites minus Yoona stood around Rhena, who was smiling like today was the best day ever, not a trace of worry.

I grabbed Ally's hand and crossed my fingers.

Ally sucked in a breath, her knees bouncing, and Jackson reached over and patted her back.

Mr. Scoggins unfolded the paper.

"Drumroll, please," Turner said.

"Hmmm," Mr. Scoggins said, his face scrunched. He looked over at Coach Crosby and Mrs. Sinoway. They both nodded.

"Come on!" Tank shouted. "Tell us!"

Ally squeezed her eyes shut and crushed my hand in her grip.

I smelled the tangerine scent first.

"Hey, girl."

Then my stomach dropped to my socks. The green-eyed girl held her clipboard and smiled at me.

"Whaaa—"

"Oh, whoops." She scanned the notes on her board. "I'm not here for you. I'm here for her."

She disappeared and I swept my gaze around the room. Where had she gone?

"Wow," Mr. Scoggins said after pausing to huddle with Mrs. Butler, Coach Crosby, and Mrs. Sinoway. "With one hundred percent of the vote in their favor, the seventh-grade team of Rhena Thornsmith and

Jackson Litner are your new Spirit Week Captains."

A combination of gasps, applause, and confused chatter surrounded us.

"Huh?" Wigglesworth said, clapping and sounding puzzled at the same time. "How is that possible?"

My head spun.

Ally opened her eyes and gaped at our circle. "None of you guys voted for me and Megan? I mean, I can understand you, Jackson, but Megan?"

"No. I did," I said, scanning the cafeteria again for the green-eyed girl.

"So did I," Mia said.

"You bet your rosy rutabaga I voted for you," Erin said. "I demand a recount!"

"Yeah," Noelle said. "No way that's right."

Across the room, I spotted the green-eyed girl handing her gold fountain pen to Rhena. Rhena signed the scroll.

My skin went clammy, but I knew exactly what I had to do. Even though eating fire sounded like a better option than public speaking, I stood.

"Excuse me." I walked toward Mr. Scoggins, waving noodly-feeling arms over my head. "Excuse me," I called from across the crowd. "Excuse me."

The applause quieted. It felt like forty million eyes were staring at me. "That—" My voice caught and I cleared my throat. "That result is statistically impossible. Do you mean ninety-nine percent? Because I voted for Ally."

Mr. Scoggins looked at Mrs. Sinoway. She shook her head. "It was a unanimous vote. One hundred percent for Rhena and Jackson."

The delivery girl was gone. Rhena crossed her arms and smiled. But her confidence no longer intimidated me. "Well," I said in the firmest, surest voice I'd ever heard leave my mouth, "that's inaccurate. Because I voted for Ally. And I'm certain others did, too."

"Perhaps you made a mistake. Checked the wrong box," Mr. Scoggins said.

"Even if I'd made a mistake, and even if Rhena had enough votes to win, I'm still certain a lot of students voted for Ally." I turned to the crowd. "Am I right? I know ballots are meant to be private, but can we agree there's no way Rhena won with a hundred percent of the vote?"

"Accept it's over," Rhena said. "I won. You lost, and—"

"I voted for Ally!" Turner hollered over Rhena.

"Me too," said Haleigh and Zoe together. They rose to their feet and three friends stood next to them. "Us too."

"Me too," said Erin, Noelle, Mia, Karen, Ellie, and a bunch of others.

"This is ridiculous." Rhena's voice screeched. "Nobody cares what you have to say, 'Fun-meister.'"

I froze.

"Yeah," Rhena said. "It's not hard to search social media. Newsflash, everyone. Megan wasn't known as anything except a dorkjob at her last school."

I could feel my cheeks turning red, but I forced myself to stand taller. I had nothing to be ashamed of. "So what?" I said. "I can be dorky. I can be dorky to the tenth. Big whoop. It's more fun than being fake." I turned and smiled at my friends in the crowd. At Jackson, Ally, and Yoona. Tank, Erin, and Wigglesworth. Turner, Ellie, Karen, Mia, and Noelle. They all smiled. None of them were giving me a judgy look. I turned back to Mr. Scoggins, held my fist in the air, and said, "Re-vote! Re-vote!"

"Re-vote!" Jackson join in.

"Re-vote!" Turner chanted.

Then Ally and Erin and Mia and Noelle were saying, "Re-vote! Re-vote! Re-vote!" So were Wigglesworth and Karen and Ellie. "Re-vote!" The cafeteria filled with the chant.

"Okay, okay," Mr. Scoggins said, trying to get everyone to calm.

"Yo," said one of the jocks, standing and gesturing to the group near him, "we all wrote in Turner's name when we voted."

Turner jumped up and saluted. "Captain Turner at your service."

Mr. Scoggins, Mrs. Sinoway, and Coach Crosby huddled. After a few moments, the coach blew her whistle. "Okay, people. We're not sure how the confusion happened, but we are going to do a revote for the position of Spirit Captain."

"Hey!" Rhena shouted. "That's not fair. I already won."

"Um, excuse me," said a girl, whose voice nobody would have noticed had she not whistled and stood on top of one of the tables against the wall. It was Yoona. "Before you say anything else, I just want to speak up and say I voted for Ally and Megan, too."

"Yoona?" Rhena said, followed by the loudest sneeze I'd ever heard.

"Ahhhhkkkkk!" Shelby screamed and pointed at Rhena.

Three large, angry welts had popped up on Rhena's nose. She scratched at her arms and looked at Shelby. "What?"

"Ewwww," Shelby said, taking backward steps. "What's happening to you, Rhena?"

Rhena kept scratching. Her nose grew redder and redder and a fifth and sixth bump popped up on her cheeks, bigger than a quarter and large enough to see from any angle in the cafeteria.

More voices echoed the shock.

"What?" Rhena demanded "Wha—*Achoooooo.*" She let out another huge sneeze, snot flying. And then a swarm of fleas burst from her hair. Her eyes grew wide and her hands flew to her head, scratching like crazy, and suddenly her hair lifted like a titanic case of instant static electricity, bristling way worse than a surprised cat.

The cafeteria exploded with laughter and chatter.

"Whoa!" a kid from my Spanish class shouted. "How is she doing that?"

I kept my hand pressed over my mouth. Clearly this was the consequence of a cheater's wish.

Rhena buckled.

"We should help her," I said.

"Yeah," Jackson said. "Come on."

Jackson, Ally, and I hurried across the room.

Rhena swatted Ally and me away as if this were our fault. Then she leaned into Jackson's arms, and he held her up as they walked out of the room.

"What a cataclysm," Ally said, confused.

"Yep," I agreed. "Couldn't have said it better myself."

CHAPTER 41

I was in English class when I was told to gather my stuff and go to the office. When I arrived, Dad was standing at the doorway, anxiously watching for me. Before I had a chance to get worried, he said, "She's fine. She's absolutely fine."

I fell into his arms, burying my face in his starched shirt and letting worry tumble from my shoulders. Sure, I had the clock and his text, but having Dad confirm the news in person made everything truly okay again.

After a few moments, Dad said, "I couldn't get any more work done. I figured you might be feeling the same way, since we're pretty similar, you and I. I hope you don't mind me saying so."

I smiled at him. "I love being like you, Dad."

"How about I sign you out and we go for smoothies?"

"Can we?" I said. "Let's get Piper, too."

Dad signed a form to release me from school, and I hoisted my backpack to my shoulders.

"Hello," Mrs. Matthews said, coming through the doorway with a stack of papers and a bag of Doritos. "Well played, Megan. An exponential flashmob was the perfect gimmick to get the school interested in math club. And thanks for announcing our first competition."

She turned to Dad.

"Your daughter is something else."

"Yes, she is," Dad said.

She went on to tell him about the cartwheeling and said, "In addition to the math component, the technology and engineering clubs managed the sound and lights." She clasped her hands together. "It was spectacular. In fact, I'd like to talk about mingling the groups more often. Perhaps if you have time, Megan, you could start a STEM club."

"Science, technology, engineering, and math," Dad said. "Sounds like my daughter." He smiled at me. "What do you think, Megan?"

"Yep. That sounds perrrrfect." This time the purr was on purpose.

Mrs. Matthews laughed. "Okay. Let's chat on Monday."

We said good-bye to Mrs. Matthews, grabbed Piper from the elementary side, and then drove to Nèktar for celebration smoothies.

We were the only customers in the tiny, citrus-smelling café and took our time with the menu. Piper and I ordered Berry Banana Bursts, and Dad ordered a smoothie made with kale, pineapple, spinach, banana, coconut butter, and coconut water. Our drinks were poured into clear plastic cups. We took them and sat on orange chairs next to a tall, sunny window.

"Are you sure you can have coconut butter, Dad?" Piper asked, swirling her straw in her cup.

"Girls." Dad folded one arm over the other. "I am healthy. I plan on staying healthy. My diet is ideal. Furthermore, I'm joining a gym tomorrow, and I am committing to you that I'll do a good job managing my own well-being. I appreciate your concern, but it's time for you to stop monitoring me."

"You'll stay on top of checkups?" Piper asked.

"Yes, Piper. But no more of that from you. Do you understand? I'm the adult. You're the child." He tucked his chin and looked over the top of his glasses, smiling. "Or I should say, you're the tweenager."

I loved how nerdy he sounded.

"Your job is to enjoy this time, do well in school, make friends, and stop worrying over my nutrition. Okay?"

"Okay," Piper said, but I could hear the hesitation in her voice. It would take her some time to get used to this new mind-set.

Dad took a sip of his smoothie and asked, "What else?"

I crumpled my napkin and shuffled it from hand to hand.

"Come on, Megan," Dad urged. "Something's on the tip of your tongue."

I sighed and met his gaze. "Can we . . . ?" My voice hitched as I looked between Dad and Piper. "We never talk about Mom, and I miss her. I know it's hard for you both, but I don't want to pretend her away anymore. I want to talk about her again."

Dad twisted his watch and remained silent. Piper glanced at him and stayed quiet, too, but then she leaned against my arm. "Me too."

Dad didn't move or talk.

Running water and soft music were the only noises in the small space. Even my breathing had stopped, but I let go of an exhale and said, "It's like you want to protect us from the pain, Dad. But it hurts more not talking about Mom."

Dad swallowed. The lump in his throat moved up and down. Then he lifted his chin and said, "You're right."

Tears pricked the back of my eyes, then Dad's eyes

filled with puddles, and I couldn't hold back the flood. Suddenly my cheeks were wet.

"Meggy-Meg," Dad said, sounding like Mom. He dabbed a napkin to my wet cheeks, and then Piper blubbered a laugh and said, "Now we're all crying." Instead of wiping her tears, she grabbed my hands and gave me a double-fisted squeeze. The magic in this moment was bigger than anything wishing could've given us.

"I'm sorry, girls," Dad said, choking on the words. "Losing your mother was the greatest loss of my life. I didn't want to burden you with that, but it seems I ended up creating a bigger burden."

"You know what Mom used to say?" I asked.

"What?"

"She'd say, 'Just like celebrations, losses are meant to be shared.'"

He swallowed and piled his hands on top ours. "We're in this together." Then he smiled. "Monopoly tonight?"

"As long as I get to be the dog and the banker."

"No way!" Piper said. "I'm the banker this time, and instead of money we're using gum and Skittles."

Dad laughed. "How did the election go today?"

"This kid Turner ended up winning with write-in votes. He announced Math Monday right on the spot and said that would be our first spirit day and 'three' will be the magic number. Anytime anyone says 'three' they have to sing thirty seconds of 'Three Little Birds' by Bob Marley."

"Wow," Dad said. "I suppose Spirit Week is a big deal around here."

"Yeah," Piper said. "And third-period classes have to sing the whole song together. Good thing we already know the words, huh, Megan?"

"Yep," I said. "Also on Monday, everyone has to dress as their favorite equation or mathematician, or bring pie to lunch. I think I'll go as Florence Nightingale. Everyone knows her as a nurse, but she was a statistician, too."

"I'm definitely going as pie," Piper said. "Apple."

Dad laughed. "What else?"

"That's all I know for now, except Friday will be all about Star Wars. Star Wars trivia, robot-building competitions, and the hall monitors and crossing guards have to dress as Stormtroopers. Everyone else gets to dress as their favorite Star Wars character."

"Is Ally bummed about losing?" Piper asked.

"A little. Turner told her she could be his assistant, but Ally said she'd be the Chewbacca to his captaining or nothing."

"I think I'd like her," Dad said. He stood and headed to the restroom. "I'll be back."

Piper turned to me and said, "I knew you'd pull off something great today."

"Thanks, Pipes." I smiled. "I couldn't believe my eyes when I saw you playing the guitar for me. Where did you even get it?"

"I borrowed it from the school band room. But I plan to dig out Mom's when we get home."

"Really?" I looked at her closely.

"Really. It felt awesome to play again." She smiled. "Megan, I'm sorry about yesterday with Rhena. I shouldn't have told her about you and Hannah."

"That's right. You shouldn't have. And if Mom were here, she'd tell me to whack you good with a pillow." I paused. "But I forgive you." I reached into my pocket for Mom's guitar pick and handed it to Piper. "Here. I've been holding on to this for you."

"Thanks." Piper closed her fingers over it. "It felt like Mom was with us today."

"I know, right."

As if cued, "Better Together" played from the overhead speakers.

Sheer luck? Maybe. Most people don't realize that luck has everything to do with odds, like the chance of being called to "Come on down" in *The Price Is Right* is one in thirty-six. Pretty darn good! That's what it felt like when Mom's song came on. Pretty. Darn. Good.

Dad returned from the bathroom shuffling a dance and singing a bit off tune, "Mmm, it's always better when we're together." He twirled in front of our table.

Piper and I almost busted a gut laughing.

After smoothies, we stopped at a music store to purchase new guitar strings. Then Dad drove me back to school to pick up my homework.

Dad and Piper waited in the car while I ran inside. It was weird to be in the halls, so quiet and empty, lacking that usual drumbeat of noise and shuffle. I stopped at my locker and loaded the books I needed into my backpack. Then I made my way to the history classroom.

The sun slanted down through the tall windows, and the little flecks of dust rising in the air seemed like sparkles of something enchanted. The room was silent. I clicked the door shut, unzipped my backpack, and pulled out the brown paper bag with the magazine. I rolled the Smart Board aside until I could see the clock. The cat eyes ticked back and forth, back and forth.

I cleared my throat. "I just wanted to say hi." Swallow. "And bye, sort of. I mean, I'll still be here, and you'll still be here, but I'm not wishing anymore." I pulled in a long breath and then sighed it out. "It's not that I'm not grateful. But I'm ready to be on my own. So I'm returning this." I held up the magazine. "I'm not accepting the September edition or any others, which means I'm done with the 'some magic' part of our deal. Okay?" I waited for a sign like lightning or thunder or the green-eyed delivery girl or anything. Nothing happened. The tail just swished, the eyes moved, and the whiskers clicked in time like it was any old clock.

"Okay, so . . . I'm going to put this in here so you can see me not accepting it." I bent down to the trash can and pushed on the magazine until it was deep inside. Then I wiped off my palms. "And also the Marilyn quote from the other magazine." I found the torn page in my backpack and waved it at the clock. "I'm throwing this away, too, and replacing it with a fortune I got from someone a little wiser. His name's Dr. Seuss if you're wondering."

The rattle of the door handle sent my heart to my throat.

"Hello, Megan?" Mr. Kersey said. "Odd to find you here at this time."

"Hi." I bit back the temptation to make up an excuse for being in the room. My new voice wasn't going to be wasted on lies.

Two elderly men walked in behind him—twins. Their gray hair was wild just like Einstein's, and their eyes twinkled like a movie star Santa. Even though it was over a hundred degrees outside, they both looked perfectly comfortable in their three-piece wool suits.

"Megan. I'd like you to meet my uncles. Uncle

Giuseppe, Uncle Remy, this is Megan. She's one of our newer students."

"Hi. Hello. Uh . . . Wow." The cat clock's tocks echoed in my ears.

"My dear." Uncle Giuseppe walked closer, his shiny black shoes clacking across the floor. He narrowed his twinkly eyes and took a better look at me. "Do we know each other?"

"Yes, do we?" Uncle Remy said, also stepping closer. A silver pocket watch dangled loosely at his side.

There was a 100 percent chance he didn't know me, but he did know someone else in my family. "No," I said. "Will you excuse me?"

As I bolted into the hallway I heard one of them say, "As you wish, my dear."

ACKNOWLEDGMENTS

It is thanks to the magic of many minds that *The 11:11 Wish* sparked to life. Thank you to my agent, Jennifer Rofé, who spent countless hours helping me get this story right. Thank you to my editor, Maria Barbo, for your sense of humor, brilliant editorial eye, and enchanted pen. Thank you to assistant editor Rebecca Aronson, production editor Emily Rader, and the amazing marketing, sales, and publicity teams who spent a day wearing cat ears around the office!

To my extraordinary critiquing partner, Jerilyn Patterson, thank you for reading 11^{11} versions of this story. I truly value your friendship. Thank you to my Boulder critiquing groups: Elaine Pease, Penny Berman, Sally Spear, Will James Limón, David Deen, and Barry Solway. A triple-sized thank-you to Stephen Mooser and Lin Oliver for starting SCBWI forty-seven years ago, and to my tribe Todd Tuell, Denise Vega, Anna-Maria Crum, and Hilari Bell. Special thanks to

Ida Olson, and my oh-so-gifted mentor Lindsay Eland. Also thank you to Aspen Nolan and Celia Sinoway for reading every draft of this story. Thank you to beta readers and/or brainstormers Jason Gallaher, Kayla Heinen, John Christenson, Hannah Gibbs, Elizabeth Butler, Madeline Butler, Monica Butler, Lori Berberian, Leni Checkas, Charles Rakay, Janet Mountain, Jackson Mountain, Ellen Tarver, and Courtney Sutherland. Thank you to Dave Howard and Dr. Ana Law for your expertise in math and medicine, and to Scott Isaksen at the Creative Problem Solving Group.

To my family, thank you for your enthusiasm, support, and love: Noelle Tomsic, Cayman Tomsic, Marlo Berberian, Ally Adkins, Renée and Paul Berberian, John Provost, Joseph and Susan Provost, and extra thanks to Katie Salidas for early edits and advice. Finally, thank you to my husband, Steve Tomsic, for living with scattered papers, index cards, and Post-it notes, for taking long walks around the lake, and for offering smart ideas when I ran into story problems. Your support was everything.

MORE MAGICAL MAYHEM AWAITS
IN KIM TOMSIC'S NEXT BOOK:

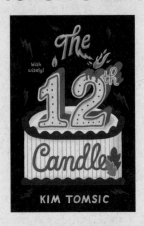

Sage Sassafras's life is cursed! No, really. Since birth, Sage has been plagued by the Contrarium Curse that's set her at odds with classmate Priscilla Petty. Every time something goes right for Priscilla, it goes terribly, horribly wrong for Sage. And things *always* go well for Priscilla. Sage blames the curse for *all* her middle school misery—from losing a friend to failing gym to gaining a reputation as the girl whose daddy's in trouble. So when Sage is given a magical candle on her twelfth birthday, she seizes the chance to turn her luck around—with a wish to reverse the curse. But when the consequences of her wish take a terrible turn, Sage has to team up with her worst enemy—before she's doomed to a life of opposites forever.